Pride Publishing books by M.C. Roth

Single Books
The Drumbeat of His Heart

I0658944

THE DRUMBEAT OF HIS HEART

M.C. ROTH

The Drumbeat of His Heart
ISBN # 978-1-83943-997-1
©Copyright M.C. Roth 2021
Cover Art by Erin Dameron-Hill ©Copyright July 2021
Interior text design by Claire Siemaszkiewicz
Pride Publishing

THE DRUMBEAT OF HIS HEART

Dedication

For Q

Chapter One

Rain splattered against the slim fabric hood that was pulled over his head. The water leaked through the flimsy fabric and pressed into his hair, making the strands clump and drip down the back of his shirt. The sky was the colour of dusty ash left too long in the fireplace and the air was thick with ozone.

Trent shivered and pulled the hoodie closer as he tried to keep some semblance of warmth against his skin. The forecast had predicted a beautiful, sunny spring day with a temperature of twenty degrees centigrade. The sun had lasted until he'd stepped out of the office to go home after a nine-hour shift trapped behind a dusty window. He'd touched the pavement and the clouds had loomed in as a virtual monsoon opened above his head.

Walking to work was as much of a blessing as it was a curse. He had no car payments, but he was stuck walking through any storm that decided to roll in.

Clouds had a habit of waiting until he left the safety of the building before they unleashed their wrath.

The cracked sidewalks were stained dark with pools of water gathering in every dip and cranny. The few buildings around him were lit up bright against the grey sky, and their signs beckoned anyone who happened to be passing by. Their brick was antique, with lines of grout that had crumbled over time. It gave them more character than the new-builds in an actual city. Their bleached Christmas lights, that were meant to be spring decorations, were charming and the most modern thing about them besides the updated espresso machine in the café.

A burst of yellow swerved along the slim street, and its tyres splashed through the puddle of a blocked storm drain. Water burst up like the landing of a flume ride and smacked against Trent. Gravel and bits of sodden leaves struck him, sticking and clinging to every light hair on his naked shins. A trail of sand curled down his forehead and dripped into his eye.

"Dammit," he spluttered as thick mud trailed down into his mouth. The taste of tainted water and decomposition made him gag and he spat into the swirling mass around his feet that was searching for a way through the cracked sidewalk. He stopped to watch as the yellow Corvette straightened and swerved back away from the kerb where it had struck the puddle that had completely drenched him. It was a manoeuvre he might expect out of a teenager who might deliberately try to soak unsuspecting pedestrians.

Instead of pulling straight along the thin road, the Corvette kept turning as it lost control on the plane of water. It looped back to the other side of the street and directly into oncoming traffic. There was no squealing of tyres or frantic running as doom approached, only the patter of rain on his soaked hood.

A rusty feed truck, tracking towards the light in the opposite lane, cleared the Corvette by a few centimetres, blaring its horn as the car crossed its path. The yellow machine swerved again, its tyres finally catching and squealing as they threw off bits of black rubber. Trent could just make out the frantic movements of the driver through the dark, tinted windows. His stomach clenched and the hairs raised on the back of his neck as he watched the scene unfold.

Sounds gurgled together as metal struck metal. The pop of tyres burst against his eardrums, accompanied by the squeal of aluminium and the snapping of glass. The muffled thud of airbags joined the fray a second later, then a shout as the bumper of the Corvette crumpled into a parked suburban van.

Trent was moving before he'd fully registered the crash. The mud and leaves were forgotten as his hood fell back and the rain pounded against his face. One of his sandals, slick with slimy water, slipped from his foot, nearly sending him down in the middle of the road. He managed to recover, running lopsided with one foot aching as it slapped against rough pavement.

The vibrant yellow handle was slick beneath his hand as he pried at the passenger door. The cracked window blurred his view so that he could only make out the shape of a person pressed between a white air bag and a black seat. There was no movement inside, not even the frantic flailing he'd seen just before the car had crashed. The handle was locked tight, resisting every pull that he made.

Trent leapt over the hood of the car, neatly avoiding where the two vehicles were entwined in an angry embrace. The adrenalin coursing through his veins gave him the boost to make it almost all the way across before his naked calf snagged on the car's wet surface. He fell over, narrowly managing to keep from falling to the pavement on the other side.

Despite the terrible noise that the crash had made, the hood of the Corvette had hardly any damage, except a pressed curve along one headlight that folded both the fender and the hood. Shattered glass was strewn along the road, hidden beneath the murky puddles. The suburban had been crushed where it had been struck along its broadside. It was one of the only weak points in the gas-guzzling tank.

Trent stumbled as he found his balance on the other side of the car. There was a coffee shop only a few feet away, and people were gathering at the window and pressing their curious faces against the glass. A handful of customers made it outside, shouting questions over the din of pouring rain. Phones were up, hopefully calling the police and not taking a video of his failed leap.

The pounding of his heart washed away any more sounds of the gathering crowd and their calls from behind the window. The handle of the driver's side was slippery under his hand and it took two pulls to realize that it too was locked tight. Luckily, the window on this side was broken and scattered like a thousand glistening waterdrops. Rain poured through the gap and onto the driver, spreading across the seat and floor of the vehicle.

Trent's gaze flickered back and forth as his senses pulled in every detail in a quick assessment. Sleek black leather was polished to a perfect finish, and the smell of sweet, smoky cologne mixed with just a hint of copper. A song was humming on the radio, dark and thick with the promise of love. In the seat was someone who made his staggered breathing come to a halt.

The man looked nearly crushed beneath the wide, white airbag that was pressed to his chest. His eyes were closed, with his head tilted back to reveal a split lip that was quickly swelling. A drop of blood smeared down his lips to a sharp chin that was shaved clean except for a few stray hairs just under his lower lip. His head was as smooth as his chin, with the dark outline of ink against his skull.

The driver fluttered open his blue eyes, dazed and staring as he gazed slowly around the inflated interior. They settled on Trent before going wide with panic.

"Are you okay?" the stranger asked him, his voice strained with his chest still tight to the airbag that was slowly starting to deflate.

"You're asking me if *I'm* okay?" asked Trent. "Buddy, you were just in a car accident. Is anything broken?" There was blood on the man's forehead, but just a small smear. He could just be concussed and confused.

The man paled until he was almost the same white as the airbags. "I lost control and almost hit you," he said as he looked around the interior of the ruined car, apparently taking in the pierced leather and damp veneer. "I swerved, then I don't know what happened." He pushed at the airbag and it sprang back like a child's bouncy castle at the local fair.

Trent reached through the broken window, trying to avoid the prickling glass that stuck up from the ruined frame. He grasped the door lock from the inside and opened it with a quick jerk.

"Can you stand? We should get you out of there," said Trent as he pulled the door open. There was no smell of gasoline, only ozone and fresh rain, but he still expected that the car might explode at any moment. The airbag now hung like a shrivelled grape, revealing that the man was still buckled into his seat. His legs were folded, even with the spacious legroom, and his body was thick, filling every bit of available space.

"I think so." The guy took in the gathering crowd as he finally managed to get free from the airbag. He reached for the seatbelt buckle, but his shaking hands skimmed uselessly off the button.

"Here... Let me." Trent moved in close and hooked his hand around the belt, sliding down until he met the buckle. The scent of cologne and something else masculine filled his nose as he pressed close enough to feel the heat of the driver through his sodden clothing. His stomach flipped and his face flushed hot as he looked away from blue eyes. He felt for the little red button on the buckle and pushed hard. It was stiff in his trembling fingers and resisted his thumb.

He took a deep breath and couldn't suppress the shudder that made its way up his spine. The man smelled so good that it was going straight to his groin and shutting down what was left of his thoughts. His body responded against his will and he became aware of the press of his peaked nipples against sodden fabric, so sensitive and ready.

A second shiver wound up through his shoulders. His hand slipped from the buckle to touch the smooth fabric of the man's pants. It was soft and sturdy under his fingertips and looked more expensive than his entire soaked ensemble.

"You okay?" the stranger asked into his ear, so soft that it made his hair stand on end. He met blue eyes, watery and streaked with red, along with the strain of fear. It was the fear he saw that gave him the strength he was missing from his fingers.

"Just soaking wet and freezing. Sorry." He finally found the clasp again and the man was free with a persistent push. Trent drew himself out of the car and back into the beating rain. The heat left him as he pulled back, and he shivered in earnest this time.

"Yeah, sorry about that." The stranger grimaced and leaned forward as he grasped the yellow roof to pull himself out.

The car must've been sitting lower on the road than Trent had first realized. The man was absolutely massive. Trent was just under six foot himself, but he was still half a head shorter than the hulking figure. The stranger wasn't skinny either, but thick and broad like a football player who still had his pads on. Trent couldn't believe he'd managed to fit into such a fancy vehicle at all.

"I called the cops. They should be here soon," called one of the onlookers who had managed to wiggle in closer. Trent turned to the voice, giving her a nod of thanks when he recognized her as a local.

The stranger cursed as he looked back at his car. "This is why I shouldn't get new cars," he said with a shake of his head. He smoothed his hand over the hood, down to the crinkled corner that now looked more like an accordion than a fender. There was nothing of the headlight left except for a shell of plastic lined with metal and a shattered bulb.

"I really don't know anything about cars, but it doesn't look as bad as it sounded," said Trent as he followed him to look at the damage. Bits of glass dug into his bare foot as he made his way around. He glanced down to find his sandal floating just a few meters away, slowly making its way down the road in the streaming puddles. After he scooped it up, he slid it back onto his bruised foot.

"You're really lucky, though. I thought that feed truck was going to cream you," said Trent. Other than the dented corner, broken windows and smashed headlight, the car was in good condition. The SUV looked okay too, with just a hefty chunk out of the side.

"Is that what that was?" the stranger asked as he looked back along the road. The feed truck had pulled over to idle on the side of the road just before the light. The driver was already making their way back towards the Corvette.

"Shit." The stranger glared at the approaching driver. The man was short and round with a coat that was much too thick for the weather. The colour of his jacket ran dark from the rain.

"Everybody okay? I can't stop that quick with that old truck. New brakes, but the tyres are shit." The driver stepped closer. There was the underlying scent of wet cigarettes clinging to his clothes and his meagre hair was flecked with bits of unidentifiable soggy fluff.

"We're all good," said Trent. He looked at the Corvette driver, expecting a reply, but the man was silent. His hands were clenched into fists behind his back and he had drawn up to his full towering height.

"Okay, well, I'll take off then if everyone is fine. I'm already behind as it is." The driver took a step back as he looked between the two. Trent offered a weak smile before taking a half-step towards the group of gathering people.

"Yep, no problem. Thanks for stopping," said Trent as the driver turned away. He looked up to the man who was still bristling beside him. "Are you sure you're okay?"

The stranger deflated and turned to Trent with a grimace. "Yeah. I was expecting a fight."

"What? Why would he want to fight?" Trent looked around in confusion, then back to the retreating truck driver. He hadn't seemed threatening in the least. The stranger shrugged.

"Some of the places I've been, there's usually a fight when something like this goes down." He smoothed his hand back down the car and frowned again at the crushed light. He was completely drenched now, with every inch of black fabric clinging to his chest and biceps as if he were wearing nothing at all. Trent forced his eyes away from the clinging cloth.

"You aren't from around here then, I guess. Small town folks don't really care much for a fight unless they're getting paid for it." Trent looked to the license plate, noticing the strange image and lettering for the first time. "Wow, you really aren't from around here. Did you drive the whole way?"

"Three of the best days of my life," the man said with a smile. "Name's Ian. Thanks for your help, man. I appreciate it."

"Trent," he replied as he grasped the outstretched palm. Ian's hand felt so warm against Trent's, which was slippery from a mix of rain and a sheen of sweat. He was sure that his face was beaming red, hopefully hidden by the downpour.

"I'll stick around until the cops show up, just in case they ask any questions," said Trent. He leaned back against the side of the suburban and winced as his freezing shirt pressed against the only remaining warm spot on his back.

"Do you know any place I can get this baby fixed up?" asked Ian. "She's a custom, so I usually wouldn't let just anybody work on her, but I'm a bit out of my area here." Blue eyes glanced around and his lips pulled into a frown at the sight of the meagre buildings, looking from the cracked grout to the crumbling brick.

"There is an auto shop about one block that way." Trent pointed to the other side of the street. "It's after six o'clock now, though, and I don't think they're open again until tomorrow."

"Shit." Ian cursed and kicked the thin rubber tyre. "Any hotels then? I don't exactly know anyone around here either."

"Uh no, no hotels. No taxis either," Trent added. He crossed his arms and stuck his freezing hands under his armpits.

"I could just call a ride share." Ian reached back into the car to withdraw his phone from where it was stashed in the centre console. Trent risked a quick peek—just a peek—as the man bent over from the waist. His pants had started to cling as they soaked through as well, and they left very little to the imagination. Trent bit back the noise that tried to escape and forced his gaze away.

"Yeah, good luck with that," said Trent after quietly clearing his throat. "Welcome to the middle of nowhere. This coffee shop"—he pointed at the glass window that had mostly emptied of its patrons since the bustle had died down—"is the best one for fifty kilometres. I can say that because it's the *only* one within fifty kilometres."

Ian groaned and sank down along the side of the car until he was hunched on the kerb. "I think I took a wrong turn about two hours ago. I was supposed to be checking into the Marriott tonight."

Trent couldn't honestly think of the closest hotel that wasn't a small operation instead of a chain. Even they were few and far between. Most were closed until the summer began to ramp up.

Ian looked utterly defeated, and it was pulling at Trent's heart strings uncomfortably. His car was trashed, his body was bruised and his lip was still dribbling slow drops of blood. Ian's eyes closed and he leaned back against the car, *thunking* his head into the side.

Trent shifted from foot to foot before shoving his hands deep into his pockets. He could hear his mother's voice in his ear, telling him to make the situation right.

"You can stay with me for the night if you want," said Trent with a shrug as he tried to downplay how much he liked the idea. The eye candy alone could last him for a decade. Christ, he would have to give Ian some of his pyjamas. That ass inside of a pair of too-small track pants would be drool-worthy.

Trent shook his head and tried to clear the image from his mind before it could spiral out of control. "I'm just a few blocks away. It's only a one bedroom, but I can pull out the old air mattress." He would happily sleep on the air mattress and give up his bed to Ian. *Christ.*

"You don't have to do that. I mean, I almost hit you with my car," said Ian as he stared at Trent like he had sprouted a few extra limbs.

"But you didn't, and it's kind of my fault that you hit the suburban." Oh God, he sounded eager...way too fucking eager.

"That's a bit of a stretch," said Ian. His eyebrows couldn't get any higher at this point, and he had started to lean back with a touch of caution.

Trent shrugged, glancing away and trying to play it off as much as possible. "It's up to you." He sighed as he had the strangest craving for a cigarette. Stress and excitement did strange things to him, especially brief grazes with his mortality. He hadn't smoked since a one-week stint as a teenager. Every once in a while the need struck when the situation called for it.

"You know what? Sure. I'll take you up on that." Ian nodded.

Trent couldn't stop the smile that went wider as Ian smiled back. That simple gesture made the man's face light up in a way that went straight to his eyes. What was Trent thinking? A sexy hunk of a man in his house for the night? He'd never be able to keep his hands to himself. Well, he would, because consent was sexy, but it would be the hardest night of his life...literally.

"I'm gay though," said Trent. He blushed as soon as the words left his mouth. "If that's a problem, no big deal. I just don't want you to feel awkward."

Trent saw the sudden blanch, even as Ian tried to hide it, and it made his gut clench. Trent was out and proud of it, but every so often someone had a reaction to the news. Most people didn't care, but a select few did. Those few always managed to get under his skin and keep him awake at night.

"You don't have to stay with me. I'm sure you can find other arrangements," said Trent, backpedalling quickly to avoid any sort of awkward confrontation.

"No, sorry… I didn't mean…" Ian trailed off as he pushed himself off the kerb. "You just surprised me, that's all. Most places, you don't really say that to a stranger."

Trent opened his mouth, not really sure what he was going to say. Where the hell had this guy been where he fought random truckers and people had to hide six feet into the closet? He couldn't judge too harshly, though. The population of his tiny town was miniscule, and there were four churches smashed into it. Up until twenty years ago, no one would've announced it here either.

His thoughts were cut off by a piercing flash of lights as a police cruiser came around the corner and headed their way. He held out his hand to help Ian the rest of the way to his feet. The contact sent a wave of heat up his arm and under his jacket.

He bit back a sigh and turned to greet the officer.

I am so screwed.

Chapter Two

"What seems to be the problem here, gentleman?" asked the officer as he approached them. The officer looked from the corner of the Corvette to the dent in the parked car with a grim frown, before he looked to the two of them standing there. He faced Ian as if he somehow knew that he was the one who had caused the accident.

"Hey, Dan," said Trent with a small wave. "Long time no see." He smiled as he realized who it was. Dan was a good cop and a good man, who had moved up from Boston twenty years before in the pursuit of the quiet life. His wife, who hadn't seen a cow before in her life, had quickly fled back to her home in the city, leaving Dan with the mortgage and their two teenage children.

"Trent," said Dan, before reaching out to shake his hand. "Good to see you again, son. Does this machine belong to you?" He looked back to the yellow beast, his eyes moving along the sculpted edges that screamed money.

Trent shook his head and looked to Ian. The man had gone silent, his arms crossed defensively. Ian's eyes were narrowed and his forehead furrowed as he looked from Trent to the cop in confusion.

"He a friend of yours?" asked Dan as he looked at Ian with a raised eyebrow, obviously not impressed by what he saw.

"We actually just met," said Trent with an awkward laugh. "Uh, Dan, this is Ian. He owns the Corvette. And Ian, this is Dan. He came to my work when I accidentally called nine-one-one." Trent's mouth hung open as he struggled for what to say next. As for introductions, it was one of the strangest of his lifetime, but he wasn't willing to say any more than he already had.

"Ian," said Dan, taking control of the situation as his voice snapped into a professional tone. "My name is Officer Lorne, or you can call me Dan if you prefer. Can I have your first and last name, please?" He pulled a notepad and pen out of his pocket that looked like they had seen better days. The frayed edges of the paper soaked up the pouring rain in moments, spreading the ink across the page.

"Ian Reynolds." Ian answered in a clipped tone as his hands gripped into fists where they were tucked under his elbows.

"Okay, Ian... Is it okay if I call you Ian?" Dan waited for Ian's nod before he continued. "What happened to cause this situation here?" He motioned between the two cars, both of which had seen better days.

"I hit the puddle along the side of the road there," said Ian as he pointed at the spot where he had drenched Trent. It had filled back into a brimming pond as the rain continued to pour down on them. "My tyres must've lost traction because I just spun out of control. I turned the wheel and hit the brakes, but nothing seemed to work." Ian shuddered and closed his eyes for a moment.

"How fast were you going?" asked Dan, not even looking up from the damp pages this time.

"About twenty-five," said Ian. "Miles per hour." He added a second later.

Dan's pen paused and he looked up in confusion. Trent wondered when the last time was that the officer'd had someone answer in miles instead of kilometres. Probably during his time in Boston, but not since.

Dan lowered the notebook and took a step closer to the car, leaning over to examine the plates. "It's been a while since I've seen Florida plates. You here visiting family?"

Ian shook his head. "No family, not here at least. I just went for a drive."

Trent watched as the officer paused as if waiting for Ian to continue. Dan chuckled when Ian remained silent.

"That's one hell of a drive, son, but you've got the ride for it for sure. Trent, was there anything you wanted to add to Ian's statement?" Dan looked at Trent and Trent felt his stomach clench tight.

"No. That's what happened." Trent felt guilty as soon as he said it, even though it was the truth. Ian's gaze snapped to him with a look of surprise before he covered it with a frown.

"Well, I'll go track down the owner of the other vehicle. I expect he's in there doing the crossword puzzle," said Dan as he looked to the coffee shop. "I'll call in a tow truck to take your car over to the garage so you can get it fixed up." He nodded once and stepped past them to the coffee shop.

"Why did you lie for me?" Ian asked, pinning Trent with a gaze that pierced into his soul.

"I didn't." Trent took a step back and thought back to what had happened. It was true…every word.

"I almost hit you, but you didn't say anything." Ian leaned against his car and his whole body seemed to deflate against the surface.

"You aren't gonna get charged for splashing me with a bit of water," said Trent as he shook his head and let out a small laugh. This guy was unreal. "But I appreciate the concern." He walked over to the kerb and sat down on the solid surface. It was cold and wet, like everything else around him. A steady stream of water poured down the little valley and washed over his sandalled feet.

It didn't take long for a tow truck to arrive from around the block and hitch up the yellow convertible. Ian had tried to insist on driving it over himself, but Dan had waved him off. The airbag was still sitting deflated in the front seat, so the car was unsafe to drive. The suburban driver was surprisingly nice when he followed Dan out of the cafe with a half-drunk cup of coffee and bits of ice cream clinging to his thin upper moustache. The whole thing was like a slow-motion sitcom.

The rain petered off to a thin drizzle as the officer finally pulled away with his sodden notebook full of likely illegible writing. The rest of the crowd had cleared, and the suburban drove off in the direction of home. It left the two of them, Ian standing and Trent sitting, on the drenched deserted street.

Trent sighed in relief. "I hate talking to cops. It's like talking to a minister. Even if you didn't do anything wrong, you still feel guilty." He was soaked to the bone and shivering steadily. He tried to keep his teeth from chattering. The sun was starting to plunge along the horizon behind the thick wall of clouds, taking the last bit of warmth with it. His stomach grumbled and his eyelids were heavy from adrenalin withdrawal. "I'm going to head home. Are you still coming?" Trent asked as he turned to Ian.

Ian was watching as the last hint of yellow disappeared around the corner on the back of the tow truck. His short-sleeved shirt and long pants still clung to his soaked frame, only making the size of him stand out more. Trent suddenly felt much more awake.

"Yeah, I'm coming," said Ian as he finally turned. "I'm just trying to figure out how I got out of this without any charges." He shook his head as if he still couldn't believe it.

"Come on. I'm only a few blocks away. You must be as cold as I am." At least Trent had the hoodie, but even with that he was still chilled after being soaked. Ian was in nothing more than a T-shirt and long pants, but he hadn't complained once. Trent glanced at Ian's arm as he stood, to see if there were any goosebumps, but he got an eyeful of muscle instead. He gulped and looked away, focusing on the sidewalk beneath his feet.

Ian stepped in beside him without a word and their feet splashed in the small lingering puddles as their paces matched. Ian moved with a grace that was too smooth for a man of his size, and he was nearly silent except for the splashing water.

They turned a corner to the street that led to Trent's home. Most of the lawns were neatly clipped and their porches freshly painted crisp white, but one neighbour pulled down the property value of the entire street. His grass was higher than Trent's knees and the stems had gone to seed already. Beneath the blades were the leaves from the previous fall that were still clumped and unraked. The porch was made of crumbling concrete that had once had a green rug along the surface. All that remained were the frayed edges of black fibre that had been worn down by hundreds of feet.

There were only a few streets in the tiny town, but every single one of them seemed to have one bad egg. It was unfortunate that Trent had to pass this one every day on his five-minute walk to work.

Trent glanced up at Ian, who was looking ahead with a slight frown on his lips. The tattoo on the side of his skull swirled around the back like dark shadow etched permanently in his thoughts.

"Did that hurt?" Trent asked as he continued to stare at the ink, trying to figure out what it was exactly. The lines were faded with an outline of dark green that he imagined must've been black originally. He could see red and blue, but not much else.

Blue eyes cut towards him. "The accident? Nah, just my lip hurts where the air bag hit me." Ian puckered his lips then grimaced as the split started to seep again.

"I meant your tattoo. I've never had one before, but it looks like it would've hurt." Trent could picture the needles piercing into flesh in such a sensitive place with no padding between skin and bone.

"Oh, yeah." A large hand swept over the beads of moisture on his skull in a practised move. "Hurt like a motherfucker, but I was drunk off my ass, so that helped."

"Oh." Trent bit his lip in thought. He'd been drunk before, sure, but not enough to walk into a tattoo parlour and let someone permanently mark him. "I didn't think you could get that done if you were drunk—just like you can't get married if you're drunk."

"Money paves the way for most of that stuff." Ian said with a sudden sad smile. "I would've got it either way, but the alcohol just sped up the timeline."

Trent narrowed his eyes, finally able to see what the image was—a flag, twirling and rocking in an imaginary breeze. "An American flag?" He snorted.

"I'm patriotic." The sad smile lifted into something more generous.

"Do you think I'd look good with a maple leaf on my forehead?" asked Trent. He hoped he came out joking and not sarcastic. Sometimes his brain-to-mouth filter malfunctioned.

Ian's eyebrows rose as he pondered it for a second. "I don't think anyone would look good with that."

Trent laughed, a full-bodied thing that made his face flush and his eyes water. It wasn't even that funny, but he was relieved that he hadn't managed to insult someone he'd just met.

"You're right. There is something sexy about an American flag. This is me," he said as he pointed to his house. It looked tiny from the outside and was even smaller on the inside. 'Cosy' was how the real estate agent had described it. Trent preferred to call it 'easy to clean'. It had a large back yard, though, which more than made up for the lack of space within the house.

"I just have to check on something. Do you mind?" Trent looked back to Ian, who had stopped at the end of the pitted gravel driveway. Ian's eyes flitted back and forth over the house, from the long cracks in the siding to the worn stairs at the entrance. The lawn was trimmed, though, and the gardens were mostly weed-free.

"You live here?"

Trent felt his hackles go up at the tone and he turned to the man. "Yes, I do. Is that a problem?"

"No, it's just..." Ian trailed off. "Tiny. Sorry, I'm an asshole, forget I said that. I'm just tired." He looked down at the ground and hunched his shoulders as he kicked a toe against a bit of loose gravel.

"It's fine, just give me a minute." Trent said, his voice harsher than he'd intended. He knew it was tiny. Hell, he'd known that before he bought it. Ian's car was probably worth more than the purchase price of the house. It still wasn't nice to point that out, especially when he was going out of his way to help the guy. The potential eye candy was looking a little less drool-worthy.

Trent circled the house to the back yard that was hidden behind a towering eight-foot fence. The fence was crisp and new, each board painstakingly and perfectly placed — and so unlike the rest of the house. He grappled with the gate's slick latch before he managed to open it with a flick of his wrist to tug the tiny rope that fed through a hole in the board. His feet were soaked again from walking through the grass, and little blades stuck to every crevice in his toes.

"Hey, ladies!" he called out as he peeked into the back.

"You got a chick back here? I thought you said you were gay."

Trent started at the voice that came from right behind him. He turned to Ian with a smile at the wording. "Yeah, I guess you could say I've got a chick back here. Three, actually." The gate gave a rusty screech as he pushed it open the rest of the way.

The setting sun sent a trickle of light through the trees to sparkle on the dew-dropped grass. It was a good-sized space that was complete with a garden, a shed, as well as with his 'chicks'. Trent spent most of his time back here, sprawled across the lawn chair on the small stone patio.

The moment the gate opened, two feathery blurs darted towards them. Trent bent down to scoop the nearest one into his arms and she greeted him with an excited squawk before she tried to wriggle free.

"Hey, girlie. You're all wet." Her silver feathers were clumped to her thin neck, giving her an appearance similar to that of a turkey vulture. Her tail feathers somehow remained fluffy though. Dirt from her claws scraped against his already-soiled hoodie. "Someone's been digging in the garden again."

"You have chickens in your back yard? Holy shit, I am trapped in the boondocks." Ian's eyes darted around the space in something akin to terror.

Trent chuckled as he kissed the top of Lavender's head before releasing her. Pourquoi was already pecking at his exposed ankle bone, while Cadbury, the third chicken, was in the back corner of the yard, rooting in the compost pile.

"You want to pet her? She's super friendly," he asked Ian. Ian's terror had morphed into wide-eyed surprise and his hands were gripped into fists at his sides.

"Are you supposed to pet chickens? Don't they have diseases and stuff?" Ian shifted from one foot to the other as he looked at Pourquoi, who was already moving in close to inspect the unfamiliar shoe laces. He took a step back as she came within pecking distance.

"Here," Trent scooped up Lavender again and held her out. "Hold your arms up like you want to cradle a baby. Yes, like that." He moved in close before slowly lowering her into Ian's arms. His hand brushed against the warm, vulnerable skin inside Ian's wrist, tingling at the point of contact. With a tiny gasp, he pulled away as if he'd been bitten.

It was unlike anything he'd ever experienced. Trent had met and slept with attractive men before, but none of them had made him feel so out of his element. Trent was usually the suave Dom who could flirt and pick up any guy in a bar, while completely keeping his cool. Now, he felt like he might pop wood at any moment.

Dexterous fingertips carded through the damp feathers and tickled the tiny beard under Lavender's chin. Ian turned to him in shock. It was like the man had never seen a chicken before, let alone been to a petting zoo.

"She's so soft." Ian's voice was so deep and warm that it sent a thrill down Trent's spine. That tone was something that should've been reserved for the bedroom.

"Yeah," Trent cleared his throat. "That's Lavender. She loves pets. Pourquoi would be happy to peck you all day and Cadbury is a loner." He pointed off to the corner of the back yard, where Cadbury had found something layered in the dirt. "Can you hold her while I check on the horses?"

"Shit, you have horses too?" Ian cried, his eyes going wide before skimming around the yard again.

Trent burst out laughing, a bit of awkwardness disappearing. "Nope. I totally had you, man." He shook his head and wandered over to their small coop.

With Lavender sufficiently petted and their food topped up, Trent headed back around the house and inside. Ian followed him, looking back every few seconds to catch another glimpse of the birds.

Trent sighed as he finally set foot inside the warm, dry house. Without a second thought, he pulled his sweater and T-shirt over his head in one motion. Water flew from his hair as he tugged his shirt free, soaking his damp back and chest. The shirt was dripping onto the floor already, leaving a spreading smudge on the blue mat. He would have to wring it over the sink before he hung it over the back of his kitchen chair to dry. Or maybe he would chuck it straight into the laundry and hopefully the grit would come out.

The door clicked shut behind him, knocking him out of his train of thought. He looked back to Ian, who was still standing just inside on the mat, his soaked shoes leaving an imprint on the rug. Ian was staring at his naked chest with open surprise.

Trent bit his lip to smother a groan. Stripping at the door was something that he would do normally if he came home wet or gross from work. Dropping his clothes then heading for the shower was the highlight of his bachelor life. He was so tired that the move had been completely automatic.

Ian's eyes were burning bright, leaving him feeling completely naked as his gaze wandered up and down. There was a hint of pink on Ian's cheekbones that could've been real or part of Trent's exhaustion-induced imagination.

"Sorry," Trent said, unsure why he was apologizing. It was his house, after all. "I'm gonna have a shower. I'll make dinner once I'm out, and I'll see if I can find something that will fit you." There had to be something in the depths of his closet that would fit those shoulders.

"Did that hurt?" asked Ian. His eyes flickered down Trent's chest, where the silver barbel passed through his nipple.

"Like a motherfucker," said Trent, borrowing the phrase from Ian. The blush on Ian's face deepened into a rosy red.

"Were you drunk?" Ian's eyes flickered up to his face before going back to the piercing. Blue bled away to black.

The small bit of exhibitionist in Trent was loving the attention, and his dick twitched beneath the sodden layer of clothes. He shifted to angle away slightly, hoping that Ian hadn't noticed. *Talk about awkward.* "Stone cold sober. My sister convinced me to get it done on my thirtieth birthday."

"What if it gets caught on something? Ouch, man." Ian shook his head, winced and brought his hand up to touch his chest.

"I've only got it caught in somebody else's teeth, which really isn't that bad. Trust me." Trent wanted to smack his palm to his forehead in embarrassment. He looked up at the ceiling, willing the flush off his face. If a hole opened up in the earth right now, he would gladly jump in. "Do you want a drink?" Trent asked, trying to change the subject, but somehow still making it sound like a pick-up line. Getting changed was the priority, but he wasn't about to offer to get naked in the kitchen.

"I, um." Ian cleared his throat and seemed to shrink back a few steps. "I don't drink." He dipped down to tug the shoes from his feet, setting them at the side of the mat when he noticed the tray was already full.

"I meant water," said Trent, holding back a laugh that threatened to escape. He watched as Ian flushed and shrugged.

"I thought you meant something else. Usually when someone offers to buy me a drink, it's on the rocks." Ian shook his head and smiled.

"I would definitely buy you one if I had the chance, but I'll give you the free stuff from the tap for now, if that's okay." Trent turned away and nearly ran to the kitchen to get away from the words that he had just said. His mouth was running away from him and he couldn't seem to get it back under control.

Ian didn't look like he wanted to punch him when he came around the corner, but he certainly wasn't at ease either. He glanced from the old cupboards that squeaked every time they opened and closed to the blue speckled countertop that didn't match any kitchen decor in the known world. The small gas stove, which was Trent's pride and joy in the room, was stark white, but matched the fridge, at least.

Ian took the offered glass and polished it off in a few quick swallows. A bead of moisture dripped down his neck and his throat bobbed as he did. The sight made Trent suddenly wish he'd poured a glass for himself. He leaned back against the counter instead, still clutching his sodden shirt.

"Do you get offered drinks often?" asked Trent. Ian looked like a man who would have anyone flocking to him at the first sign of availability.

Ian looked Trent up and down as he set his glass on the counter next to the double sink. "Do you?" His eyes settled back on the piercing and he drew his lips tight.

"I always leave room for one more drink," said Trent. He needed to stop or there was no way he would get back to this side of sanity.

"Anyway, I'm heading to the shower. I'll be out in a few. Make yourself at home." Trent gripped his wet clothes tight to keep himself from doing anything he would regret later.

Christ, the way Ian was looking at him, with his eyes dark and his shirt stretched so tight across his chest, made him want to drop to his knees and start worshipping. But that would probably mean that he would start off his weekend with a broken nose, which was not the way he wanted it to go. Best to just shower and try not to think of the hunk of a man on the other side of the thin door.

Chapter Three

Trent pushed his back against the bathroom door and slid down the wooden surface until he was sitting on the cold linoleum floor. His head hit the door with a soft *thunk* as he let out a loud sigh. The room was tiny, with just enough space for a toilet, a sink and a small shower. The walls were light yellow — a colour he had picked out of a magazine. The countertop was a deep black speckled with silver tones that had been taking up space in a clearance section before it made the trip to his house.

"What the hell was I thinking?" he whispered into the quiet bathroom. The humming fan answered him with a steady warble. Ian was so far out of his league that he may as well have been on another continent. And by his reaction, the guy was definitely straight. Trent had no dinging gaydar, just forlorn longing for Ian to keep him company in the cold bathroom.

He pulled himself to his feet and peeled his wet pants off before letting them slide to the ground. They splattered on the fake tile.

He moved to his boxers next, pulling them down to let his cock free with a hopeful bounce. He was half-hard and well on his way to full mast with the way his thoughts had been turning. He could imagine Ian pulling his shirt over his head, revealing every inch of damp skin. Trent would've dropped his shorts right there in the hallway. He would've let Ian push him against the wall and slip his hand down the front of his boxers.

"Christ." Trent gripped his cock in his hand, now hard with a pearl of milky pre-cum at the tip. He tugged it once, hissing at the sensation before he forced his hand away. He couldn't jerk off with a stranger on the other side of the door — a stranger who was waiting in wet clothes that were cold and uncomfortable, wet clothes that clung to thick biceps like they were the best thing that they'd ever felt. They probably were. Those arms looked strong enough to lift Trent as though he weighed nothing. Something about that sent another thrill of desire down to his groin.

A six-foot figure like himself, strong and tall with deep brown eyes, was always expected to be the top and the leader in the bedroom and out. He was usually fine with that when he picked someone up at a bar or club. He would push into them and they would grip him like the best kind of home. He would set the pace and bring his partner to orgasm before he had his own, because getting them off was important to him.

Just once, he wanted someone to take care of him, to want him, to dominate him.

Trent shook his head and forced himself into the lukewarm shower spray. He longed to turn the temperature warmer but didn't want to empty the small hot water tank. It held just enough for him in a rushed onceover but would leave nothing behind for his guest. The water felt especially cold against his sensitive cock, which throbbed and twitched under the assault.

"Go away," he hissed through his teeth as he stared down at his cock. It didn't listen, simply bouncing along as he scrubbed with body wash. He gritted his teeth and tried to imagine a plethora of disgusting things, but his mind kept coming back to the stranger in his house.

The way Ian had blushed when Trent pulled his shirt over his head, and how his throat had bobbed as he swallowed long and hard... There was a look there, one that Trent hadn't imagined. For a brief second, there seemed to be interest...or at least curiosity.

He needed to get laid more often. He was obviously long overdue if he was imagining reactions like that to a little bit of skin.

"Shut up." He pressed his face to the cold shower wall. "Even if he's gay, there is no way he would be interested in you." He'd never been called sexy once in his life. Big...yes. Powerful...yep. But never attractive and never sexy. He was just a touch too gangly and his hair just a bit too brown to be anything but average.

The soft knock at the door was nearly lost to the sound of water pounding next to his head. The knock came again as Trent plunged his head under the stream of water, so while he thought he'd heard something, it really didn't amount to anything to pay attention to. When he pulled back, he nearly screamed at the sound of a voice so close.

"Was that an invitation?"

Trent peered past the grey shower curtain towards the sound. He clung to the fabric just to see if he was still awake and not in a dream. Ian was standing there, blocking the doorway with the width of his shoulders.

The top of his bald head was just shy of skimming off the door frame. His dark, clinging shirt was gone, leaving a stretch of bare skin behind. He looked like a fucking sculpture.

The tattoo on his head was not the only one. There was a dark swirling rose over his left pec and a smattering of words along his ribcage. The words were the freshest, still black and without the faded green quality the others had. Below the tat was a long scar that was still curled and angry red.

He could only be described as beautiful—but in a masculine way. Every bit of skin was tanned, with muscles spreading underneath, tight and strong. A full minute of open-mouthed staring passed before Trent realized that Ian had asked him something. Ian had shifted back in the silence and looked just about ready to close the door before Trent finally managed to speak again.

"Yes," he said, slow and slurred as if he was four quarters on his way to being drunk.

Ian smirked, stepping fully into the room and pulling at the buckle of his belt. There was no shyness or hesitation…only smooth confidence. It was like that word had changed something fundamental in the man, and Trent was finally seeing him for the first time.

Trent ducked behind the thin curtain and pressed his back into the cold wall. His cock throbbed at the mere thought of the man undressing on the other side. He couldn't bear to watch for fear of coming with the slightest touch.

A tightness settled into his gut at the same time. This was a stranger—a much larger and stronger stranger. He was fine with picking up guys who were smaller than him, as he always felt safe that he would never be forced. He knew nothing about this guy other than the car he drove. And now he was naked with nothing more than a five-dollar shower curtain between them.

"Is it okay if I come in?" Ian called from the other side of the curtain. His hand was already curled around the corner of the plastic, ready to pull it open at a moment's notice.

"Yes," Trent managed.

The curtain ripped back with a screech of cheap metal on metal. His vision was filled with tanned skin and curved muscles. Ian's chest was almost hairless, with a smattering of thin dark-blond curls between his pecs. The hair trailed down in a thin line to a neatly trimmed groin. His legs were covered in the same fine blond hair.

Trent settled on the prize that he had avoided looking at on the first pass. He always liked to save the best for last. It was the same reason he saved his red Smarties and green Skittles.

Ian's jutting cock was perfectly nestled within the blond hair. It was thick, hard and completely proportionate in every way. He was cut, and the mushroom head was already flushed bright red. The thick vein along the bottom of the shaft pulsed as it rapidly inflated.

He looked back up to Ian's face. The man was doing his own assessment, with his gaze trailing up and down Trent's body. He paused at Trent's hard cock and the looping piercing through the crown.

"Did you get that one before or after the nipple piercing?" Ian asked as he took his first step into the shower.

"Same day. They had two people working on me at the same time. They were afraid that I was going to pass out." Trent moved back along the wall and out of the way. It would be a tight squeeze with the two of them in the shower, but he would happily let Ian invade his space. Heat was rushing to his skin and painting his whole body a flushed rose.

"Shit, that's cold." The first spray of water hit Ian and he shrank back. His nipples went rock hard and his skin peaked from the sudden chill.

"Sorry." Trent reached for the tap and turned the temperature up to where it would normally be if he were alone. The move put his back to Ian, who was quick to move in.

"Were you thinking about me in here as you were taking a cold shower?" Ian mouthed at his ear as his chest met the length of Trent's back. Ian settled his large hands at Trent's waist before wrapping around and moving lower along the slick plane of skin. The man was a wall of heat and strength behind him.

"Yes." Trent bit off a moan as Ian went straight for his cock with a callused palm. The man held him with the perfect amount of pressure that was just on the right side of too much. One slide from base to tip and Trent was arching his back and thrusting his hips into the grip.

"I was thinking about you too when I was standing there out in the cold," said Ian as he moved down to mouth at Trent's neck. "You telling me on the street that you're gay and want to shack up for the night. Next thing I know, you're getting naked when we're just inside the door. I've never got so hard so fast."

"Fuck, please," said Trent as a hot mouth bit down on his shoulder. His cock throbbed and his stomach fluttered as he grew closer to the edge. "Can we go to the bedroom? Please?" He said the words that were usually being said to him.

He groaned as the hand lifted off his cock and reached for the knob. The water spluttered to a stop a moment later.

"Lead the way," said Ian as he moved.

Trent had never moved faster in his life. Not bothering to dry off, he grabbed Ian's hand and dragged him from the bathroom, careful not to slip on the linoleum. He rushed from the room and around the corner to the bedroom. It was a quick trip, of only a few short steps, but it seemed much too long.

The bedroom was just large enough to fit his queen bed, a single nightstand and a tall dresser that held most of his clothes. The bed was topped with a plethora of pillows and a fluffy duvet that only covered the far half of the sheets. Over the floor was an old carpet that had gone soft and thin from the abundance of foot traffic in its long life.

Turning to face Ian, Trent settled on the edge of the bed. Water soaked into his sheets as it dribbled down from his hair. He was sure that he looked like a wanton mess, completely drenched and hard, but he couldn't bring himself to care, not with Ian looking at him like he was.

Ian leaned down and Trent arched and tilted his head back to meet Ian halfway. It was sweet and light, a contrast to the heavy hands that had wrapped around him in the shower. The barest hint of moisture was left on his lips and it was enough to slick the way.

Ian swept a hot tongue along the seam of his mouth, begging for entry. Trent granted access with a deep groan. Ian swirled it into his mouth, tracing every inch with that smoky sweetness he thought was Ian's cologne. There was also the taste of distant cigarettes that had lost their bitterness and a natural flavor that was ripe like a fresh apple sliding across his mouth. Ian pushed in deep, forcing Trent to submit, even though he gave in willingly. His cock twitched again, lonely and forgotten against his belly.

Trent fluttered his eyelids open as Ian pulled back. Christ, the man was an amazing kisser. Ian's lips looked bruised already and tainted red where the split had opened just the barest hint. The sliver of a pink tongue crept out and licked the bead of moisture along his lower lip. His eyes were wide and so dark that there was almost no blue left. Ian groaned once before he leaned back in for more.

Their lips met, hard enough to bruise, and a wave of heat curled in Trent's mouth at the point of contact. He could see himself becoming addicted to this — the perfect touch, slick and domineering, and the perfect taste.

Trent lifted his hands to thread into the other man's hair. It was an automatic move, although he was usually the one pressing down from above. He met slick skin instead of the locks that his mind had been expecting. He jolted, sliding his fingers along the flesh, but unsure of what to do. The skin was soft, surprisingly so, with no scratch of stubble against his fingertips. There was no anchor to hold on to, to keep himself from becoming lost in the sensations. He could only feel and will himself not to become overwhelmed.

He dropped his hands back to his own naked thighs to hold the soft spot just above his knees. Ian had moved in between them and was pushing him down and back into the mattress. His stomach muscles screamed from the strain, but Trent wasn't willing to be the one to break contact to flop back on the bed.

"Put your hands around my neck," said Ian as he pulled back to nibble on Trent's lower lip. He licked along the seam before he sealed their lips together again and pushed back inside. His hands were braced on either side of Trent and holding his bulk just out of reach.

Trent shot his hands up to the man's neck and grasped his own wrist around the sturdy column. It was exactly what he'd needed. He pulled Ian down to him, matching every thrust of his tongue and pushing their chests together. Naked skin met with a flash of heat and tingle of sensation.

Ian moved his warm hands from their place against the sheets to slide along his legs. The man was strong enough to hold them both partially aloft with no effort at all, even as Trent tugged hard at his neck. Those callused palms started just above Trent's knees, before twisting underneath him and sliding back to his ass. He grasped the cheeks softly, spreading them apart to expose Trent's sensitive hole. The comforter shifted and brushed along his seam, making him moan at the tickling sensation.

The groan seemed to snap something in Ian, who went suddenly still against his lips. He pulled back, licking the string of spit that still connected them, his eyes dark and wanting.

"Scooch up along the bed," said Ian in that low voice Trent had only heard once before.

Trent relaxed his hold and hurried back, scrambling to follow the order. He fell against the comforter, which soaked the last of the water from his skin. Ian was flushed red across the bridge of his nose and all the way down his chest to his curved cock that was now leaking steadily. Trent's dick throbbed, needing those hands back on him, but he was terrified that a simple touch would make him come. He'd never been more turned on in his life.

"Eager?" Ian smirked, already knowing the answer. "Do you have any stuff?" His hand went to his cock and stroked a few times, smearing pre-cum across the mushroom head and slicking the way for his palm.

"In the side table," said Trent. His legs trembled as it finally sank in. He was going to have sex with this stranger in a way that he'd never had sex before — the first man to top him, and he only knew his name. His legs shook harder, no longer a chilled shiver but getting closer to outright panic.

"You okay?" Ian paused on his way to the drawer, eyeing Trent's trembling with concern. "We don't have to do anything else if you're not comfortable. I'll stop if you need me to."

"No, I want you," said Trent, needing this man more than ever. "Just go slow. It's been a while." A partial lie. He'd never been penetrated, not even with toys. He'd never found much appeal to the feeling of plastic in or around his ass. It was too cold, too impersonal and never managed to replicate the feeling he really desired. Even his own fingers had lost their appeal after a few tries. He was too focused on the pressure against his fingertips and how he squeezed around them, to notice the sensation of being penetrated. And he'd never been able to reach his prostate, even when he was buried knuckle-deep.

The drawer rattled as Ian swept through it, searching for the lube Trent kept there and the few foil condom packets crinkled together. Trent hoped that they weren't expired. He usually went out and stocked up if he was in the mood, and that hadn't happened for a few months.

"Disappointing," said Ian as he shook his head. His hand swept through the drawer again, adding to the already disordered clutter. "You can usually find some pretty cool stuff in a bedside drawer — vibrators, toys or at least some porn mags." He pulled out a few items and tossed them to Trent. "Condoms, lube and earphones. Seriously disappointing, Trent. Where's the kinky shit?" His smirk widened as he crawled to Trent. He grabbed the lube on the way, glancing at the bottle as he moved closer.

"This stuff isn't really great for what I want to do," said Ian as he turned the label over to inspect it.

"What do you mean? Lube is lube." Trent grabbed the bottle from his hand, before looking at the label. "There's nothing wrong with it. It works great." For jerking off at least. He'd bought the stuff on sale a few months before when he was just looking for something to ease the way of his hand.

"Maybe for jerking off." Ian moved in closer as if he had read Trent's mind. He dragged a hand up the inside of Trent's thigh, chuckling as Trent twitched and stifled laughter. "You need long-lasting stuff for good sex. This stuff will dry out too quick."

"Oh," Trent trailed off as lips pressed against his. His reply was left unsaid. He'd never brought anyone back to his place, as he preferred to go to a partner's. They always had the right kind of lube, apparently, and Trent would bring his own condoms. It made them feel safer with him, and he didn't have to worry about them tracking him down for a second date. Ian was the first man, other than himself, to ever see inside that drawer at all or touch the bottle. The condoms were there, simply because there was no space left in the bathroom drawer to store them.

"Don't worry. I'll go slow and keep you wet."

Trent groaned and surged against Ian's sweet lips. The man pushed him back until he was fully pressed against the comforter. A larger body covered his with a damp slide of sweat and heat. One hand threaded through his hair, but the second was absent.

Trent tried to track it, but he was overwhelmed by heat and pressure. Ian pressed his hips between his splayed thighs and lined up their cocks. The first touch of smooth, hot skin against his own had him letting out a startled cry. It was so good, and so much better than grinding down from above, where he would set the pace and pressure.

The heat disappeared as Ian lowered his lips to Trent's neck and latched on to his collar bone with sharp teeth. Trent thrust his hips up until his cock was rubbing against the smooth skin of a toned belly. The skin was flat and hard, but there were no mounds of defined muscles that could be found in a body builder. If Trent rutted hard enough, he could feel the dips and peaks of the hidden six pack beneath the thin layer over the top.

Trent didn't even realize that his legs were being pushed wider until he was completely exposed. His mind was set on a simple goal, and between nipping teeth and the press of his cock, he couldn't focus on anything else.

Ian bit at his nipple before his teeth snagged at the edge of his piercing. He arched into the sensation as he gripped Ian's head and pulled him closer. He slid his fingertips over the smooth surface of his skull and the even skin where he knew the tattoo lay.

The teeth latched on harder, fed by his enthusiastic encouragement. At the same time, a slick finger swept over his exposed hole.

Trent jumped at the sudden and unexpected assault. He hadn't even heard the tell-tale click of the lubricant lid when Ian had opened it. His legs pressed on either side of Ian as Trent tried to close them, feeling suddenly embarrassed and exposed.

"Shhh, it's okay, T. I'll go slow." Ian's lips snagged against the piercing as he spoke. "I'm getting the appeal of the nipple piercing now. You're so sensitive for me."

Trent hummed in reply as he loosened his fingers where they'd dug into Ian's neck. He pulled back to tongue over the metal bar, flicking the budded nipple back and forth.

"I fucked this girl once who had her nipples pierced," said Ian as he moved to the other side of Trent's chest. This nipple was unpierced, but peaked and hard already. "She wouldn't let me touch them at all. It hurt her too much."

"Feels good," Trent slurred and forcibly pulled the man back to the piercing. "I like it when you bite it." He groaned as Ian did just that.

The finger that had circled his pucker for the last minute suddenly pressed inside. The slide was smooth from the ample slick and Trent's overall relaxed state. It was wholly and completely different from when he'd tried it on himself.

He could feel everything, from the light scratch of Ian's nails to the ridges and bumps along the thick girth of his finger. The finger was hot, maybe even hotter than his body temperature, and it felt almost scalding inside him. It pressed in slowly until it gradually buried itself all the way in.

"Fuck, you're so tight," Ian mumbled against his chest with a groan. "I'm not sure if I'm gonna fit if you keep clenching like that."

"Sorry," said Trent automatically. He took a deep breath in the same way that he had told so many men beneath him to. His body relaxed and the strange feeling started to fade.

"Don't apologize. It's a good thing, really good. Nothing worse than fucking a loose slut."

Trent tensed under the words, his body going tight again. The single finger inside suddenly felt too big for him. *Slut.* That wasn't what he was at all.

"Relax, T, and take another deep breath for me." Ian moved up and pressed his lips to Trent's. He forgot the harsh words as the man started to move.

Ian curved his finger and pressed along his walls in a slick motion that made him burn. The slight drag along his rim was startling with how good it actually felt. The digit pulled out and returned a moment later, dripping with slick gel. It slid in so easily that the burn completely disappeared, leaving a vague pleasurable feeling of fullness behind.

"That's better. You're doing so well. You're so tight for me, T."

Ian dragged his teeth down Trent's chest to nip at the soft expanse of skin just above his belly button. He wasn't toned the way Ian was, but he had managed to stave off the paunch that affected so many men as they approached their mid-thirties. Next to Ian's body, though, he looked skinny and soft.

A slick tongue slipped into his belly button as a second finger joined the first. It slid in slower, matching the leisurely licks on the sensitive divot of his belly. With a twist and a press, Ian slid up to his knuckles with two fingers.

"Now if I can just find it," the man mumbled as he twisted his hand. Ian flexed his forearm and bunched his tanned shoulders with a seemingly single-minded focus.

For a moment Trent forgot what the man could've meant. A second later, heat fizzled at the base of his belly and he arched up with a cry.

"Found it. It's deep, real deep, baby. Bet no one's been able to reach it for you like this before." The words brimmed with confidence as they were growled into his skin. Ian's smile revealed his teeth at the sound of Trent's cry.

"No, never." Trent cried out again through his bitten lips. He gasped for air as the sensation came again when Ian's slick fingers slid over his sensitive prostate. He'd taken men apart under him by doing the exact same thing, but he'd never felt it for himself. The rush was so sudden that he was instantly on the edge of coming.

"I'm gonna come." Trent gripped the blanket hard in one hand and Ian's neck with the other.

"No, you aren't," Ian chuckled as he tapped against that spot inside over and over.

Trent groaned as his cock twitched and jumped, but his release stayed just out of reach. He bucked his hips, but Ian had moved up to hover over him, so he only met air. He was so close, but Ian was right. There was something there that was blocking him from taking that last step. It was so good that it nearly hurt.

A third finger slid home with a slick twist. Ian pulled back just a bit, so he was too shallow to continue his steady assault. Trent let out a sigh of relief, which quickly turned to a wince. The three fingers were broad. Almost as broad as Ian's cock. They stretched him farther than he'd even been stretched before. His body was opening, but it was resisting and refusing to relax under the pressure.

His breath hissed through his nose as he tried to let go. It stung like an itchy wound on his most vulnerable area. Even with all the lube in the world, it was still too big to be comfortable.

But Ian persisted. He spread his fingers and curved them against his walls, lighting up his nerves until he was relaxing again. The sting faded to an ache, then to an overwhelming pressure. Before he realized it, he was rocking back his hips onto the digits as he tried to press them deep to move against his prostate again.

"I'm ready. I want you now," Trent found himself saying as his cock started to throb in time with his heartbeat.

The crinkle of foil was followed by the barely audible click of the bottle of lube. The fingers retreated as Ian moved up his body to hover over top. Ian brought his hands up to his thighs and pushed him wide open. Trent revisited his natural urge to try to snap his thighs shut, but just managed to resist.

Ian pressed his lips against his as a blunt slickness pressed between Trent's cheeks. He flexed as he braced himself over Trent's body and started to push.

Impossibly, Trent's body yielded as if it was made for this. There was pressure at first as he clenched down, but Ian's cock was unyielding. It pressed in, and in, until Trent could hardly think, let alone do anything but feel. Just before he thought it might break him, Ian settled his hips against Trent's.

"Fuck, you're so tight, T. Ease up a bit for me," said Ian as he leaned back to hover over him. His eyebrows were knitted together in concentration. "That's it. You're doing so good. Are you ready for me?" Ian grabbed the lube and dribbled another stream where they were connected.

Trent nodded then gasped as Ian pulled almost all the way out before pushing back in to the root. When he pressed back inside, Ian flexed his hips to bury himself as deep as he could go, then ground up as his cock jumped inside. The head of his cock slipped past

Trent's prostate as he pulled out for a second time. When he slid back inside with a quick thrust, he nailed the bundle of nerves head on.

Trent shouted as he was brought to the edge of pain, awash with toe-curling pleasure. His body clamped down, milking Ian as he tried to withdraw again.

"Fuck, T, ease up. Fuck." A tinge of pain drifted through Ian's voice as he withdrew.

"Sorry," said Trent as he trembled from the absolute overload. His legs were shaking hard and he swore he felt tears at the corner of his eyes.

"It's okay. You're just so tight. I didn't think you'd be that sensitive. Is this your first time or something?" Ian's dark eyes, which were blown wide with lust, narrowed in concern.

Trent nodded and turned his head away from the man as his cheeks blazed.

Ian let out a wounded groan. "Why didn't you say something? I could've made it so much better for you. Hell…" He trailed off, dragging a hand over his scalp as he rocked back on his heels. He eased his cock out of Trent, leaving an empty ache behind. "Roll over. It'll be easier that way."

Ian nudged his hip and Trent found himself rolling. He grabbed a pillow and pressed his face gratefully to it. It soaked up the tears that had managed to fall and muffled a small sob. His cock was still throbbing, so painful and neglected, but his mind was racing. Being called out like that in the middle of something so intimate… It was something horror stories were made of.

"It's not my first time. Not really. I'm always the one on top," said Trent, struggling to get the words out past the pillow. They sounded weak, even to his own ears.

"It's okay." A warm kiss settled in the middle of his back as two hands swept down his sides. He spread his legs as the hands urged him wider so the heat could settle behind him. The position made the hairs rise on the back of his neck, so he pushed himself up to his hands and peered over his shoulder.

Ian was spreading another layer of lube over his covered cock and lining himself up. His eyes were half-lidded and so dark that there was hardly any colour left at all. He simply stared at his goal with a dazed look and bit his lip hard enough that the freshly healed split began to bleed again.

Ian pressed in with a single smooth motion. It was so much easier in this position that Trent let out a sigh of relief. He felt more open and relaxed with the angle, and it didn't threaten to hammer against his prostate again. Instead, the large cock slid safely by with only the barest hint of toe-curling heat. When Ian settled deep, Trent could feel every inch of him against his sensitive nerves, but the pain was gone.

Ian grasped his hips and pulled him back as he thrust inside again. It drove a small grunt from Trent and a gasp as the sensation sweetened. He suddenly wanted it harder, deeper and hotter. He rocked back, meeting the next thrust with full force. Their skin slapped together with a startling noise in the quiet bedroom.

"Harder," said Trent as he dropped his head down between his arms. Ian responded instantly and snapped his hips to drive himself deep. Trent felt the first part of his orgasm start to unravel as the cock twitched within him. He snuck a hand between his legs to grasp his cock, but it threw him off balance with the force of the thrusts behind him.

Ian moved with the fall, grabbing Trent's leg and lifting it up. Ian's cock slipped out of him and he groaned from the loss. Ian straddled one of his legs and brought the second one up until he was forced to roll onto his side. After a moment of fumbling around the sheets, the blunt head was pushing back into him, slicked again with fresh lube.

The position was good. It let Ian thrust deeper into Trent and brush slightly harder against his bundle of nerves. It wasn't the brutal onslaught from before, but the perfect combination of power and pleasure. Even with his legs splayed so far apart, Trent didn't feel a single moment of shame or embarrassment. His face was flushed with pleasure instead.

"I'm going to come. You ready for me, T?" Ian's hips stuttered against him.

Trent's cock flexed at the man's words, so close that it actually hurt. Ian crept a large hand down his thigh and skimmed across his groin to his cock, circling him with his fingers and jerking twice before he started to shoot.

"Fuck," Ian cursed above him as he pumped his hips and tightened his grip.

Trent clamped down on the large cock inside him as it thrust deep one last time. He could feel every vein and bump as the cock twitched and poured into the sheath that separated them. He ground back against it to move it over his prostate and prolong the pleasure.

Ian pulled out with a sigh and fell to the side of the bed with a muffled grunt. Trent winced at the sudden emptiness. He reached back, his fingers prodding at his loosened furl. The edges were hot and sensitive to the touch as he skimmed along them. He could dip inside so easily with his fingertips. It was smooth and warm, and it still tingled from the overload. His hand came away dripping with thick lube that was already drying on his fingertips.

He let it fall away and collapsed to the side on the queen-sized bed. The orgasm had drained the energy from his limbs, leaving him loose and warm in the chilled room. His heart was thudding as it tried to catch up, but his breath was calm. He watched Ian through half-lidded eyes as he waited for the man to say something. Now that it was over, a looming force was making itself known. If Trent were in Ian's position, this would be his cue to get cleaned up then head out. Something about that terrified him.

Ian grimaced as he pulled the condom off his softening cock. He tied it off and looked around the room for a second before he set it on the bedside table. A little frown settled on his face as he performed the movements with automatic precision. Trent wondered dully if he was just another notch on this man's bedpost. He'd certainly made a point of expressing his experience.

"Crap," Ian's frown deepened as he looked over at Trent, his eyes settling on his groin. "I forgot to play with that." He motioned to the piercing. "Next time."

The weight lifted from Trent's chest as he broke into a laugh.

Chapter Four

He showered again in record time, only lingering to remove the thick lube and cum that had dried on his chest and thighs. The water still ran cold and almost immediately leached the blush from his skin. When he stepped back into the bedroom, Ian was scrolling through his phone with a dim smile. His discarded clothes were on the bed next to him instead of on the floor in the hall, but he'd made no move to put anything on.

"You're up in the shower. If you give it a few minutes, it should be warm again," said Trent as he pulled a dry T-shirt over his head. He skimmed through the drawer, looking for something that would fit Ian. "Wait! Didn't you have a suitcase with you or something if you were traveling?"

"No, just a day bag, and I forgot that in the trunk." Ian glanced up from his phone. "I wasn't really expecting to take a trip. I just got in the car and drove. Hotels have laundry services, toothpaste and all that crap. I didn't need much else."

Trent swept to the bottom of the drawer, pulling out a shirt that he knew didn't fit him. It had been from his mother for his birthday the previous year. She had bought something that she knew to be a size too big, declaring that he could simply grow into it during his next growth spurt. He would always be a growing teenager in her eyes.

He tossed the shirt to Ian, who caught it with his left hand without looking, while he continued to scroll though his phone with his right.

"You right-handed or left?" Trent asked as he crouched down to his pants drawer.

"Ambidextrous."

"How does that work for jerking off then?" Trent smirked as he pulled out a pair of too-large sweat pants and threw them at Ian.

Ian laughed, tossing his phone across the bed and catching the pants with his right hand this time. "Maybe I don't have to jerk off."

The heavy feeling settled back into Trent's gut, but he quickly shrugged it off. "Even married guys jerk off. They probably jerk off more, actually."

"Not married." Ian grunted and pushed himself off the bed. He stepped up to Trent, pushing him back and crowding him against the dresser. He pressed his lips to Trent's smiling ones, then he slipped his tongue into Trent's mouth with no preamble.

Trent groaned, going to his tiptoes and wrapping one hand around Ian's neck to pull him closer. The man pulled back with a smile that lit up his eyes. "You saved me from having to jerk off tonight. My hands appreciate the break. They were starting to get calluses."

Trent remembered those calluses and how they felt against his cock. "I'm not complaining."

Ian pulled away and disappeared around the corner and into the bathroom. Trent watched his ass disappear then wiped a drop of drool from the corner of his mouth. Maybe he should just hide the clothes while Ian was in the shower.

"Towels are under the sink," Trent called. He couldn't help but follow the man's path, peeking at him as he slipped behind the curtain. His dick twitched again as it recovered in record time. He considered pulling his shirt back off and ducking behind that curtain to slide up behind Ian. He was already open and it wouldn't take much for him to get fully hard again.

His stomach grumbled, ending his train of thought before he was half-hard. He needed food if he was going to be up for the promised second round. He turned away, pulling on a pair of pants and tucking himself safely away before he stumbled to the kitchen. He managed to throw together a quick dinner before he heard the shower turn off. By the time Ian appeared, looking damp and utterly delicious, Trent had a meal on the table for them.

"That smells so good. What is it?" Ian peered down into the bowl, taking the spot that Trent usually reserved for himself. Trent stopped the immediate retort and went to sit at the end of the table instead. It was awkward sitting in a chair with a new view of the same kitchen that he'd known for years.

"Pad Thai." He lowered his eyes to his bowl before taking his first bite. "It has peanuts. Sorry, I didn't think to ask if you had any allergies." Ian was already chomping down on a second bite and hopefully not going into anaphylaxis.

"No worries. This is freaking good, T. I thought you said there weren't any restaurants around here. Where did you get it?" Ian spoke through the noodles as he shovelled a third bite into his over-full mouth.

T. Ian had called him that once before, and he hadn't minded. Now, with Ian's mouth overflowing and bits of rice noodle sticking to his chin, it grated on Trent. It was fine to be called something else in the bedroom, although anything demeaning was a huge turnoff for Trent, but Ian hadn't even asked if the nickname was okay. He took a deep breath before taking another bite. He was getting hangry.

"T?" Ian paused, swallowing a big gulp of food. The sauce glistened on his slightly-swollen lower lip. It made him look kissable, even if he was being borderline rude. Trent gave in to the need to feel those lips again, leaning forward and pressing firmly against them. He swiped his tongue through the sauce, dipping inside for a split second to taste the sweetness mixed with Ian's natural taste. He laved at the raised bump where Ian had split his lip on the airbag. It was hot and metallic.

"I made it," said Trent as he pulled back. Ian flushed red from the simple kiss and his eyes went dark. The Pad Thai was apparently momentarily forgotten.

"Any other hidden talents I should know about?" Ian whispered as he moved back in close. Their lips met again in a sloppy kiss, their teeth clacking from the awkward angle.

It was Trent's turn to blush. Pad Thai wasn't a talent. It was one of the easiest things he knew how to make. There were a lot of recipes that came through his kitchen, and this one had stuck around, changed and quirked, until it was perfect.

"You'll just have to find out," said Trent, who immediately flushed hotter. That made it sound like he expected Ian to stay longer than just one night. "I mean, not really. It's not really a talent. I mean, I can sing—not well or anything—but I'm good at remembering lyrics. Usually I can hear a song once and be able to remember all the words, even months later. Same with movies. I'm crazy good at remembering movie lines." Trent stared down at his bowl and forced his mouth shut so he didn't start another round of word-vomit.

"So, you're good at charades and copyright infringement." Ian rocked back and arched one eyebrow.

If Trent's face got any hotter, it might be permanent.

"You aren't very good at taking compliments, T. Just relax. Dinner is good, really good. Thank you." Ian smiled, scooping up another forkful of the cooling dinner. He wrapped his lips around the fork and sucked it clean with a slurp.

The man's messy eating habits and slutty remarks were forgotten with those two beautiful words. A smile spread across Trent's lips as he glanced up through a short curtain of hair.

"Your welcome."

They ate quickly, urged faster by their awakened hunger, before they gravitated to the living room. The space was oblong and just large enough to fit a two-seater couch and a modest television on the other side of the room. The couch only had one end table on the side that Trent usually gravitated towards. The other side was crisp and as squishy as the day it had been delivered.

Ian took a seat, guessing the side right this time. Trent had to smile as the man bounced gently against the padded cushion before feeling the smooth leather.

"A gift to myself when I got a new job," said Trent as he took his seat. He moved his hand along the leather, petting down the conditioned surface. It was smooth and perfect but had cost him way too much. He'd almost walked away from it in the store, but it was literally the most comfortable couch he'd ever sat on. He could melt into it after a long day at work, and his headache would simmer away to nothing.

"What do you do?" Ian perked up, glancing around the room. There were a few paintings on the wall that were cheap things from discount sections and garage sales that had caught Trent's eye at the time.

"Network administrator. Sounds fancy, but it really isn't. I mostly fix other people's computer disasters all day," said Trent as he shifted on the couch. Their legs were touching from hip to calf, and there were only a few inches to breathe between their shoulders. He noticed that the pants he'd given Ian were too small and had ridden halfway up his ankle like flood pants. The T-shirt was better and not quite stretched to its breaking point across his broad shoulders.

"What do you do, Ian?" Trent grasped the remote from the side stand drawer, flicking on Netflix.

"Oh," Ian shifted uncomfortably, glancing up at Trent strangely. "I thought you knew. That's why you invited me back to your place."

"What? Why would I know you? I mean, we don't even live in the same country. I don't even know my neighbours all that well." Trent gave Ian a confused look before he noticed the tension in the man and focused on the screen instead. Ian's name had sounded familiar now that he thought about it. Lots of names were familiar, though. In his hometown, most people were distantly related and many shared the same last name.

"Just kidding, man. My mother always told me not to bring home strangers, but you must've missed that lesson." Ian smiled, but it didn't reach his eyes. The tension in his shoulders didn't relax either. "I'm a percussion specialist."

Trent heard the vague title and imagined a group of people hammering nails with different items to determine their quality. "Sounds interesting." It really didn't. It would explain the delicious amount of muscling that Ian had though, and why he had such a great tan.

Despite just finishing dinner minutes before, Trent excused himself to pop up some popcorn. As the microwave started to hum, he heard a distant ringing coming from the direction of the bedroom.

"Ian, is that your phone?" he called into the living room. Ian had shifted on the couch and brought up the recliner while he searched through Trent's library for something to watch.

"Just let it ring. I'm ignoring my boss right now," he said without looking up from the television.

"If they are anything like my boss, good luck," said Trent. "He is the most persistent bastard on the planet. Can't even get a day off without going through the gears a dozen times. And when I finally do get a day off, he's calling me the whole time, asking me to fix shit when I'm not even there." Trent poured the steaming popcorn into two bowls and brought them back to the living room.

The dull hum of a movie was already playing in the background. Trent took a quick glance at the screen before shuddering. This was definitely not on his watch list or anywhere remotely near it.

"This okay? I've been meaning to watch it, but I haven't had time lately," Ian asked before turning up the volume. The suspenseful music started to peak and a woman screamed on the screen. Ian had moved again to sprawl across the couch, taking up enough space that they would have to be touching completely to sit side by side.

"Yeah, I guess. I don't usually watch horror movies. I get too many nightmares." Trent handed him a bowl of popcorn and squeezed onto his side of the couch. He leaned on the arm, giving Ian more room to sprawl without having to plant awkwardly against his side. Ian gave him a side-long glance, before shifting further into Trent's space.

"I can put something else on if you want," Ian said with a playful smirk as he rested his hand across Trent's leg. The heat of his palm was scorching through the fabric.

"No, it's okay, just, yeah." Trent gave up on keeping his personal space and leaned into Ian. He fell against the other man's chest and let his head rest at the level of Ian's collar. It should've been awkward, as snuggling usually was for Trent. Then again, he'd never actually wanted to snuggle with anyone before.

They'd already slept together, so hopefully Trent would be less embarrassed when he inevitably got hard from the proximity to the delicious man. Even after using Trent's body wash, Ian still managed to smell exotic.

"I'll keep the nightmares away tonight," Ian said before he pulled Trent even closer. "You really don't know who I am?" Ian whispered against his scalp. The words were so quiet that Trent wasn't sure if he was supposed to hear them or not, so he let them slip by. He set his popcorn on the ground so he could snuggle in closer. Ian set his own bowl next to the couch so his hands were free to roam.

The movie picked up with screaming and jarring music, but Trent could hardly hear it, let alone focus on the screen. Instead, the steady thump of Ian's heart grounded him, taking away the utter terror he would normally feel the moment a horror movie appeared on the screen. Even the commercials would usually keep him awake at night, lurking under every shadow.

Ian dipped his hands down Trent's back to hold his hips, and soon he was stroking slow circles over Trent's skin. Ian dipped callused fingertips beneath the hem of his shirt and moved up. He broke out in goosebumps and shuddered against Ian's chest.

"You sure this movie's okay?" Ian mumbled against his hair.

"Yeah." Trent's voice was scratchy and he suddenly longed for a glass of water. His popcorn was just out of reach but he didn't think he would be able to swallow it anyway. Ian only hummed in response.

A problem was circling with every pass of warm hands over him. At some point, from the lingering touches and the warmth of Ian, Trent had gone from interested to fully invested. He'd shifted down until he was half lying and half sitting against Ian, and his groin was pressed right against Ian's leg. He'd managed to roll his hips back and keep from pressing into the beckoning warmth, but the pressure was mounting fast. As Ian dipped warm fingers beneath his waistband, Trent let out a groan and his hips humped forward of their own accord.

Ian froze before he looked down at him with surprise. His eyes went dark as they noticed the obvious flush on Trent's face and the tent in his sweatpants. There was nowhere to hide under the flexible fabric.

"I don't know if I can go again so soon," said Ian as he glanced between Trent and the screen. He was already moving a hand down to cup one of Trent's cheeks in a firm grasp while he splayed his legs wide, inviting Trent in.

"Only one way to find out," said Trent, biting his lip in embarrassment at his lewd words. Something about Ian forced words through Trent's lips that would normally remain silent.

Trent shifted and brought his leg over Ian's lap so he was straddling him. He sank into the soft cushion as he settled over strong thighs that could easily support his weight. The recliner snapped down and Ian was suddenly much more solid beneath him. The position put Trent at the perfect height to bring their lips together.

He moaned into the kiss that went from innocent to filthy in seconds. Ian sucked Trent's tongue into his mouth, twirling it with his own before he retreated to nip at Trent's lips. Trent gripped the base of Ian's neck, now used to the smooth surface instead of the expected hair.

Ian flexed a heavy hand on his ass before dipping it lower and brushing against his hole with unerring accuracy. He pressed two fingers just inside the slight gape, unable to go far without lube. Trent threw his head back as he ground his hips down and back into the fingers while his cock bumped against Ian's. Ian wasn't fully hard, but he seemed to be swelling quickly as Trent rubbed against him.

Ian pushed the waistband of Trent's pants down and his cock sprang free with a slight bounce. The small piercing shimmered in the low light, along with the few drops of pre-cum that had started to leak from the head.

"I'm not going to forget to play with you this time." Ian grinned into his mouth, eyes flickering down to the piercing. "Are you clean? I want to go down on you."

Trent took a deep breath before he was able to answer. "Yeah, I got tested after my last relationship. That was about a year ago. I can get a condom if you're more comfortable."

"I think I trust you," said Ian with a strange look on his face. "And I really want to taste you." If he had any thoughts about Trent being celibate for a year, he kept it to himself.

Soon Trent was seated on the couch and Ian was sliding down between his thighs. He tugged at the sweatpants, slipping them off the rest of the way. Another scream in the background was drowned out by Trent's moan as Ian licked the head of his cock with a slightly pointed tongue.

He swirled along the head of Trent's cock before he dipped the tip of his tongue into the small slit, flicking the piercing and setting nerves alive all the way down the length. A few drops of pre-cum welled up, only to be lapped away.

He tongued at the head, slurping and licking like it was his favourite candy, before he suddenly dropped farther down his cock. Trent was expecting him to stop about halfway, which was the spot where most tended to pull away. He wasn't massive, but he was generous enough that he worried about his partner's gag reflex and was always careful to hold back.

Ian didn't stop, though. He kept pushing past the point where Trent bumped against the back of his throat—and farther still. He didn't stop until his nose was pressed against the trimmed hair on his groin. Ian's throat pulsed around him as he swallowed.

Trent trembled as he tried to maintain control and not buck his hips up into Ian's mouth. He'd never been deep-throated before. No one had even come close to taking him that far. Most of his so-called relationships had lasted a few hours at the longest, but Ian showed a familiarity with his cock that long-term couples would beg for. He seemed to know exactly where to press his tongue, scrape his teeth and suck.

"You have such a pretty cock," said Ian as he pulled off to lap at the head. "The first time I saw it, I knew I had to get my mouth on it." He popped a finger into his mouth, licking it briefly before he pulled it out and dropped his head back down again.

Trent slid his legs open to give Ian more room, and Ian took every advantage. A slick finger slid easily inside him with no more than a slight pressure. His rim ached slightly from the penetration, but it was nothing to the feeling of Ian being back inside him.

"You're still so open for me, T. Just begging me to slide my cock right back in. You'd let me, too, wouldn't you? I could just turn you over and push you into the couch and you'd let me fuck you right here." The press of his finger deep inside punctuated every sentence.

"Yes," said Trent, trying, and failing to keep his hips still. Ian went silent again as he slid down Trent's cock to the base before he pulled up then hummed around the head. "Get the stuff, Ian. I want you to fuck me again."

"It might hurt, T. You were so tight last time. Your body needs time to catch up. I can just blow you if you want. I'm good." Ian frowned with concern. Trent could see the tent in the other man's pants and knew he wasn't 'good'. The sentiment was very nice, though.

"I don't care. I want you again." Trent shuddered as Ian pulled away. Trent eyed the bulge hidden by a thin layer of fabric and his breath caught. Had he really taken all that inside him before?

Before he could second-guess himself, Ian returned with a single condom and the half-empty bottle of lube. He stripped his pants with no ceremony and rolled the condom on with one hand while popping the tube of lube open with the other. Who knew that being ambidextrous was on Trent's kink list?

"Roll over, T. I'm gonna fuck you from behind and make you feel so good," said Ian as he slicked his cock.

Trent knelt on the couch and faced the wall. The first touch of slick fingers made him jump as they swept across his entrance.

"Shh, it's okay, T. I'll take it slow again. You tell me if you need me to go slower or stop, okay?"

Trent nodded before he pressed his face into the top of the couch. The fingers disappeared and the heat of Ian's body pressed up behind him. The throbbing cock slid between his spread cheeks and brushed against his opening. Ian steadied his hips as he kissed the back of Trent's neck. Then he was sliding inside.

The strange feeling of fullness that was quickly becoming familiar was the first thing to strike him. There was no pain with the stretch this time, only a dull ache at his rim. His body relaxed of its own accord as

Ian slid all the way home. The position pushed the man's cock against Trent's prostate, but not so hard that it hurt.

Ian paused to allow Trent time to adjust, trembling with the effort of keeping still. Trent wasn't having it, though.

"Please fuck me hard. Show me what it's like," said Trent as he rocked back on the thick cock inside him.

Ian sucked in a breath and his hands went tight where they were braced on his hips.

"I don't want to hurt you." Ian kissed the back of his neck again before nuzzling against the damp locks.

"Just don't hold back."

Ian pulled out and the cock slipped from his body. He groaned with loss, which turned into a moan as Ian slipped inside again. The strokes were longer and deeper than before, but not rough enough to actually hurt him. The speed was building as Ian slowly lost control.

Trent groaned, pushing back to match each thrust as it slid home again. The new position took some time to get right, and a few times Ian slipped out completely. As much as he hated the loss, Trent loved the feeling of Ian lining himself up and pushing inside to the hilt in one go.

The sound of skin slapping and breathy moans overwhelmed the movie that was still running in the background. Ian kissed up and down Trent's neck, scraping his teeth before latching on and sucking a bruise into his pale skin.

"So good," Trent said, his voice muffled by the couch cushions that were barely supporting him. The couch was rocking hard, with springs squeaking and the bottom thumping against the ground as they moved closer to the wall with each hard thrust. Ian must've heard him over the noise, as his strokes only got harder.

"T, you're so hot tight. It's like you were made for me. I'm not gonna last." Ian's teeth snagged against his neck as his hips started to stutter. "I'm gonna come in you, baby, and mark you up." He bit harder against Trent's skin as he started to shoot.

Trent knew that there was a condom between them, but the thought of having Ian naked inside him and filling him up made his cock jerk and his toes curl. He was right on the edge as Ian thrust one last time inside, his cock twitching as he drained himself.

Ian only waited one beat before he pulled out and a hand gripped Trent's hips and urged him to turn over. He landed awkwardly on his ass, staining the leather with a smear of lube. Ian bent down until he was on his knees between Trent's legs before he leaned over and took Trent's cock back into his mouth.

The sensation of Ian swallowing, and the sudden emptiness inside, had him coming immediately. It hit so fast that Trent didn't even have the ability to warn Ian, but the man was already swallowing him down. Ian hummed as he drained Trent's cock until he was twitching from overstimulation.

Ian disappeared while Trent was still panting from his release, returning seconds later with a wet cloth in his hand instead.

"I wash my face with that cloth, you know," said Trent with a slow smile. His skin was prickling from the sudden loss of heat, and he held back a shiver.

Ian chuckled as he wiped Trent's groin before dipping down to swipe the lube from between his thighs, ignoring the mess on the couch cushion.

"Cum makes a great face wash. Micro scrubbers," said Ian, laughing as Trent's face twisted.

"I am never going to be able to get that image out of my mind. Just gross." Trent shifted, and another dribble of lube leaked from his hole, quickly swiped away by Ian. Ian sighed, tossing the cloth and sitting on the unstained seat.

"Come here, T," said Ian as he patted his naked thighs.

"Am I too heavy?" Trent asked as leaned back against Ian's chest and settled in his lap. His naked skin rubbed against Ian's in the most deliciously damp way and Ian's spent cock lined up with his hole as he shifted. The simple touch shot a line of heat straight to his gut, and his cock twitched almost painfully.

"I want you again," said Trent as he leaned back to rest his head against Ian's shoulder.

Ian nodded, his eyes going even darker. "I want you too. It's weird. Usually I can go once a day, maybe twice, but I already want to fuck you again. If I could get hard now, I would just slip inside and hold you there so you couldn't move away. I would come so hard that you'd be dripping for days. Fuck, I've never wanted someone so much before."

There was a beat of awkward silence when Ian's arms pulled Trent even tighter. The tip of his soft cock brushed against Trent's open entrance, threatening to push inside.

"I'd let you."

Chapter Five

Trent woke on Sunday morning to a warm mouth on his cock and a tongue flicking at the thin piercing through the head. He was close enough that his balls were drawing up tight and his stomach was clenching. There was no transitioning from asleep to awake, just a sudden realization that he was—and seconds from coming.

He ran his hands over the smooth, tattooed scalp that was surely sweating beneath the blankets. He dug his nails in after a particularly hard suck, and Ian groaned, sending a hum along his cock that pushed him over the edge.

"Fuck." Trent came with a single cursed word and snapped his body tight around the three fingers inside him. They pushed against his prostate, gentle but firm, forcing his pleasure even higher. Ian swallowed and there was a slurping noise Ian made as he tried to gather every drop.

This wasn't the first time that Ian had sucked him off. It wasn't even the second. It felt like the man couldn't get enough of his taste. Just as Trent couldn't get enough of the feeling of that cock thrusting inside him to the hilt.

Thursday, soaked and filled with adrenalin, felt more distant than just a couple of days. The rain had long since cleared to an unseasonable warmth, but they'd spent most of their time inside as they tested out every available surface of Trent's tiny home. Trent had even managed to get half of Friday off work to spend more time with his insatiable lover.

The stove was not a fun place to fuck, at all, though. Trent had accidentally hit the igniter switch when Ian had him bent over to thrust a tongue in his ass, and Trent had almost lost his chest hair to the sudden flame. He'd ended up with a bald patch the size of a quarter, and the nasty smell of burnt hair had stuck in his nose for the rest of the day.

His exercise mat was an excellent place to fuck. He'd pushed Ian back onto it, using his pants as a pillow. Then he'd ridden Ian's cock like he'd never see it again. It had brushed inside him perfectly as he rocked his hips and settled so deep that he saw stars.

The wall was an impractical place. Trent had managed to stay upright for about a minute with his legs wrapped around Ian's waist. The man could hold his weight, but his grip had loosened as his thrusts grew deeper. Luckily, they'd landed on a thin stretch of carpet when Ian's legs finally gave out.

"T, baby, I need you so bad. Can you take it now or are you too sensitive?" asked Ian as Trent's cock slipped from his lips. He moved up and pressed between Trent's thighs. Trent opened wide, letting Ian in. He grasped his chin, pulling him up in a dirty kiss.

They both tasted of morning breath, mixed with the remnants of arousal.

"I can take it. Just go slow, Ian. I like how you feel inside of me after I come." He didn't even blush at his own words this time. A week ago, he would've gone bright red before hiding in embarrassment. But he'd done a lot in the last couple of days — some things that he'd never even dreamed of.

Ian pulled back just long enough to slide a condom and lube over his cock. Then he was pressing in, all the way in one long thrust. Trent arched up, clawing at Ian's shoulders as he was stretched wide. Even after days of fucking, it still felt like the first time when Ian slid home.

"Fuck me hard." Trent changed his mind the moment Ian was inside him. Trent's legs were pushed up until his knees rested just shy of his ears. His back protested as he was contorted beyond anything he'd experienced before.

Ian pulled back and slammed back in. His cock slipped out just a bit to nudge against his rim, before pushing in again. It was something Ian had confessed to loving after their third time together, and Trent had agreed. Going from completely empty to full in just a moment was so overwhelming that it always made him want to shoot, and the stimulation along his perineum was an added bonus.

After that, Ian repeated the move as often as possible. It made Trent feel like he was opening up, body and soul, to make a place for Ian. He tried to deny the pangs in his chest that the thought gave him.

Ian's groin smacked against his ass as the man pushed. He gripped Trent's ankles, forcing them even farther back. It let him go deeper and harder, exactly the way Trent wanted it, no matter how sore he was.

It wasn't long before Ian's hips started to stutter. "You're so tight, T. I can't even help myself. You're just so good."

The praise went straight to Trent's groin, making his hardening cock twitch. He reached down between his legs, finding that he was leaking and ready. He'd hardly noticed it compared to the satisfaction of being filled yet again.

When Ian noticed his jerking movements, the man groaned and moved in for a heated kiss. Their breaths combined, and they slid their tongues together briefly before Ian pulled back.

"I fucking love it. You can't get enough, can you, T? Yeah, me neither. I could do this all fucking day if you'd let me." Ian's hands gripped tight on his ankles, pushing them to their limit.

"I'd let you," said Trent. With one last harsh pull, he was coming between them. His seed splashed against Ian's chest and his own stomach. It was a pathetic dribble compared to what he was usually capable of, but he'd never come this often in his entire life. His body clamped down even harder after the second orgasm, milking Ian's cock as his walls went tight.

Ian went rigid, thrusting to the base before he tensed and ground against Trent's ass as he pushed himself even deeper, trying to claim Trent despite the barrier between them.

It wasn't the first time that Trent had wished that there was no condom. He wanted to feel the heat of Ian's skin as he came and the rush of cum that would flow deep. He wanted to touch himself after and sweep a finger inside before bringing it to his mouth.

He knew Ian wouldn't let him. He'd flat-out refused a blow job when Trent had gone to his knees.

'Not without a condom. I don't want you catching anything from me. I haven't got tested in a while. Too long,' Ian had said with a frown and a shake of his head, pushing Trent away, despite his aching cock.

Trent had raced to the bedroom and back, smoothed the condom down on Ian's cock, and sucked the tip into his mouth. He barely suppressed the gag that erupted from the terrible taste of latex and spermicidal lube. Ian had laughed at his expression before pulling him up for a filthy kiss. Trent had ridden his lap instead, clinging to his neck and rocking his hips like a porn star.

In the bed, Ian collapsed next to him with one arm stretched across Trent's heaving chest. Trent rolled into the touch and pressed his cheek against Ian's sweaty chest. Ian looped his arms around him to pull him close and press his lips to the top of his head. There was no urgency, even with the stickiness seemingly everywhere on Trent's body.

Trent's eyes were just starting to drift shut to the sound of Ian's heart when a rhythmic knock sounded at the front door. The sound travelled through the tiny house with unerring accuracy.

"Shit, shit, shit," said Trent as he pushed himself up and lunged for his phone to check the time. "It's nine o'clock already. Crap." He scrambled out of bed, nearly tripping over the tangled sheets at the foot. Ian was sitting up, looking more alarmed by the second.

"Who is it?" Ian asked as he looked down the hall towards the sound. His flush had died away to a loose-limbed relaxation, but he was instantly on edge and ready for a fight.

"It's my mom. Christ, I forgot to call her. She gets all protective if I don't check in with her. She'll start calling hospitals if I don't answer the door." Trent pulled a pair of sweatpants on while grappling with a T-shirt over his head. Any fluids that hadn't dried already, soaked into the T-shirt and pants, leaving an obvious stain behind. "Get dressed, and please don't listen to anything she says." With one last look at the beautiful man in his bed, Trent raced to answer the door.

The knock sounded again, just as his footsteps stuttered to a halt on the mat. He flushed as he opened the door to reveal his mother.

She was tiny, all of five feet, but every inch of her was filled with bright fury. Her hair was still naturally blonde — at least, she'd convinced everyone else of that fact — and her narrow hips fit neatly into a size two. Trent was utterly terrified of her.

Her piercing blue eyes, which always managed to see too much, looked up and down his form once before a knowing smile broke over her lips.

"Well at least somebody is getting laid in this godforsaken town." Her smile widened to reveal perfect white teeth. "And from the looks of it, that was some mighty good dick. But I still don't forgive you. I can understand two days, maybe even three, but not four. Four days since you called me, you little punk. I thought I was going to come down here to find a corpse." She pushed her way past him into the tiny front hall.

Trent gaped at her with his mouth hanging wide as she pushed him to the side like he weighed almost nothing. There was nothing he could say or do to stop her, either. She was an unstoppable force. She paused in the doorway to the kitchen, tilting her head back to smell the air.

"It still smells like sex in here. Do you not know how to open a window? You aren't in college anymore, sweetheart." She stomped into the kitchen and grappled with the stiff window over the sink. She had to perch up on the tips of her toes, but she managed to open it.

Trent shuddered. She was the reason he had no brain-to-mouth filter. It was directly genetic.

"Mom, he's still here. We were just sleeping. Could I maybe call you later and we can catch up?" Trent followed her into the kitchen, where she was already pulling a frying pan out from where it was stashed in the oven.

"Nope. Four days, Trent. Four." She turned and jabbed his chest with a tiny, manicured finger. Trent felt the tiny bruise form under the woman's wrath. "And obviously you're a caveman and haven't even made your guest breakfast. Now go wash up and fix your shirt. It's inside out. If it's not too much trouble, you can chat with your mother over breakfast and introduce me to your friend. It must be someone special if you brought them home." She turned away abruptly, obviously without any doubt that her orders would be followed.

Trent ducked back into the bedroom and pulled the door shut before his mother could peer around the corner. Ian was pulling on the clothes that he'd worn when Trent had first met him. They'd long since been washed and dried, but Ian had stacked them on the dresser instead of putting them on, lounging in Trent's clothes instead. Trent had to pause and shake his head when he found himself eyeing up the way the trousers slid over Ian's hips, and the way the shirt hugged his thick chest and biceps.

"Please tell me that you didn't hear that," said Trent as he leaned back against the door, just in case his mother tried to break through. Ian turned to him with a soft laugh.

"Every word. It's okay though, T. I'm glad your mom is accepting of you. I wish my family was cool with it." Ian shrugged and turned away to grab his socks from the dresser.

Trent wrapped his arms around him from behind and pulled the man into a hug. "Sorry. She means well. She just gets over-excited for me sometimes."

"She's proud." Ian turned and pressed a kiss to Trent's lips. "It's a good thing. Trust me."

There was a darkness behind those words that Trent didn't like. Ian had been tight-lipped about his life and family over the weekend, and Trent hadn't pressed him. He'd only mentioned one person—his best friend Mac, who also happened to be his boss. Trent didn't want to ruin the time that they had together by trying to dig up anything more.

A tongue slipped into Trent's mouth and he had to bite off a groan. The smack of lips was loud in the small room, matched only by the sound of their breathing. Trent pulled Ian close, slipping his hands along his neck and shoulders before cupping his waist. Ian followed the motion, until they were touching from chest to hip. An answering twitch met Trent's hardening cock.

"You two better not be fucking in there!"

They broke apart, more winded than they should've been for such a short kiss.

"We're not, Mom. We'll be right out," Trent yelled back through the door before he sighed and pressed his face to Ian's chest. He took a deep breath. The scent that he had thought was cologne still lingered, now mixed with the scent of Trent's body wash. He forced himself away before he did something he would regret later. His mother would have no qualms about interrupting them.

"Come on." Trent slipped his hand into Ian's. He'd half expected the man to let go but was pleasantly surprised when Ian only tightened his grip. Trent pushed through the door with a small smile on his face.

"You didn't fix your shirt, honey." His mother's piercing gaze picked up every detail. She flitted over to Ian, her eyes going wide with surprise. "Well, look at that. You are just gorgeous—and one hell of a man." Her gaze flicked up and down, taking in Ian's towering height and thick build. Trent winced when she obviously eyed Ian's groin.

"It's a nice change, Trent, honey. I didn't know you were into that kind of thing, but it's a good look on you." She flipped something in the pan, before grinding it against the flame.

"Oh my God, Mom, please stop," said Trent as his face flamed hot. He glanced at Ian out of the corner of his eye, but the man was unreadable.

"It's nothing to be embarrassed about, honey. Being a bottom is just as great as being a top." She smiled sweetly as she flipped the pancake again. "Now, don't be rude. What's your name, dear?" She turned towards them, brushing off her front with a few sweeps of her petite hands.

Trent visibly wilted as he glanced over at Ian again. Ian's mouth was open in shock, but his eyes were sparkling with intense humour. His grip was tight on Trent's hand.

"Ian, this is my mother, Betty. Mom, this is Ian, my..." Trent trailed off, biting his tongue before he could utter another word. What could he say? Weekend fuck buddy? They certainly weren't boyfriends...or partners. They hadn't gotten close to having any sort of conversation about any of that.

"Lover." Ian leaned forward to shake Betty's hand with his free one. He made the embarrassing term sound sexy enough that Trent flushed even deeper. "It's nice to meet you. I can see where T gets his sense of humour."

"T?" Her eyebrows hit her hairline as she smirked at Trent. "Well, this just keeps getting better and better. Have a seat, Ian. My son may not know how to feed you, but I won't let you waste away."

Trent hardly raised his head through the embarrassing debacle of breakfast. Ian was obviously enjoying himself as he laughed at Trent's expense several times as Betty divulged childhood secrets.

"That's nothing," Betty chuckled as she patted Ian's shoulder. Ian was laughing so hard that he had tears in the corner of his eyes. Trent wanted to drown in the syrup on his plate.

"When Trent came out of the closet to us, he thought he was so clever. I'd known for years, ever since I caught him looking at the male underwear models in my catalogues."

"That was one time, Mom," said Trent as he sank lower in his chair.

"Shush, honey. Mommy is talking to your lover. Anyway, Trent calls this family meeting with me, his two brothers and his father. We're all sitting there and he just comes out and says it. *'Mom, I'm gay.'"* Her voice went high and squeaky in her imitation of his pubescent voice. "And I tell him that I'm so glad that he's happy. We're just one happy, gay family. He looked so upset that we weren't getting it, and his father was just trying to stop laughing. So he says, *'I like guys, Mom.'* So, I told him that it was just fine to have friends that were girls and friend who were guys." She laughed, wiping a few tears from the corner of her eyes.

"So little Trent, he's getting so upset and he's bright red. He just yells out, *'I want to fuck guys. How hard is that to fucking understand?'* We just smiled, nodded and I told him that it was about time he told me."

She stood, still shaking with laughter as she started to clear the plates from the table. Ian was hiding behind his hand, obviously trying to keep his laughter in check, but as Trent glanced up, he burst into a new round of giggles.

"And now you know why I am the way I am." Trent mumbled into the placemat as he let his face finally fall all the way down.

"Oh, honey, I love you, you know that, but a mother only has so many opportunities to torture her children. I have to take full advantage. It's payment for three years of no sleep. Hell, you still keep me up at night."

"It's all good, T," said Ian as he slid his hand over Trent's shoulder. "I wish my family was anything like yours." A frown tugged at the man's lips and the sparkle in his eyes dimmed.

"Oh dear, did they not take it well when you came out to them?" Betty asked. Her humour fell away to a stance that Trent recognized as 'protective mother mode'.

"Well, I never told them. Any of them," Ian said quietly. "They've made their feelings about homosexuals abundantly clear. I only have one friend who knows, and it was really hard for him to accept. I'd rather not go through that again."

The kitchen went silent except for the tap running into the sink. Trent shot his head up as he went through a dizzying array of emotions. He couldn't imagine hiding such an important part of his life from everyone he knew. It would break him.

"Well, Ian, honey, you're part of our family now too. We accept you one hundred percent, no matter what." Betty dropped a kiss on Ian's head and Ian tensed, looking at Trent with a heart-breaking sadness. The tears that had been from humour shone with grief instead.

"Ian," said Trent as he reached out to grab his hand.

"The ladies haven't been fed yet, have they? I'll go take care of that and you can help Betty dry dishes," said Ian as he pushed himself to his feet. The chair squealed from the sudden movement and it nearly tumbled over. "It was nice to meet you, Betty." He didn't wait for a reply before he grabbed his shoes and disappeared out of the front door.

"Mom." Trent sighed and rubbed his hands over his face. His stomach burned, and it wasn't from his mother's cooking. Seeing that look on Ian's face brought back so many memories of every person who had ever looked at him like he was a freak.

"He is an excellent man, honey. He's damaged and hurt, but I think he needs someone like you in his life." She wrapped her soapy hands around him and pulled him over to the sink.

He could peer into the back yard from the window. Ian was back at the coop and the chickens were already rushing around his ankles in excitement. Cadbury, who usually didn't even look up when Trent was in the back yard, leapt into Ian's arms and tilted her head to the side for a scratch. The two had bonded while Trent had been at work during the morning on Friday. He'd been terrified to leave a near-stranger in his home alone for the day, but when he'd returned, Ian had been passed out in a lawn chair with three chickens curled up on his legs.

"Oh, honey, you are so gone on him," said Betty, shaking her head. "It's okay. I know that look. It's the same one that your brother has for his wife and that I had for your father."

"He's leaving today," said Trent. "He was just staying here while they were fixing up his car, and it took a while longer than we'd initially thought it would. The garage called last night, but he was going to head out this morning." Trent sighed as he brushed the plate in his hands with a dishtowel. He had known that he was developing something for Ian, but he'd thought he'd buried it under several layers of lust and denial.

"That's okay, honey. He can't live that far away. You can always visit each other on weekends." She passed him another plate without looking away from the adorable scene in the back yard.

"He lives in Miami." It was the same continent, but more than a twenty-three-hour drive away, and Trent didn't even have a car.

"Oh, honey, I'm so sorry." She wrapped her arms around him, pulling him close.

Trent held back the tears, refusing to let them fall. He didn't want to ruin the last morning with Ian by having a breakdown. He was going to enjoy it until the moment that Ian stepped out of the door.

"I'm going to head out, honey. You call me later if you're up to it." She left the sink half-full of dirty dishes, already pulling her shoes on.

Outside in the yard, Ian looked back to Trent standing at the window. The man waved, ignoring the protesting clucks of the chicken in his arms. Trent broke out into a smile. He was going to enjoy the rest of his morning to the fullest.

Chapter Six

Trent fumbled with a stack of CDs as the door slammed shut a second time. The old door was slightly warped from years of transitioning from hot to cold, and the wooden frame was just a touch too small. A strong slam was the only way to close it.

There was a rustling of fabric and the distant thump of shoes being thrown down on the mat. There were probably bits of dirt and mud on the wall from their haphazard landing, but Trent couldn't bring himself to care. Ian hadn't commented when Trent had moved a pair of sandals to make room for Ian's size twelves, but he always made sure to aim for that little spot.

"What are you doing?" asked Ian and he came around the corner. He leaned against the wall and crossed his arms over his chest, all semblance of tension drained away. Ian's cheeks were rosy from the brisk morning, and his scalp was damp with the barest hint of sweat. He filled the room with his smell, mixed with the perfect scent of sunshine.

"Don't make fun of me. I know everyone else in the world just downloads music, but I like CDs." Trent flipped through the stack, looking for something to play. He steered away from his collection of heavy metal, as he was unsure if Ian would like it or not. He didn't want their last few hours together to be awkward because of his music choice, but he didn't want silence either.

"It's cool, T. I have a record collection, so I get it. Sometimes you need to hold something in your hands to really make sense of it." Ian wiped a hand over his scalp as he glanced down at the mess.

"Exactly," said Trent. "I couldn't have said it better myself. Any preferences? I've got the classics and some new stuff too. Anything you don't like?" He held up a few different cases, squinting at each one as he named them off.

As Trent turned to show Ian one of the cases, he accidentally collided with the haphazard stack he had created. The clear plastic holders, filled with their square paper labels and shiny circles, tumbled to the ground. One case tipped and flung open as it hit the ground. The sensitive underside of the CD dragged along the vinyl floor as it slid to Ian's feet.

Trent grabbed the case at the same time Ian went for the silver disk. Both of them froze.

Trent settled on the paper insert. When he was young, he would open the little pages and read along to the lyrics as he listened to the songs for the first time. Now he usually ignored them and went straight for the disk.

On the case, above the track list, was a picture of the band members, all wearing smiles and classic band T-shirts. One of the five members, the tallest of them, had a set of drumsticks in his hand. He stood out like a beacon of fire in the middle of a thunderstorm. It was Ian.

Ian had flipped over the disk in his hand to look at the label. His eyes widened as his body went tense, and he looked as if he was almost crushing the disc in his hand. His eyes flickered over to Trent as his look darkened and narrowed into a glare.

"I thought you said you didn't know who I was," said Ian, his words low and laced with something dangerous.

"I didn't —"

"Did you have fun touching the real thing this weekend?" Ian took a step back. "I knew it was too good to be true. I finally found someone who I couldn't blame on the drugs or the drinking, and of course they turn out to be a lying groupie. Fuck you, Trent."

Trent tried to stand, and the empty case fell from his fingers. His stomach surged at the thought of meeting someone famous, especially so intimately, but the feeling dropped into numbness at the brutal barbs of Ian's voice.

"I'm not like that," said Trent. He tried to say more, but his voice clogged on everything that was trying to stumble forth from his mouth at the same time.

"I guess we both have our own dirty little secrets then. Just do yourself a favour… Don't go to the press or I'll fucking bury you." Ian threw the disk at Trent's head as he whirled out of the room.

The round plastic disk slapped against Trent's cheek, knocking him back a step as he cried out in surprise more than pain. It shocked him out of his momentary stupor, sending him after Ian as he fled to the door.

"Wait, Ian. I swear I didn't know. I recognized your name, but I couldn't figure it out. Please believe me." He grabbed for Ian's shoulder but was shrugged off. "Ian, please." His voice trailed down to a whisper.

"Fuck you," said Ian without looking back, his shoes still in his hands. The door slammed loud enough to shake the plates in the kitchen sink.

Trent would've done anything to go back to the moment where he was still standing above the sink, looking at Ian as he played with the chickens in the back yard. Why the hell had he needed to play music suddenly? The silence hadn't even been that bad.

He crumpled to his knees in the front hall. A stray pebble dug through his pant leg and pressed a bruise into his kneecap as a tear rolled from his eye and dropped to the mat. It disappeared into the acrylic loops in seconds, leaving no trace behind. His sobs peaked, then faded to nothing.

He struggled to his feet, preparing to follow Ian. He would chase him down the street if he had to. He knew the destination. There was only one place for Ian to go.

He ran out of the door with tears still running down his face, and his eyes probably red and swollen for anyone who cared to look. His neighbour, Cindy, could look through her curtains and judge him right now and he wouldn't give a fuck. Nothing mattered except reaching Ian and making him listen to reason. He couldn't part on bad terms…not like this.

He was breathing hard by the time he reached the garage parking lot, but it was empty except for the smashed remains of an old Volvo that was covered in a thick layer of dust and scraggly leaves. The beautiful yellow Corvette was gone. There wasn't even a single tyre track left in its memory.

When Trent got back home, he numbly stacked his CDs and placed them back in their usual spot beneath his television stand. The stray disk was scratched beyond repair, but he placed it back in its case and stacked it along with the others.

His shoulders drooped and his swollen eyelids pulled shut. He crawled back into bed and pulled the blankets to his face. There was still that sweet scent that hadn't belonged there before Thursday night. His tears started again, against his will.

He spied something on the bedside table that gave him a thread of hope. Ian's phone was there, still connected to the small charging cable. The screen was open and unlocked with Instagram flashing across the screen. Ian had probably scrolled through his messages before he decided to wake Trent up in the best way possible.

Trent grabbed it, careful to avoid the power button to keep it from locking. He opened the contacts and skimmed through the names with determination. Over the entire weekend, Ian had only mentioned one name to him — Mac, his best friend in the world and his boss, who he was expertly avoiding.

Trent scrolled down the list of contacts and clicked on the name. He deleted the last conversation before he could read it, doing his best to salvage privacy. Wiping the tears from his face, he typed in the only thing that might be able to heal his broken heart. It was a lie, but one that Ian would know if the message ever made it back to him.

Hi, this is T from Marvin's auto. Ian was just here to pick up his car and he accidentally left his phone on the counter.

Would you be able to let him know when you see him next?
TIA

He pressed send before setting the phone back delicately on the bedstand. A second later he scrambled to pick it up as it vibrated with a response.

Please ship it to…

Trent ran to the kitchen and pulled out a pad of paper before scribbling down the address. It was Miami, in an area that Ian had mentioned once or twice. It could be his address or Mac's. Trent didn't know. His meagre plan hadn't worked at all. Ian wouldn't be coming back to get his phone so Trent could make him listen.

He was about to turn off the phone when inspiration struck. He added his own cell number as a contact, saved simply under T. He saved Ian's number in the contacts on his own phone as well. Then he opened notes and added one to the main screen. He tapped against the surface as he typed out a short letter.

Hey, Ian. I really didn't realize who you were until I saw that picture. I am a fan, but I am definitely not a groupie. Just ew.

Trent paused with his finger hesitating over the backspace. He ploughed on through the note.

I had a wonderful weekend and I'm glad I met you. I put my number in your contacts if you ever want to call and have someone to talk to. What my Mom said is true. You are part of the family now, and there is always an open door and an open ear here. I wish you would come back just so I could kiss you one more time. I think I'm falling for you, and I thought maybe you felt something too. I've never had this kind of a connection with anyone before. I know we hardly know each other, and I want to get to know you better. Please call me.

T

Trent saved the note to the home screen and hit the power button before he could back out. He could mail the phone tomorrow. If he used express shipping, it might even beat Ian home.

He wiped the tears from his face and ground his teeth in determination. A seed of hope threatened to blossom in his chest, no matter how hard he tried to suppress it. He kissed the phone and set it in the centre of the table. With a sigh, he headed out to the back yard. His feather babies always made him feel better.

Chapter Seven

"I swear I didn't break it," said the blonde woman next to Trent. She tapped her nails against the plush office chair before she spun around once while looking at the tiled ceiling. Her feet, which were wrapped in strappy blue sandals that matched her blouse, slipped over the carpeted floor.

"I'm sure you think that." Trent sighed as he skimmed through the vague code of the computer before him. It was the third time he'd heard those words today, but that didn't make them any truer. A headache had formed behind his eyes, which made the numbers and letters on the screen flow noisily in front of his face, and his back ached from bending low over the desk.

The office had a surprising number of employees for being in such a small town, but most of them drove in from the surrounding areas that had a smattering of houses. The builders had taken an old brick mansion and converted it into a tasteful building that used the tiny rooms as employee offices instead of using cubicles. He was currently in one of the larger rooms, which had been painted bright blue by the current occupant, who was committed to driving him insane.

"I don't understand how you manage to crash your computer just by using Excel. Your skill is astonishing," said Trent as he tried to smile. The curl of his lips felt heavy and false on his face. "It's okay though, Candace. I get it. Your hands are made of magnets."

"Nope, just my bracelets. They help with my carpal tunnel." The blonde flicked her hair back over one shoulder and rolled her eyes. She flung her chair aside as she stood to hover over his shoulder.

Trent held back another sigh and pinched the bridge of his nose. Candace was a good person — she really was — but sometimes she just got to him. She had an abundance of energy that was just sucking him dry on the hot summer day.

"You okay, Trent? You've been awfully quiet for the last few weeks. Longer than that, now that I think about it. We haven't even gone out for drinks lately." She shouldered her way past him so that Trent had to meet her eyes. Her bright red lips were turned into a frown as she looked him up and down. He could see her mind turning as she searched him like a geological map.

Trent shook his head and tried to focus on the screen. "I'm okay, Candace. Just tired." Work…that, he could handle. He didn't want to think about anything else, including the reason he was up every night.

"Did you want to talk about it?" She stepped into his line of sight again. Her hand came up to rest against his shoulder and he deflated under the soft touch.

"Can't fool you, can I?" asked Trent as he flopped down in her chair, giving up on the computer all together. She rolled a second chair up close and sat.

Their knees knocked together and she smiled, pressing her hand on his kneecap.

"I'm not your best friend for nothing." Her smile was genuine.

He didn't know what to tell her. He'd told Candace, and only Candace, about what had happened between him and Ian. He'd thought he'd be able to put it behind him as the weeks turned into months, but obviously not. If he could just forget about it, then the pain in his chest might disappear.

"Would you date me, Candace?" He asked, fixing her with a stare.

She looked at him with narrowed eyes, as if she were seeing him for the first time. She patted his knee twice before she withdrew and crossed her arms.

"Not unless you have the superpower to grow a cunt," she said with a straight face.

"Shut up," Trent hissed before he slapped his hand over her mouth to stifle her laughter. He glanced over his shoulder to make sure that no one had walked by. "Someone could hear you. That is not a work-friendly word."

"This isn't a work-friendly conversation. Tonight. Nine o'clock. Get ready to get fucking plastered," she said as she pushed his hand away. Her eyebrows waggled and she licked her lips.

"It's Wednesday," Trent deadpanned.

"And you're boring," she threw right back at him.

Trent knew she meant the words to be light-hearted, but they carved in deep. "Is that it? I'm just too boring to keep a man in my life?" He didn't have much besides his usual routine, after all.

"Trent, don't say that." She pulled him into a quick hug and the smell of her floral perfume overwhelmed him. "Come to my place tonight and we can talk. There will be a two-drink minimum."

He found himself smiling for the first time in weeks. Even if things weren't great, Candace always knew how to make them at least a little bit better. He had something to look forward to that wasn't an empty house and a quiet phone.

He fixed her computer, threatening her with certain doom if she crashed it again. He knew he'd be back by tomorrow at the latest.

When their shift ended, Trent met Candace back at her desk. She packed away a few pieces of paper into a small filing cabinet, before she grabbed her purse and they were out of the door. Trent squeezed himself into her compact Toyota, dreading his aching knees by the end of the ride.

"So, what's your problem?" she asked as she started up her car. Straight and to the point. No wiggling around in the mud, looking for a lost pig.

"You know, I've never actually dated anyone," Trent mused as he clipped on his seat belt. "I've fucked lots of people, but in thirty-plus years, my longest standing relationship was two months."

"Two months is totally dating," said Candace as she wheeled out of the parking lot. "Two months is enough time to figure out if it's good dick or not – or pussy, in my case."

Trent glanced at her as her hands gripped the steering wheel tight. She hadn't put on her seatbelt and the alarm was beeping. She waved her hand as if that would make it disappear. He reached across her and expertly threaded the belt over her arm and across her waist before he buckled her in.

"See? That's my problem. That's all we did for two months," Trent sighed as he leaned back and rubbed his sore forehead. "We hooked up a couple of times a week, then I would end up heading home. I never asked to stay over and he never asked me to stay. When I finally asked him out to dinner, he turned me down." He knew she'd heard the story before, because she was the one who had gotten him out of his slump when it had happened.

"Allergies?" asked Candace, catching him off guard. Outside, the edge of town fluttered past, and fields stretched out on either side.

"What? No. He already had a boyfriend." Trent gave her a strange look. "Why would someone turn down dinner because of allergies? I'm not going to force-feed him shellfish."

"I dated this chick," Candace said as she rifled around in her centre console, taking her eyes off the road for way too long. "Every time we went out, she was running to the bathroom after. I thought she was bulimic, but her teeth were too nice. When I called her on it, she said that she was allergic to restaurant food."

"You can't be allergic to all restaurant food," said Trent shaking his head. This was a story he hadn't heard before, but Candace didn't talk too much about her side of the fence…unless it was to cheer him up.

"Well, that's what I thought too." She nodded and flipped down her visor so she could apply a thin layer of balm over her lower lip. She swerved to miss the barn cat on the road without looking. "So, I followed her into the bathroom the next time we went out. Just curious, right, not super creepy. That was our last date."

"She was lying?"

"Nope." Candace shook her head. "But I can't date someone who shits themselves every time I want to go out. It took me a day to get the smell out of my hair, and I was only in the bathroom for a minute."

"You are so shallow," said Trent, shaking his head. The best thing about his friend was that she always made him feel better about himself. It was like starting a diet, then watching *My Six-Hundred Pound Life*, before realizing that an extra ten pounds wasn't that bad.

"Hey," she said as she reached over to smack his chest. "You weren't there. It was bad, like rotting corpse mixed with dead worms." Her laughter died off. "Things were ending before that, though. She was in the closet, hard. She wouldn't introduce me to friends or family. We always had to drive forever to go on a date, and she would cancel last minute, sometimes, if she got nervous that we were going to get caught. I couldn't live that kind of life."

Silence settled between them and Trent shifted in the small seat, his knees knocking the dash that was keeping him partially paralyzed. He ran his hand through his hair, massaging at his temples as his head started to throb harder.

"Is that what this is about? You're dating someone who's in the closet?" She looked at him and completely ignored the road. He grabbed the wheel and steered them back into the correct lane.

Trent shook his head. "Not dating, no."

"But you want to," she said, sighing as he nodded. "Just promise me that you'll be careful, Trent. Guys like that...? Sometimes they never come out, even if they make promises. I don't want to see you get hurt."

"I wouldn't mind getting hurt, if he would just call me," he said as the car rocked to the right when

Candace took a sharp corner. They passed a herd of cows that had a blanket of white around their middle. A calf ran along the fence as it chased something Trent couldn't see.

"You talking about Ian?" she asked, taking his silence as an answer in itself. "Well, as far as I'm concerned, that guy is just another famous prick. He used you too, Trent, but then he has a freak out and just leaves you like that? What a dick." She shook her head. "You need a nice guy who you can take care of, not one who's going to break your heart like that."

"But that's not what I want, Candace. It felt real. For the first time in my life, it actually felt real. I wasn't trying some move that I'd seen in porn, and I wasn't going down on a guy because I thought that was what they wanted. For the first time, I did it because I wanted to — and not for any other reason." Trent let his head fall against cool glass. His head pounded ever tighter.

"How much vacation time do you have saved up?" asked Candace. She pulled into her driveway and hopped out of the car. Trent followed with much less enthusiasm. After a nine-hour shift, she was still like the Energizer Bunny.

The flowers in the front bed were completely dried and wilted, and the grass was just a touch too long to be safe for small animals. The house itself was massive compared to Trent's own, but it lacked the polished shine of care.

"I don't know, like three or four weeks." He shrugged. "I didn't book any time off this summer." Her driveway was gravel that was still fresh enough that he sank into the stones as he made his way to the porch. It drained the energy from him even faster.

"You are calling in sick tomorrow and taking next week off. I know the boss loves you, so it shouldn't be a problem." She twisted the key in the lock and pulled the handle hard to open the latch.

"What? Why?" Trent shook his head as he followed her into the house.

"Well, after you told me about Ian, I may or may not have done some research," she said as she threw her keys into the bowl at the door and flipped off her sandals.

"Invading his privacy, you mean." He shook his head, denying that he had done the exact same thing. He set his shoes neatly on the empty boot-tray before following her.

"Google is not an invasion of privacy. Besides, it was the band page I was looking at." She disappeared into the depths of the house and Trent tried to keep up.

She was in a suburb that had been sold and resold over five times to different development companies. The houses were old now, some barely standing and sparsely placed around empty lots. Her neighbours were dicks, too, and wouldn't hesitate to grab what they needed from her house if the doors were unlocked.

"Okay. That still doesn't explain why I am wasting my vacation." Trent looked around the house as he tried to track her voice. It was three times the size of his, with more bedrooms than he would ever need in a lifetime. She was waiting for him in the kitchen with her hair down and sprawling around her shoulders.

Everything inside the large room was perfectly colour-coded, except for the line of dust on top of the fridge. Even the mugs were arranged in order behind the glass doors that were smudged with fingerprints. He moved to the table, which was pushed off to the side of the room and piled with a stack of flyers that looked to be a few weeks old. He took a seat on a hard, wooden chair after swiping a bit of what looked like egg off the seat.

"Well, I had a plan if Ian got in contact with you, but I put it on hold, because he's a dick." She paused, waiting for some sort of response from Trent. "Your boyfriend is playing in Toronto tomorrow night."

Candace brought him a mug that was filled to the brim with something dark. He took a sip, suppressing the shudder from the pure taste of whisky as it washed over his tongue.

"And I happen to know somebody who knows somebody." She trailed off and waggled her eyebrows.

"Meaning you had a threesome with somebody just so you could fuck their girlfriend," he said, taking another sip.

"Oh, did I ever, but that's not the point. I owe you a birthday-Easter-Christmas gift this year anyway. I could get you front-row tickets, easy-peasy." She slurped at her own mug before she sat across from him. "I'll go with you because you are a great wingman for chicks. If we play our cards right, we might both get lucky."

"I don't know if he even wants to see me, though," Trent groaned and dropped his head into his hands. "I left him my number and that note, but he never called — not even a thank you for returning the phone."

"Let me ask you something," Candace slapped her mug to the table with a *thunk*. "If you thought someone was an asshole then found out you were the one in the wrong, how would you feel?"

"I dunno. Guilty, I guess." He stuck his finger in his mug, then licked the drop of whisky from the tip before plunging back in.

"Don't do that. It's disgusting," she said as she slapped his hand away. "If you were feeling super guilty, and maybe a bit ashamed, would you want to face that person again?"

"Probably not," he conceded.

"So that's why we have to show up and make him apologize in person. It's an ice breaker. A little apology here, a little tongue there. Next thing you know, you're on stage getting a blow job."

"Yeah, I don't think that's how it works," said Trent, shaking his head.

"I already told you that I know a guy." She downed the rest of her glass with a gulp and a sigh. Her cheeks flushed bright as a wave of intoxication started to take her. "Now let's get fucked up."

For the first time in weeks, Trent felt a bit of hope replace the loneliness.

Chapter Eight

"I expect a fashion show," said Candace as she passed Trent a silver bag. Her hands were on her hips with one cocked out as she tapped her foot against the plush white carpet.

They'd checked into the hotel two hours before and Trent had marvelled at the view and the room. He could see a hint of the lake through the massive glass windows that stretched from floor to ceiling. The room itself was entirely too posh. The bathroom had actual marble floors and the countertop was a deep black granite. The shower was big enough to fit five people comfortably and had a rain showerhead that they'd both tested out. The bed was a huge king that took up most of the real estate in the room. But of course, there was only a single bed.

Trent peered down into the opaque plastic bag with a shudder.

"I'm not wearing this." He pulled out the item that was at the top of the concealed pile. The texture was smooth under his fingertips, like silk, but with the subtle stretch of spandex. They were baby-blue boy shorts that looked to be about five sizes too small for him. The legs were decorated with a thin, delicate lace, and a looped ribbon circled the top. "What the hell is it?"

"Oh, shit," Candace grabbed the panties from his hand with a fierce blush. "Those are mine. These are yours." She fumbled around in the bag for a second before she retrieved the exact same item, only several sizes bigger. "I thought it could be fun to match."

"I'm not wearing those," said Trent for the second time. "I'm not some twink looking for a Daddy to take me home tonight."

"But twinks are hot." Candace smiled while holding the offending item up to his groin. "See? Look? It would fit perfect. You can't tell me that it wouldn't make you hard if Ian slipped his hands under your jeans and found those underneath. He would smooth over the soft lace, pushing your pants down so he could take a peek. He could peel them off real slow with his teeth. You'd be damp and leaking—and straining against the fabric as your cock tried to escape."

"Okay! Fuck, stop." Trent adjusted himself while ignoring Candace's knowing smirk. "I think it would be the same with any underwear, though. I'd get hard for him no matter what I was wearing."

"Don't say underwear again, you heathen," she said as she poked him in the chest. "These are panties. Panties are meant for fucking. Underwear is for grandmas and grandpas who sleep in separate beds. Just try them on. I want to see. They were expensive, too, so you have to at least try them."

"Why did I agree to this?" Trent grumbled as he messed with his belt buckle. A trip with his best friend was one thing, but he hated being her human doll. He slid his jeans off his hips, followed by his boxers a second later.

"Hey, little Trent," said Candace as she waved at his groin.

He'd spent most of his adolescent life playing a live model to her whims. He'd honestly been surprised when she'd come to work with him instead of pursuing her dream of fashion design. Her excuse at the time had been that she knew how to dress people to look fabulous, but she had difficulty of thinking of new ideas on her own. Inspiration was not her thing. But it had struck her at his work, where she was now the general manager of the entire operation.

He grabbed the panties and slid them over his ankles. They felt different as soon as he started sliding them up his thighs. His boxers were soft and stretchy, but these were silky and smooth. The material stretched obscenely as he settled it on his hips. His package was just barely covered by the fabric, and his pubic hair was poking through oddly. The back was already sliding between his cheeks until the seam settled against his rim. He looked massive stuffed inside the tight panties.

"They don't fit right, and they're giving me a wedgie." He pulled the fabric at the back and tried to release its hold from between his cheeks. As soon as he let go, the slick fabric slid right back in.

"It's supposed to be like that," said Candace as she slipped her own pants and thong off and slid on the booty shorts. "Oh, they feel nice." She slid her hands along the fabric to cup her ass then slide along her front. She was shaved clean expect for a tiny strip of hair just above her lips. It left a finished aesthetic when the panties slid home, with no bulging or unsightly hairs.

"You just have to adjust yourself. Here, let me." Candace grabbed his package and arranged it under the small shorts without a second thought. When she pulled her hand back, his sac looked more normal and his cock was outlined by the fabric, instead of seeming like a bulging mess. She poked at a hair and hummed. "How willing are you to shave?"

"I already trimmed. I will *not* shave." There were some lines he was not willing to cross.

"No fun. Seriously, they look good on you. I'd definitely fuck you if you had a pussy or if I wanted a kid." She dipped back into the silver bag, pulling out the next item. "I got us matching shirts too. Here, try yours on. I guessed the size."

"Of course you did," said Trent. She knew his size better than he did. "Oh, I love this band." The shirt displayed the band's title with white and red lettering against a black background. The lettering surrounded a skull with antlers twisting out through the eye sockets. It was all topped with a delicate rose.

"I know you do. You can't wear the shirt of the band you are seeing, so I went second best." Candace pulled her own T-shirt on. It fit snugly and hugged all the appropriate areas. "And they had women's sizes." Hers was slightly more delicate, with blue instead of the stark red, and the skull was a pale green with red roses curling from the eyes instead of antlers.

"Almost done. Try on the pants next." Candace tossed a pair of black jeans at him that she pulled out of the suitcase. The silver bag went back in the case, still heavy with things for later.

He slid them up his legs, having to tug hard to get them the last few inches until they settled around his hips. He looked back to the mirror behind him. His ass had lifted in the jeans, giving more definition than was actually there, and taking him from a six-and-a-half to a solid nine.

"Good. No muffin top." Candace poked the hint of visible skin at the top of his jeans.

"You calling me fat?" Trent swatted her hand away and smoothed the fabric down while tilting back and forth in the mirror.

"Everyone over a size double zero has muffin tops if they're not careful. I know it's hard to believe, but it's even happened to me. You look good." She stared at him in the mirror for a second before her hand dipped obtrusively into his pants to arrange him slightly. He grimaced as she showed no care for poor little Trent. "There. Now you are perfect. Can I do your makeup?" She perked up hopefully.

"No." He had to draw the line at that one. "When should we head down?"

"I'm thinking twenty minutes." She called back over her shoulder as she made her way to the bathroom with a brush in hand. "You can buy me a twenty-dollar drink as a thank you for the clothes and the ass they'll deliver to you."

It was still sunny when they made their way to the hotel elevator together. They'd ended up booking only a single hotel room, despite the chance that one of them would come back with company after the show. They'd seen each other fuck before. Candace had even participated in a threesome with him when he'd had a two-week stint with a bisexual guy. She'd told him that it was what had made her realize that she thought guys were hot, but she would rather fuck a woman.

The concert venue was only a quick walk from the hotel. The hotel itself was still relatively new, and the price matched the chic look. Trent's jaw had nearly hit the floor when Candace had told him how much his half was going to cost. She'd ignored his protests and flat out refused to take a subway or bus. Personally, he didn't mind the giant metal tube that would bend around the tracks with the distant smell of long-lost pennies.

They were still early when they arrived at the venue. It was an outdoor stage that was smaller than Trent was expecting. In his mind, he had visualized a massive stage that would have had enough space for four bands to play at a time. The crowd would be enormous as it stretched out into a formless sea of faces.

Instead, after a quick bag search through Candace's purse and a beeping metallic wand, they weaved through layers of concrete walkways. It was a giant circular maze, obviously meant to confuse so concert-goers would have to pass by vendors multiple times. With each loop, the forty-dollar T-shirts looked better and better.

He spotted something from the corner of his eye that made his chest pull tight and his stomach lurch. Of course, he'd been expecting to see Ian, but not until he was up on stage. He was wholly unprepared to see that handsome face on a life-sized poster in the back of a booth. The airbrushing and touch-ups from the professional photograph made him look almost too good to be real. But it was missing that sparkle that lingered every time he told a joke or buried himself deep inside Trent.

He shivered and forced himself to look away from the band poster. Candace was already ten steps ahead of him and hadn't noticed his absence yet. She was chatting away in a non-stop babble that she tended to do when she was nervous. He rushed to catch up and slid next to her again without her ever noticing his absence.

They rounded another corner and stepped up to a ramp. They passed through a second wave of security and ticket checkers before a helpful someone motioned them down the final pathway.

When they rounded the bend, Trent's excitement sank just a little bit. The stadium, if it could be called that, was terribly ugly and outdated. Little blue plastic fold-up chairs were bolted in rows that made a gradual semi-circle on a slanted concrete pad. A simple roof of metal and netting was above them, but the sides were open to the air and breeze. The stage was relatively tiny compared to the one he had pictured.

Candace moved past the chairs to a guarded entry way for floor ticket holders. Another guard looked them up and down and inspected their tickets before they were allowed past. They joined the steadily growing group in the small area. It was quickly becoming crowded.

"Do you feel like a terrorist right now?" Trent asked her as he looked back and forth across the stage. It was bigger up close, with only a thin sectioned-off path separating the stage from the onlookers.

"What do you mean?" She pulled her purse over her head before slipping it around so it was strapped across her body.

"Every time they looked in your purse, I was expecting them to find bombs or something. It's worse than going to the airport. They make you feel so guilty, even though you didn't do anything wrong." Trent shuffled closer to the front of the crowd as a space opened up. Candace sidled in next to him like a slippery worm.

"They were just looking for drugs. They did a shit job about it too." She shrugged with a little smirk. "You want?"

"No, I'm already freaked out enough. I don't want to lose control too." He shook his head almost violently and his stomach clenched. He couldn't stop her, and it wasn't his place to bitch about it now.

"Suit yourself," she said. She rummaged around in the tiny purse before she slipped a small pill out between her fingertips. In a second it was between her lips and her purse was closed again.

By the time the first band was ready to start, the floor space was packed with bodies. Trent was lucky that his height gave him a bit of an advantage in the crowd, but Candace wasn't faring as well. She had started to slip from his side as she was battered away by others pushing to the front. More than once he had to pull her back to him and plough their way back to the stage. He settled his arms on either side of her shoulders and pulled her against his chest. She wiggled in his arms and pushed away.

"You're supposed to be my wingman, not my boyfriend," she said as she freed herself.

"Just stay close to me. You're my ride home." He had to yell into her ear over the noise of the crowd.

"Aww, you're so sweet to me, Trent." She slid her arms around his waist and hugged him tight. "I almost think you love me."

"I don't know why." He sighed before prying her off him. "I'm just not one for crowds. That's all."

Her eyes lit up, but the teasing smile dropped from her face. "You really do like this guy, don't you?"

A flash of sound cut off his answer as the curtain pulled back with a burst of colour. The first band was already on stage, jumping up as they began to sing. The crowd around them cheered in the infectious way that only happened when half of the people were already drunk or high. The bag searches had obviously missed more than Candace's small stash.

The beat started like a pulse between his hips that tugged at his spine with each note. Trent wasn't a dancer, and he usually couldn't move to save his soul, but suddenly it was happening. He raised his arms and bounced on the tips of his toes as the songs moved from one into the next. He moved his hips in a way that he only did when he was buried deep inside someone as he searched for that perfect spot. The band kept moving, with only a few small breaks to yell at the crowd and wait for the intoxicated reply.

The singer was so small compared to the sound that came from his mouth, and he was so skinny that Trent thought he might collapse at any moment. The guitarist had long, tangled dreads, but the bassist and drummer were clean-cut. It was a mismatch of people and personalities, but somehow it seemed to work.

Trent was mesmerized, and when he looked at Candace, he saw that she was in a similar state. The funniest part was that he knew if he heard the song on the radio, he would probably change the channel after the first verse. But here, in the press of bodies, the sea of noise and the smell of sweat and fresh air, he was sucked into a different universe.

The silence was jarring when the songs ended and the band gave one final bow. With a strum of noise, the curtain swung closed across the front of the stage. Through the crack at the very bottom, Trent could see the flash of feet and equipment moving by.

He panted in the aftermath, his throat sore and mouth chalk-dry from singing along. The ringing in his ears and the murmur of the crowd were the only things that kept him on his feet. He couldn't imagine how Candace was feeling with drugs in her system on top of the rest.

"What are you going to do when you see him up on stage?" Candace asked after she pulled him down so she could yell into his ear over the constant ringing. She looked surprisingly well with only a light flush across her cheeks and a touch of sweat along her forehead. Her hair was out of place in a way he rarely saw it, but her smile was genuine.

Trent didn't have an answer. He'd had a plan, a perfect plan that they'd discussed at length on the drive to the hotel. It was absolutely foolproof, but it had disappeared like a wisp of smoke.

"You could fuck him up there." The drug slurred her voice. She pulled a bottle of water from her purse and took a long swig. "You could totally get past security." She waved the bottle at a large, balding figure on the other side of the metal fence. He was about an inch shorter than Trent, but he made up for it with lateral bulk. With more fat than muscle, he still made an intimidating picture.

"Here's your man!" Candace screamed as the curtain rustled and the lights flashed on the stage.

Then the drapes pulled wide and the black fabric revealed five figures on the stage. The light shimmered once and the vocalist shouted into the crowd. The crowd erupted in a scream of noise without words or meaning. It was pure joy for the love of the music.

Trent found himself yelling along with them, even as he searched the stage for the familiar smooth head. His eyes swept over them all, but he came up empty. It was only on the second sweep that he finally found him.

Ian was sitting behind the largest set of drums that Trent had ever seen. The stage lights were glowing an eerie red that cast a shadow over him and made him almost blend into the background. His head was covered in a plain black baseball cap that was turned around so the rim was at the back, and he wore a tight black shirt that was stretched across arms that were a size too big for the holes. The rest of him was hidden behind the drum set.

Trent rocked up to his toes as the crowd surged and the first song began. He leaned closer until he was pressed against the metal barrier. The lights changed, illuminating Ian's ripped figure. Bodies swayed around him, but he stood riveted to the spot. The stretch of muscle across Ian's arm as he moved, and the way his pec would tense as he beat the drums, drew Trent in. He could almost see the bead of sweat moving down Ian's brow.

He watched, mesmerized, as one song became two. The sound was different and on a whole new level compared to the previous band. These guys were good, and they knew how to put on a show. The band reset with each song, and the guitarist and bassist would sometimes switch places. The vocalist would shout into the crowd and the crowd would answer back as one.

Ian never looked at him. Not once. He stared off into the blank space behind the crowd where light had given way to darkness. His hands moved as if they were possessed and didn't even belong to him, and he hardly blinked except for when a bead of sweat dripped into his eyes.

Trent felt something inside him break at the sight. This wasn't the animated man who Trent had taken to bed. This wasn't even the angry one who had stormed out of the house. This was the hollow shell of a man who was in too deep to be able to see the way out.

"Ian," he shouted towards the stage. The sound of his shout was lost in the roar of music and the strum of guitars. Trent rocked back. He was so close to his goal, but it was just out of his reach, taunting him like a thieving bully.

Something pushed him from behind and he rocked into the barrier. The security guard looked at him, his arms uncrossing as Trent was jostled again. Trent shot an elbow back as he was hit again, and someone groaned behind him.

The press of bodies and the whirl of noise came rushing back. The lyrics, which he knew the moment he first heard them, were echoing around the stadium. He knew exactly when the sound would get loud, and when the vocalist would whisper into the microphone like it was a secret lover.

"Ian!" He shouted as loud as he could as the sound lulled. His voice cracked from the strain and he coughed into his hand. The vocalist sang on as if he hadn't heard a thing. The crowd swayed and rocked.

He looked up, ready for defeat and the indifferent stare off into the distance. Two blue eyes met his. The beat stuttered for the first time in the set as surprise overtook the stoic drummer.

A smile broke over Trent's face that was so large it hurt. His hand came up on its own and he waved at the astonished percussionist.

A moment later, the spell was broken, and the beat began again as if it had never disappeared. There was one difference, though. Those crystal eyes stayed locked on Trent. Ian's surprise bled away and a familiar smirk settled over his lips. His arms bulged with new power as he tore into the drums with an energy that lit up the stage. If Ian had been a star before, now he was a god.

The vocalist smiled as he glanced back to Ian. When he turned back to the crowd with a belted note, the place erupted in noise. The energy of the song and the power of the notes became almost tangible.

"Fucking percussion specialist." Trent mumbled.

"Did you see your boy? He looks so good." Candace screamed into his ear. Her hands wrapped around him from behind to pull him down to her.

"I just got it." He yelled back. He broke out into laughter, shaking his head at the title that Ian had given his profession when he'd told Trent all those nights ago. He watched as Ian's lips turned up and his smirk became a sweet smile as he mouthed two silent words.

Call me.

Chapter Nine

The second the curtain drew closed and Ian disappeared from view, Trent was already turning to leave. The crowd was dispersing as they went to get more beer or relieve themselves during the quick break. Candace grabbed him by the arm as he tried to push by and clung to him like a leech as people parted around him.

"Thank you. I have to pee so bad," said Candace. Her hands slipped down his arm until she was clinging weakly to his fingers. She stumbled over nothing as she tried to keep up to him.

"Are you going to be okay if I take off?" Trent asked. He paused to take a good look at her. Her cheeks were flushed and her pupils so wide that they took up almost her entire iris. She focused on his face for a split second before her gaze cut to the left at something he couldn't track.

"I'm fine." She smiled with a loopy look on her face. "This is so fun. I'm so glad we came together." She ran a hand through her hair with a broken giggle.

Trent pulled up short with a sigh. "What did you take?" he asked softly. "You're completely out of it."

"I'm fine. I'm fine. I'm fine." She nodded rapidly as she continued to repeat the same three phrases. "You can take off." She whirled around and started stomping away. She tripped over a small stone along the way, just barely correcting her balance.

"Wait," Trent grabbed her arm. "I still owe you that beer, right?" He let her go and she disappeared into the bathroom as he went to stand in line. His gaze cut back to the bathroom entrance every few minutes as he waited for his friend to emerge. He was almost at the front of the line when a voice broke into his thoughts.

"You worried your girlfriend is going to run away?"

Trent turned to the voice. A short brunette with a spiralling eyebrow piercing looked back at him. She popped her gum as he looked her up and down.

"She's not my girlfriend, actually. I'm just worried she might've gotten sick in there. Can you check on her for me and I'll buy you a beer?" asked Trent.

"Deal," she said, already walking towards the bathroom. "What does she look like again?"

"Blonde, cute. Amazing tits and she knows what a tongue is for," Trent yelled louder than he'd intended. More than one curious look passed his way.

"Perfect." The brunette broke into a smirk and disappeared into the bathroom. Trent nodded to himself, pleased that he had once again nailed it. He wasn't the best wingman ever for nothing.

Five minutes and forty dollars later, Trent was on his way out of the venue. Candace was already wrapped around the brunette and drinking from the wrong glass of beer. She was coming down off the drugs and sleepiness was hitting her hard. The brunette took it all in stride, slipping her tongue in with the foamy drink at every opportunity.

"Best wingman ever," he heard Candace yell before her voice disappeared in a wave of sound as the next band took to the stage. She knew how to look after herself and could kick his ass, despite her size and level of intoxication.

He forced himself to wait until the music was just a dull thud behind him before he pulled his phone from his pocket. His fingers hesitated over the screen for a second longer before he unlocked it. He pushed the contact that he had saved months before, when he had looked at Ian's phone. He lifted it to his ear with a shaking hand.

The path around him, which had swarmed with people trickling into the concert, was now almost deserted. He heard the click on the other end after the second ring, followed by the deep voice he remembered intimately.

"Hello?" Ian's voice cut straight through him.

"Hey," Trent breathed into the phone. He could hear the distant thump from the other side of the phone, louder than the beat on his side. "It's Trent."

"Hey, T." Ian's voice went quiet. The phone speaker muffled and cracked, and the sound of music dimmed.

"I want to see you," said Trent. His shoulders slumped as he practically begged into the speaker. Months of hurt and disappointment poured into those few words, even as he tried to keep them at bay.

"Me too." Ian's voice was so soft that he could just barely hear it. "T, I'm sorry."

"I'm sorry too. I should've realized who you were. I mean, you're in one of my favourite bands. I'm just really terrible with names and faces, and I hadn't listened to that CD in a while. It was—"

"T, it's okay. You don't have to apologise. I should've believed you..." Ian trailed off. The music went quiet before it started up again moments later.

"Can we not do this over the phone? I want to see you," said Trent. He looked around the dimly lit pathway. He wasn't the only person making an early exit and there were a few other stragglers heading slowly down the path. One was half-passed out in a bush and a security officer was already rushing over to them.

"I can't. I'm with the guys. We're just heading back to the bus for the night. We spend the night here, then we're heading out around ten tomorrow."

Trent's heart dropped to the vicinity of his shoes. "I guess I'm still your dirty little secret then." He pulled the phone away from his ear as the tears prickled at the corners of his eyes. He'd imagined the conversation going so many ways, but this wasn't one of them. He had to go shooting off his mouth before Ian could even say anything. "I gotta go." He hit the end call button before Ian could reply.

"Fuck." He shoved his phone back into his pocket, nearly ripping the seam open on the tight jeans. A tear trailed down his cheek and he wiped it away. A second one replaced it and soaked the same path.

He stormed down the path and pushed past the open turnstiles and out onto the sidewalk. The hotel was only a few minutes away, but it felt impossibly far. His face felt raw as tears streamed down and soaked into his collar below. He let them fall and refused to acknowledge that they were even there.

Ian might as well have ripped his heart out and chopped it into tiny pieces. He'd reached out, again, only to be shot down. He was the one who had come the extra distance, and Ian had refused to see him like he wasn't worth his time. It wasn't even a matter of being too far apart. The man was right fucking there.

His phone vibrated in his pocket, jingling against the room key there and making a terrible noise. Trent whipped the phone out, not even looking at the caller ID, knowing exactly who it was.

"You can fuck right off." He ended the call. He wanted to toss the phone across the sidewalk and onto the road so he could forget about everything on it. His phone vibrated again, jumping against his palm.

"What?" he screamed into the speaker.

"Is that any way to talk to your mother, you little prick?" His mother's voice cut through his daze. "Here I am, being a good mother and calling her son to see how his week went, and he tells me to fuck off? Well, I'll tell you something, mister. I can take you out of this world a hell of a lot easier than I brought you into it. I didn't go through nineteen hours of labour with no epidural to have my son tell me to fuck off. The cops will never find your body."

"Mom," he said, cutting into her rant. Her voice dropped off immediately.

"Are you okay, honey? You sound like you've been crying." Her voice changed to the coddling mother who existed beneath the layers of nosiness.

"How do you do that?" He wiped his eyes on the back of his hand. His voice cracked as a sob threatened to come from deep in his throat. He clamped down, pushing it back into his chest.

"I know you, sweetie. Are you okay? Are you hurt? Where are you?" Her voice lifted in panic.

"I'm fine, Mom. I'm just upset. I was just talking with Ian," said Trent. "It didn't go well." His phone chimed as a second call started coming through. "Mom, the other line is ringing. I gotta go."

"You tell him I say hi, sweetie, but If he hurts you again, I'll circumcise him." With a click, she was gone.

Trent took a deep breath before hitting the accept button without looking. He couldn't bear to see the name on the screen.

"T, don't hang up." Ian's voice cut through his grief like a knife. Trent couldn't help the small smile that lit up his lips at hearing him. "Are you there?" Ian asked after a beat of silence.

"Yes." Trent's voice came out scratchy and raw. He cleared his throat, trying again, but it was no better.

"Shit," Ian cut in and Trent heard him sigh on the other end. The music in the background had disappeared into silence. "Where are you staying?"

"I don't remember what it's called. It's that new hotel just down from the venue. It's fancy," Trent found himself saying. The lightpost buzzed as he leaned against the beam. He ducked his head as a few people passed him, giving him quizzical looks.

"What's your room number?"

Trent pulled the key card out of his pocket and squinted at the small print on the cardboard cover. "Four-thirteen."

"I'll be there in five," said Ian as he hung up with a click.

Trent looked up from his phone. He was still just outside the stadium, the turnstiles in sight behind him. It would take him more than five minutes to get back to his room from there. His stomach lit with panic. Ian would show up and he wouldn't be there.

He broke out into a sprint, clutching his phone like a lifeline. His feet slapped against the pavement in shoes that were meant for style, not use, and he cursed as his tight jeans tugged at his legs and made him slower. People dodged to the side of the thin sidewalk as he barrelled past them.

By the time he reached the hotel, he was gasping for air and his heart was thudding almost painfully. Sweat dripped down his back, which made his shirt cling uncomfortably, and his jeans felt like a disgusting second skin. The summer air, although slightly chilled, was still thick with humidity.

He pushed through the heavy glass doors and ran past the concierge desk while gripping his waistband and hiking his pants up the inch they had slid down. The hostess behind the desk looked up in alarm as he thudded by. His feet skidded and squeaked along the polished marble floors as he rounded the corner and ran for the elevators. One of the doors was ajar but closing fast.

Even in Trent's panic, he remembered the movie where the woman was chopped in half as she tried to get out of the elevator that was half-open. It hadn't been advertised as a horror movie, but it had left him terrified and shaking. Because of that movie, he never went near doors that were already closing, and he even avoided escalators for fear that he would somehow get caught and be dragged through the tiny crack. All that was pushed to the back of his mind now as he leapt towards the sliding metal.

He bashed his shoulder along the edge of the door hard enough to bruise as he tried to squeeze through the tiny space that was too small for him. The doors paused, shuddering to a stop before they slid open with a hollow ding. Trent tumbled into the elevator, unable to stop his forward momentum as he ran into the person waiting within. He registered a dark shirt and a blur of skin before he slammed into their chest.

If it had been someone the size of Candace, they both would've ended up with concussions from the force of the crash. Instead, he struck a broad chest that felt similar to hitting a brick wall at full tilt. Trent bounced off the elevator's back wall just before someone wrapped their arms around him and halted the inevitable tumble.

"T?"

The smell hit Trent first. The deep scent that he'd once thought was cologne, mixed with sweat and fresh air. The voice that was deep and soft, just how he remembered it as they spoke together for long hours. Those arms were strong enough to hold him up against the wall, or in this case, keep him from falling on his ass.

Trent snapped up his gaze at the sound of his nickname. It was a full minute before he could respond. The elevator door had long-since closed, leaving them in relative privacy that couldn't last long. His stomach lurched as he finally realized who he had slammed against.

"Ian." His voice was more breath than words. His throat ached from his repeated screaming at the concert hall and from the flat-out sprint right after. He was breathing so fast that his vision was starting to blur around the edges. If Ian hadn't been supporting him, he would already be on the ground.

"Why are you breathing so hard?" Ian looked down at him with concern. He pushed Trent back so he could scan for injuries.

"Had to run." Trent gasped between each word. "You said five minutes. Was still…at the stadium." He smiled as Ian broke out into a laugh. The sound of that laugh was better than any noise he'd heard all night.

"We could have made it ten instead," said Ian as he leaned past Trent and pressed the 'four' to take them to the floor Trent indicated. "Our bus was already parked in this lot, actually. We had just parked when I called you back. Our agent made a deal with the hotel so we could park overnight and still use the pool here."

"I thought I heard music in the background." Trent leaned back and pulled himself out of Ian's arms. The disappointment was starting to creep back in, ruining his joy at finally getting to see the other man.

"Just the radio. The guys were just winding down. Mac already left and took a taxi to some restaurant down the road that is supposed to be the best in the area. He calls himself a food connoisseur." Ian leaned back against the wall as he spoke. An awkward silence settled over them as the elevator lurched to a stop on the fourth floor.

"I missed you, T." Ian reached out and ran a hand down Trent's shoulder. He brushed his fingers against bare skin and sent a spark of heat down to Trent's fingertips.

"But you don't want to see me?" The words came out more bitter than he had intended. The elevator door swung wide and he stepped out onto the landing. There was an older couple waiting there. The woman smiled at Trent as he reached back and held the door open for her.

"Oh, thank you, dear." The woman stepped past him, her husband following close behind.

Trent looked up as the door started to close. Ian had shrunk back to the other side of the hall, his eyes narrowed in suspicion.

"Do you think they know?" Ian asked after the elevator door slid shut again. "That guy was glaring at me and I swear I heard him whisper, '*Faggot*'."

Trent turned and started down the hall and he didn't stop walking until he was tapping his card to the black unlocking mechanism on his door. It unlocked with a beep and he pulled it open wide enough to let Ian pass into the room behind him.

Trent stepped into Ian's space and pushed him back against the door the moment it closed. He reached up and gripped behind Ian's neck before forcing him down to his level. There was resistance at first as Ian tensed, uncertainly in his eyes. Then he was surging down to meet Trent.

Their lips met in a press of soft skin and the small sweep of tongue as Trent pushed inside. He pulled Ian down harder and licked into Ian's mouth to taste the sweetness that he remembered, along with the distant smoke of a long-forgotten cigarette.

Trent pulled back and licked over his lips to gather the moisture there. Ian's gaze darkened as he followed the movements. He bent down, trying to press their lips together again, but Trent pushed him back against the door.

"I'm not asking you to do that outside of the bedroom," said Trent as he trailed his hand down Ian's chest. His fingers pushed past the buckle of Ian's jeans and tangled in the trimmed hair that covered the man's groin. "I'm not asking to go down on you when you're up on stage. I'm not even asking you to hold my hand on the street. But I want something from you. When you stormed away like that, I thought I would never see you again. It made me realize that I had feelings for you—feelings that I wasn't quite ready for. I thought maybe you felt the same way, but it's been months since I sent your phone back and gave you my number. So, tell me, Ian. What do you want? Are you looking for a quick, secret fuck before you storm out in the morning…or are you looking for a lover?"

Ian's cheeks tinted and he looked at the soft carpet on the bedroom floor. He rubbed the smooth stretch of his skull in a move that Trent had seen many times over the course of the weekend that felt like a lifetime ago.

"What are you asking from me, T? I don't know what I can give you. I got your note and I wanted to call so bad, but we don't even live in the same country," said Ian as he rocked his head back against the closed door. His large shoulders heaved as he met Trent's gaze.

"Tell me what you want. That's all." Trent bit his lip and prepared himself for the worst.

"I just want you, T, even though we hardly know each other. I think I'm in love with you." Ian baulked at his own words. "Shit, I didn't mean to say that out loud."

Trent surged towards the man as heat burst from his chest at the unexpected words. He wrapped his arms around Ian and pulled him down into a kiss. Trent begged for entrance, and he was granted access without hesitation. Ian pushed him back, winning the fight for dominance without any struggle at all.

Heat filled Trent's belly and his groin throbbed into sudden awareness. His cock pressed against the limited space in his jeans. He slid his palms along Ian's chest and over the hidden nipples that strained beneath the fabric of his shirt.

The backs of his knees hit the king-sized bed and he crumpled onto the fluffy duvet. He could scarcely breath beneath the sudden weight as Ian moved on top of him.

"Sorry," said Ian as he moved to pull off.

"It's okay. I like it." Trent pulled him back down and relished the weight.

Ian smiled as he pressed Trent back into the mattress with full force. Trent let out a gasp as the friction of their rubbing cocks through their jeans finally gave him what he was looking for. It wasn't his own hand pressing against his groin as he thought of Ian. It was the real thing, with a cock that was bigger than he remembered.

They moved up the bed until Trent met the pillow that was suddenly against the top of his head. He snuck one hand up and teased at the edge of Ian's shirt. Ian panted into his mouth, going lax as Trent ran his hand over the thin strip of skin between pants and shirt.

"Fuck, I want you so bad, Ian. You're all I've thought about in months," Trent whispered against Ian's lips. He looped his leg over Ian's hips and twisted until he was flipped over onto his back and Trent was on top. Trent ground his hips into the barely trapped bulge and skimmed his fingertips over Ian's peaked nipples.

He pushed the edge of Ian's T-shirt up higher and mapped every new exposed inch with his tongue and mouth. He paid particular attention to the faded scar and the words stretching above it. The thin layer of hair tickled his tongue as he lapped over the heated flesh.

He paused as he looked at Ian's tiny belly button that was hidden behind the tuck of skin. Ian sucked in a breath as Trent leaned down and slipped his tongue into the divot. Ian shuddered under him and rocked his hips up into the empty air. Trent snaked his hand down between them to press at the hard outline of the straining cock that pushed against thick denim.

He slid his hand away from the bulge before moving up. Ian groaned at the loss and bucked his hips uselessly. Trent pulled at the offending T-shirt before slipping it over his lover's head and tossing it onto the ground. He trailed his fingertips down the rugged muscles of Ian's arms, tracing every tense line. He dipped to the small bit of softness under Ian's arms.

"Stop it," Ian laughed and tried to pull away, "that tickles."

"You're beautiful." Trent slid his fingertips across the same place a second time, ignoring the stuttered laughter. "You're so hard here," he said as his hands moved over biceps and triceps. "But this little spot under here is still so soft and sweet." He leaned forward to kiss the smooth skin. He grimaced at the bitter taste of deodorant as he pulled back and licked his lips.

"You think I'm sweet?" Ian looked dazed with his mouth wide and his pupils blown.

"Like fuckin' candy." Trent replied as he moved down to the small bump of Ian's collar bone. He kissed the hard bone before pulling back his lips and nibbling. Ian's sharp inhale spurred him on and he bit the skin, leaving an impression of teeth behind. He dipped lower again to lick a taut nipple before he scraped his teeth over the bud. Ian's back arched off the bed and Trent held on as the man bucked against him. He ground down into his lap mindlessly, so focused was he on his task.

"Your lips are the sweetest thing I've ever tasted. Even when you had morning breath, it was still like sugar." Trent surged up and crashed his lips back into Ian's. Two large hands settled on his hips before they moved lower to knead his ass.

Ian flipped them in a move that was all raw strength and pressed Trent's back into the mattress with his legs on either side of Ian's waist. A length ground down into him with the perfect pressure that was too much and not enough. Trent flinched as he was suddenly right on the edge.

"You okay?" Ian mouthed over his lips and down to his neck. "I'm not gonna hurt you. I'll go as slow as you need. I know that ass was made just for me. It must've been so lonely without me there to fill it up just perfect — and just the way you need it. You're probably so ready for me now. I could just roll you over and slide in and you'd fuckin' take it, wouldn't you? Such a greedy ass, T. I could fuck it for days."

"Fuck," Trent said through clenched teeth. His hips jerked once and the pressure snapped as he came in his pants like a teenager. He couldn't stop his hips as they jerked against Ian in an uncontrollable grind.

"Did you just...?" Ian pulled back with his mouth gaping wide in astonishment.

Trent groaned as he came down from his orgasm and covered his face with his hands as he flushed with embarrassment. He bit his lip to stutter a second groan of absolute mortification when Ian broke out into a laugh.

"Shut up," said Trent as he smacked the man lightly on the shoulder. Ian rocked back onto his knees as his chest heaved with laughter. Trent just wanted to curl up in a ball and wither away into the sheets. He hadn't had an incident like that in over ten years. The last time it had happened, he'd been fumbling around in a club bathroom, grinding for way too long against a willing body. He had a weakness for dirty talk, and with the way Ian had whispered right into his ear, he just hadn't been able to hold back.

"That is so fucking hot." Ian pushed him back as he attacked him again with a new vengeance. He swept his tongue deep once before he pulled back. "No one has ever been that responsive for me, T. So fucking good for me." He tugged at the hem of Trent's shirt and pulled it over his head.

"Love the shirt, by the way. Do you want me to get it signed for you? The drummer is a friend of mine." He tossed the bunched-up shirt to the side before he leaned in to lick a stripe up Trent's chest and flick his pierced nipple. "Just don't going falling in love with him. He is very straight."

"I won't," said Trent as he arched up into Ian's mouth. His groin was damp and getting uncomfortable, but his cock was already twitching back to awareness. Ian's presence was like a kind of natural Viagra that left him constantly wanting.

Ian dropped his hands to the buckle on Trent's pants, playing with the button before popping it open with one hand. The zipper slid down and Ian dipped inside. He paused just as his fingers skimmed inside Trent's jeans.

Trent went tense, very suddenly remembering what he was wearing beneath his too-tight pants. Ian was looking at him incredulously as his fingertips slid over smooth fabric. He played with the looped ribbon of the waistband before dipping down farther over the wet, silken fabric.

"They were a gift." Trent blurted out as Ian started to slip the jeans from his hips. Inch by inch, the blue panties were revealed, and Ian's eyes went wide, his mouth hanging open as he took in the sight.

The front was ruined with a wet stain that stretched over the otherwise-innocent fabric. Somehow, with the sprinting, grinding and an orgasm, Trent's package had managed to stay neatly encased in the thin fabric. His cock was straining in the soft fabric's embrace.

"Should I be jealous?" Ian asked as he skimmed his fingers lightly down the panties, before pressing the damp patch with his thumb. His eyes had gone dark, but his lips were set in a small frown.

"No, they were a gift for you. My friend Candace bought them and made me wear them for you." Trent bucked into the light caress and whined as Ian moved his hand away.

"Remind me to thank her." Ian moved down so his head was level with Trent's groin before he nuzzled against the straining fabric and breathed deeply. "You smell good, T. I bet you taste even better. Can I taste you? Are you still clean?" Ian looked off to the side as he asked, as if he was afraid of what Trent's answer would be.

"There's been no one since you. I couldn't be with anyone else when I was just thinking of you." Trent hadn't stepped foot in a bar or a club and had managed to avoid a heavy-handed guy at the grocery store.

Ian's heated eyes snapped back to him at the declaration. "Me too." It was so quiet that Trent wasn't sure if he was supposed to hear it at all. He did, though, and it sent a rush of warmth to his chest.

Ian gripped the edge of the panties, sliding his fingertips inside and teasing the sensitive skin underneath. Slowly, he began to slide them down Trent's legs until his cock sprang free and slapped against his stomach. It was still damp from his cum, but already red and starting to weep anew.

After tearing away the panties, Ian slid his mouth over Trent's cock a moment later. He wrapped the skilled tongue around him and swept away every drop from tip to base. Ian took him into his mouth entirely until his cock was nudging the back of Ian's throat and moving beyond. The wet heat pulsed around him as Ian hummed, and Trent struggled to keep from bucking his hips.

"You taste better than I remember." Ian slid off with a pop, licking the last remnants of cum from his lips. His voice was slightly hoarse from having Trent's cock down his throat a moment before. "I dreamed about that cock and how good it tasted. The dreams never came close." He wrapped his hand around the shaft and gave it two quick pulls as he flicked the piercing with his tongue.

Trent groaned, biting his lip as heat overwhelmed him. He was closer than he'd thought possible, especially since he had just come a few minutes prior. He really needed Ian to stop talking if he didn't want to embarrass himself again.

"Ian, I'm gonna come again if you don't slow down." He moaned aloud as Ian quickened his pace before he circled the head with his thumb and smoothed down the wet shaft, dragging slowly along the piercing.

"Maybe that's what I want," said Ian. "Maybe I want you to come so many times that you just can't anymore.

You'll be crying out for me to keep going and to stop all at the same time. That's when I'll lick you open real slow and fuck you on my cock. I won't stop, no matter how much you beg me. I know that's what you really want."

"It is. Please fuck me." Trent groaned as the hand dropped away from his dick. Ian dropped onto his cock again and he let out a strangled yell. It was so hot and so good that it brought him right up to the edge. He smoothed his hand over the bald scalp and pressed Ian even closer to his groin. He felt the heat building as his orgasm started to peak.

Ian ripped off his cock seconds before he came, making him pulse near-painfully. Trent groaned as his orgasm slipped just out of reach. He tried to reach his cock to relieve the insistent pressure, but he was batted away.

"Have you ever tried edging?" asked Ian. It was a harsh term for such a sweet thing. Ian blew over the wet, pulsing surface, but kept his hands and mouth far away.

"Not on me, but I did on someone else," said Trent through gritted teeth as he tried to keep his hips from violently bucking up. "He cursed me the entire time, even though he asked me for it. I think I understand why now."

"Is it too much for you T? I can make you come if you want instead. You don't have to hold back." Ian circled the base of Trent's cock with his fingers and pressed lightly on the shaft.

"No, it's good. It's a lot, and it almost hurts a bit, but it's really, really good too." Trent felt the edge slipping further away as the throb in his groin calmed. He met Ian's smiling face and flashed a grin of his own.

"Turn over for me," said Ian as he pushed at one hip.

Trent scrambled to turn over, loving what was coming next. He remembered clearly how talented Ian was with his tongue, and how it had felt to be rimmed for the first time. He found himself craving the sensation over the feel of fingers in his ass. Nothing could match that warm slipperiness that seemed to move everywhere at once.

"Is it okay? I ran all the way here." Trent trembled as the tongue probed at his rim regardless. Ian hummed before pulling his cheeks wide and pressing in. His slick tongue penetrated him with a smooth slide, with one finger following it a moment later. Trent clenched down on the intrusion automatically before he took a deep breath and forced himself to relax.

"Fuck, T, you're still so tight. I thought you would've bought a toy by now to fill up that bleak bedside drawer of yours." Ian dove back in like a starved man.

"I did," Trent said between gasps and moans. "It just wasn't the same. I would get distracted, and I could never get the rhythm right. It was like trying to fuck myself."

"I'm sure you're a good fucker, T. But you're right. You were made for my cock, and some piece of plastic isn't going to replace me." He drove deep with a second finger and spread Trent's cheeks wider. The scratchy stubble of Ian's scruff scraped along Trent's most sensitive place, sending him even higher.

Trent arched his back and cried out as Ian struck the bundle of nerves. He pressed back against Ian's fingers as he pushed in deep again, this time skimming along the edges of his prostate.

"So sensitive for me, T. You could come just from me inside you. I could leave you hanging there, and you would still come for me." A third finger pressed into the tight ring. "Just relax, T. You're doing so well. I could do this all night." A hot breath stroked against Trent's swollen ring.

"Please make me come." Trent sighed as the fingers withdrew, leaving him empty and open. The bed let out a soft creak as Ian shifted behind him. When Trent peered back, the man was looking around the room as if he were searching for something.

"Shit, do you have a condom and lube?" asked Ian as he leaned down and opened the side drawer. There was a bible there that was crisp and untouched.

Ian scrambled for his pants, which he had discarded on the ground while he was rimming Trent. His cock was red and curved towards his belly in a solid arch that leaned just slightly to the right. It was bigger than Trent remembered — so much bigger than just three fingers.

Ian snagged his wallet, pulling it wide before ripping a condom from the billfold. A card flew from the folds in his haste and it was quickly retrieved.

"Shit, this is expired. I wasn't expecting to get laid tonight. Sorry, T. I'm usually more prepared than this, I swear." He tossed the silver packet into the garbage bin across the room. It sailed through the brim with ease.

"Don't worry. I bought some stuff. Candace packed it all up in her suitcase for me. There should be a silver bag." Trent leaned on his hand with a smile as he watched the other man scramble for a condom.

Ian marched towards the suitcase, his cock bobbing with every step. He threw it open with such force that it turned over onto its side, tipping off the stand and spilling its contents across the ground. Ian didn't even seem to care. He snagged the silver bag, the same one that had contained the satin panties, and tossed it onto the bed. He followed a moment later before he gripped the corner of the bag and upended it so the contents spilled over the comforter.

"Um." Trent flushed bright red and whirled around as items rolled across the bed. His eyes were drawn to a bright pink double-ended dildo that stopped just shy of his knee. It was modest, only perhaps ten inches in total length, but it made up for its size in pure detail. Realistic veins squiggled along the side and over the bulbous heads that were lined with projections like a ribbed condom. It rolled to nudge against his knee, starting to vibrate.

"Oh my God, that is *not* mine," said Trent as he watched the bouncing double dong vibrate violently across the bedspread. Ian was frozen in place too, with his eyes locked on the vibrating phallus.

"You don't want to try it?" Ian's lips pulled up into a smirk and he reached for the fake cock, twisting a dial near the middle so that it stopped humming. "It would feel really good, T."

"It's probably been in my best friend. I'll take a pass." Trent shuddered. It was one thing to share a water bottle, but this was just way too personal. Even when they'd foolishly had a threesome together, Trent had always made sure to keep a warm body between himself and his friend's nether regions.

Ian shrugged. "You've got a point. What else was in this bag of wonders?" He skimmed through the foil wrappers, grasping the first condom he touched. There were another twenty spread across the bed. "Your friend came prepared."

"They aren't for her," Trent blushed even brighter. "She packed them for me. She had high hopes."

"Then I won't disappoint. Oh, and you got the good lube. This is going to feel so much better. Trust me, T." Ian peeled the wrapper off the bottle and flicked the cap open. He poured a drop onto his finger before smoothing it around with his thumb. "Perfect. And I'll take this too." He grabbed something else from the pile before Trent could see it and deposited it behind him and out of view. "Turn around, T. I wanna taste you some more."

Their mutual arousal had dimmed somewhat while they'd stared at the plastic penis, but Trent's cock throbbed back to life at Ian's words. He quickly turned back around and pressed his face into the pillow to muffle the sounds he knew he would make.

He felt the sweep of a tongue along his rim again and pushed back against the feeling. It was fleeting, slipping out of him, only to be replaced by three fingers a moment later. They slid in smooth and slick, and so much easier than they had with just spit. They pressed deep, sliding the new lube around his hole and pushing deeper inside than before.

Something else teased against his entrance as the fingers withdrew. It wasn't the blunt head of a cock that he was expecting, but something cool and slim. It slid in easily, only a small pressure before it disappeared past his rim and pressed inside. He could barely feel it as Ian pushed it deeper inside with one of his fingers. Instead, he could only feel the tiny tickle of something at his rim that connected to the object inside.

"Ready, T?" Ian didn't wait for an answer.

Trent heard a click, then his back was bowing and he was yelling out as the bullet jumped to life inside him. The finger that was still in there pushed it directly against his prostate. It wasn't a steady hum like the double-dong. It pulsed and jumped rapidly and hard against his prostate in an unpredictable and increasing pattern.

"Fuck. Ah," said Trent, barely able to get the words past his lips. The buzzing calmed to a more manageable level but was still hard enough to make him see stars. His cock was leaking so steadily that it almost felt like he was coming in a constant wave.

"Sorry, T. I Didn't know it was maxed out when I turned it on. It's good, though, right? You look so good like that, T, with your ass in the air and your face buried in the pillow. I bet the neighbours still heard you scream." He undulated his finger and the bullet circled Trent's bundle of nerves.

"Nnnnn, Ian, I can't." Drool dribbled from his mouth and soaked the pillow beneath his cheek as his face went utterly slack.

"Don't hold back, T. You can come when you need to. I'm gonna start fucking you as you do so you get tight around my cock." There was a crinkle of foil as Ian likely plucked the condom from the package and rolled it down his hard member. The snap of the lubricant cap was lost to Trent's continuous moans.

"Put it in me now, at the same time." Trent rocked back against the finger, needing more than the inconsistent buzz to get him off. He heard a smothered curse, then the finger withdrew and Ian was guiding his cock to his entrance. He pushed deep in a single drawn-out thrust that slid the bullet harder against his sensitive bundle.

"Fuck, Ian, I'm going to come." The pressure of Ian so deep and perfect inside, combined with the rumbling bullet, pushed him over the edge without a single stroke on his own neglected cock. It jumped and spurted as Ian started thrusting inside immediately, skimming over his prostate just how Trent liked it.

Ian pulled back just enough to jerk out the bullet before he was plunging back inside. Trent tried to muffle the sound in the pillow, but Ian gripped his hair to pull his head up.

"I want to hear you, T. Fuckin' scream for me." Ian's grumbled into his ear as his hand clenched harder on Trent's hair. His voice was deep and so utterly dark as he had his way.

Trent did scream. On the next stroke, a sound burst from his lips that was half-scream and half-moan. It was loud enough that he was sure that he could be heard two doors down on the floor below, but he couldn't care less. He rocked his hips back to meet each of Ian's thrusts, taking him hard and fast and deep.

"I'm going to come, T. You ready for me?"

Trent groaned, slamming his hips back hard. Ian's cock smashed against his prostate and his body went taut as his vision whited out. He felt Ian's cock twitch and go impossibly harder before his thrusts stuttered to a halt and he ground himself into Trent's ass. They gasped together as the endorphins slowly dissipated.

Trent grimaced as Ian pulled out and made quick work of the condom. His breath rushed out as Ian collapsed on top of him with his entire weight. He grunted, elbowing the man until he rolled to the side and settled onto his back. Trent crawled over him before wrapping his arms across his chest and settling his head down on the thin patch of hair between his two pecs.

"I missed you," Trent whispered before placing a kiss on Ian's chest. "More than I thought possible." Slick sweat pressed against his cheek as the air conditioning hummed to life on the other side of the room.

"I don't deserve you." Ian threaded his hand through Trent's hair, combing through the damp strands. "I couldn't bring myself to call you, not after what I said to you. I was so angry when I stormed out of your house. I kept expecting to see something on the news or TMZ, but there was nothing. Then I got my cell phone back. It took me a week before I could turn it on and another week until I could open that note. By then, I thought it was just too late and there was no way you'd ever forgive me. I couldn't believe that you felt the same way, like I'd finally met someone who just made sense. I've had a lot of people, way too many when I was high or drunk, but none of them meant anything. Sure, it was nice to blow off steam, but I never went back for more. With you, I just couldn't get enough, then I thought you'd lied. I've never felt betrayal like that."

Trent shifted on Ian's chest and turned to look at those beautiful blue eyes. "Have you ever thought that the reason I didn't know who you were is that you just aren't that popular?" Trent laughed at the incredulous look on Ian's face. "I'm joking, but I get it. Everyone but me knows who you are." He sobered. "Is it hard to live that kind of life where everything is public?"

"It's not really like that. I still have my private life for the most part, but the hardest part is being recognized. At first, it was neat going around and everyone seemed to know me and want my autograph. But it gets old really quick. It makes the little things hard, like going to the grocery store or the movies. It's great having money for a fancy car, but you can't drive it anywhere. I was ready to be done and I just took off and drove around for days. Then I almost hit you." He pulled Trent into a hug.

Trent kissed the same place on Ian's chest again before he moved over to a nipple. He sucked the pebbled bud into his mouth, smiling as Ian gasped. "Can you stay the night?" He moved over to the other nipple without waiting for an answer.

"You couldn't make me leave if you tried. I'll have to leave around ten, though, so they don't drive away without me."

Trent stayed silent and ignored the rumbling at the pit of his stomach. He knew Ian would have to leave again, but somehow, he'd hoped that their reunion might stave off the inevitable. He wasn't sure he'd be able to go back to the way things were.

He moved up to Ian's lips before dipping down and pressing against the sweet heat. He trailed his hands down Ian's body as he tried to memorize every inch. It wasn't long before Ian was straining below him and Trent was slipping a fresh condom over his heated flesh. He straddled his hips and slid down onto his length with a pleased sigh. He kept his eyes wide open and his lips sealed as he took in every noise and every sight as he brought Ian to completion. His own cock only made it half-hard, still too exhausted from the earlier romp.

He collapsed down onto Ian's chest after taking care of the second condom and wiping down both of their bellies and chests with a warm cloth. He fell asleep with his arms wrapped around Ian, holding tight and never wanting to let go.

Chapter Ten

Trent woke up slowly to the sensation of hot, sticky skin against the damp side of his face. He was warmer than usual and under a comforter that was unusually soft. The unfamiliar scents of strange laundry detergent and sweet cologne tickled his nose. There was something else, almost like a faint perfume, but it was lost beneath the smell of Ian.

He pried his eyes open and blinked down at the naked chest beneath him. There was a puddle of drool in the centre of sparse hair and a red smudge from where his face had been pressed on the rigid bumps of Ian's sternum.

Ian was still asleep, with his face relaxed and his mouth slightly open. His eyelids fluttered as he dreamed, and he twitched his fingers ever so slightly where they were gripped around Trent's hips. He looked younger than his thirty-four years, with every worry and stress line smoothed. The deep rock of his chest as he breathed was as rhythmic as a wave.

Trent's chest clenched painfully, but he pushed the feeling away. The room was still dim, with only the first morning rays peeking through the curtain. The painting on the wall, of a willow over a lake, burst with colour as the first hint of light hit it.

It was just enough light to see the tiny details on Ian's face that he had taken for granted the night before. The low light also meant that he still had time.

His morning wood throbbed to life as he peeled off Ian. He moved carefully beneath the comforter and let it fall shut so he was in total darkness. It was even warmer beneath the blankets as he settled himself over Ian's groin.

He didn't want to risk waking Ian by teasing him to life slowly, so he grasped Ian's semi-hardness in his hand and slid it straight into his mouth. He swirled his tongue as the cock in his mouth responded automatically.

Ian rocked his hips up into his mouth as a hand gripped Trent's head lightly. The corner of the covers lifted and light flashed into Trent's small cave. A sleepy, blushing face looked down at him. He smiled around the heavy cock in his mouth.

"T?" Ian tossed the blanket aside.

Cool air rushed over Trent's naked body and he sighed with relief. He dropped his hands to the bed as he prepared to crawl back up to Ian's mouth for a proper good morning kiss. He froze as his hand struck something warm and firm. His gaze snapped to the object, expecting one of the sex toys that had tumbled onto the bed the night before.

A foot peeked out instead. It was small and feminine, and the toes were painted bright purple with a shimmering glaze that sparkled in the growing light.

They curled and flexed as the cold air hit them before they disappeared under the edge of the blanket.

Trent shot up and ripped back the rest of the cover with a giant tug. He knew that the foot didn't belong to Candace, as she was a size nine. It was attached to the short brunette who Trent had briefly encountered at the concert hall. Candace and the brunette were completely naked and snuggled together on the far side of the massive bed. He had been so focused on Ian that he hadn't even noticed the shocks of dark and blonde hair peeking above the comforter.

"What the fuck, Candace?" Trent lunged for the comforter again and pulled it back over the two naked women with a startled yelp. He leaned down and used his own body to cover Ian's, sacrificing his dignity to protect Ian.

"It's our room, Trent." Candace peeked back over the blanket while blinking the sleep from her eyes. "If you can bring someone back for a fuck, then so can I."

"Not at the same time!" Trent flushed as he grabbed for any piece of clothing that might be in reach, while still trying to keep Ian covered. He found the stained blue panties beside the bed, so he grabbed them and lay them over Ian's groin. The tiny fabric did nothing to cover his generous length, which hadn't diminished in the slightest.

"We didn't." Candace rolled out of the bed with an air of nonchalance, leaving a cowering brunette behind. "I gave you dibs, and you didn't have the decency to even clean up your mess. You're lucky I didn't kick you out last night." She strolled across the room before bending over, completely naked, to root through the overturned suitcase. She grabbed a shirt before she dropped it back to the ground, meeting Ian's face for the first time. Ian had gone completely still beneath Trent, but he hadn't said a word.

"Hi, I'm Candace." She waved at Ian, her breasts swaying back and forth. "You must be Ian. Trent's told me all about you."

Ian shifted under Trent before he got one hand free and gave a half-hearted little wave back. "Hey."

"Should I go?" The brunette finally spoke up. She had wrapped most of the blanket around her so that only her purple toes and her face poked out. She looked at Ian for the first time and her eyes went wide. "Wait! Are you —?"

"Give me your number before you go," said Candace as she cut off the brunette and turned away again. She pulled a shirt and pants quickly over her frame before tossing the brunette her clothes, which were scattered along the floor.

In record time, the brunette shimmied into them while keeping under the blankets. She scrambled out of the bed, scribbling her number on the hotel pad before she took off out of the door. Trent grabbed the free comforter as soon as the door clicked shut and tossed it over Ian. He scrambled for Ian's clothes, which were scattered on the ground. The man caught them one-handed.

"I can't believe you fucked her when we were sleeping right next to you." Trent found a fresh pair of boxers and pulled them over his hips. "Isn't that some kind of rape? It's gotta be rape. Ian, why aren't you getting dressed?" He rounded on the man. Ian was still sitting in the same position on the bed with his cock tenting the blanket. There was a small smile on his lips.

"Don't want to get dressed if I'm just gonna take it off again." Ian replied simply. He broke out into a laugh when a stained pair of pants were tossed at his head.

Candace giggled behind Trent. "You know what? I think I like you. Let me buy you breakfast, after you take care of your little problem, of course — or not so little, from the look I got at it. Have you ever thought of selling a cast of your junk to sex shops? It's more than just a pretty head."

"You're unbelievable," said Trent as he shook his head and wished he had something to toss at her. Ian only laughed harder. "Both of you are."

"I want to go for a swim before we go, anyway. There's a pool on the roof. On the roof, Trent!" She pulled her bathing suit out of the tiny pocket in the suitcase. Her clothes were off again a second later, then she was pulling on the suit.

"Can you stop getting naked? Any more tits and I might go straight." Trent groaned as he smacked a hand over his face.

"*Pfft,*" Candace laughed. "I've touched your dick more than Ian has, and I have no desire to get it anywhere near my twinkle cave. No thank you." She grabbed a towel from the bathroom and walked out of the door. It shut with the same soft click. The silence was near stifling after her energy disappeared from the room.

"Your friend is…" Ian trailed off as he stifled his laughter.

"A human disaster? Someone who doesn't know what boundaries are?" Trent groaned and sat on the edge of the bed next to Ian. He'd wanted the two to meet, but he'd hoped to introduce them slowly.

Candace could be a lot. Sometimes if one pulled the bandage off too fast, they ended up ripping off skin too.

"I was going to say she was neat. Hot, too. If you were both into it, that would be a totally epic threesome." Ian wrapped his arms around Trent's shoulders and pulled him back so he was lying alongside him.

"Not happening. Been there, done that. Aren't I enough?" It came out sharper than Trent had intended. The laughter on Ian's lips died away.

"We should talk, Trent. I have six months left on this tour and this is my last day in this part of the country." His arms tightened and his hands clenched in the sheets. "I don't know when I'll see you again." The shadows of the morning light were long on his face.

"I'll wait for you. I know yesterday, when you said you were falling in love with me, I didn't say it back, but I am. It's not just about the sex, Ian, I missed the other stuff too." Trent took a deep breath of Ian's scent. It was probably the thing he missed most about the man.

Ian huffed. "What? Like how I snore?"

Trent shook his head. "It's weird, but I missed seeing you in the back yard on that crappy lawn chair with Cadbury curled up in your lap. She still looks for you, you know. Every time she sees me, I'm just a disappointment." Trent turned his head and tilted his lips back to meet Ian's in a chaste kiss. "I miss how you ate all the food I made, even if it wasn't that great. I miss how your feet hung over the end of the couch, even though it was the biggest couch the store had that would fit."

"Trent." Ian sighed and ran his hands over his arms. "I miss that stuff too…except for the couch thing. That was just annoying. We could try to make this work. I'll talk to you when I'm on the road as much as I can. If you call, I'll try to answer."

Trent turned to lay his head down on Ian's chest. There was a little divot there in the top of Ian's pec that his head fit into perfectly. He ran a hand under the comforter to the base of Ian's cock. It was soft now and rested comfortably in his hand. It twitched under his touch.

"I might hate myself for this later," said Trent, "but can we go swimming too? I love swimming and I hardly ever get to do it. And, it's on the roof." Not to mention that his ass felt like it had been split in two. *Why didn't I stop after round one?*

"Sure," Ian shrugged. "As long as I'm with you. But I didn't bring swim trunks."

"I brought two pairs. Well, Candace packed them. Thank God for that woman." Trent shook his head at the absurdity of that statement. He jumped off the bed and grabbed both pairs before tossing the larger one to Ian. They were still ridiculously tight when Ian slid them over his thicker thighs. Trent paused for a moment just to enjoy the view.

"She bought you the tickets to the show too, right?" Ian grabbed two towels from the bathroom. Trent nodded, following him out of the door.

"She's the best friend I could ask for."

The pool was just as amazing as Trent had expected, and watching Ian swim was like watching a hurricane approach a shore. His powerful arms carved through the water as he dove in and started doing laps immediately. Water swirled around him and he made an actual wake from the strength of his movements. He was quick and inevitable. The only stranger in the pool gave Ian a startled look and quickly moved to join Candace in the hot tub.

Trent was so focused on the view inside the pool that he could hardly pay any attention to the landscape surrounding the rooftop. The slight breeze was warm, but the sun had tucked itself behind a cloud with a threatening look. The lake, which was just visible beyond the glass railing, was grey but calm. The people walking on the streets below scurried like tiny ants.

"You coming in?" Ian paused at the side of the pool and hefted himself up to rest his head on his arms. He was barely out of breath from his water sprint.

"Is there anything you aren't good at?" asked Trent as he dipped one toe into the pool. The water was freezing and suddenly the air didn't seem nearly as warm.

"Lots of stuff," said Ian as he pulled himself closer to the stairs where Trent was slowly walking in. "I can't cook worth shit, for one. And I only finished grade eight for another."

Trent swallowed at the painful admission. He couldn't imagine. His education was so important to him and it was the basis for who he was as a person.

"Is there anything *you* aren't good at?" Ian turned the question back at him, successfully breaking the silence.

"Umm, I'm shy?" He toed the water and sank down to his ankles with a shudder. "I'm not brave or very strong. I take most things personally, even if they're not. I have no filter, and I am terrible at board games."

"We're even then." Ian lunged at him suddenly and grabbed him around the waist.

Trent screeched, with a noise that was much too high for his size, and clawed at Ian as he was lifted off the stairs by cold and clammy arms. Suddenly, he was falling and plunging into frigid water. Air expelled from his lungs in a rush of bubbles as he screamed again. The arms released him and he was pulling himself to the surface that was only a few inches away.

He broke the surface with a second yell as his skin reacted to so much cold water all at once. He wouldn't be surprised if his balls were the size of raisins. Ian was laughing hard as he quickly swam to the other side of the pool. The sound was deep and rich, and Trent couldn't help the smile that beamed on his face. He floated back over as Trent started to catch his breath. *Big mistake.*

Trent lunged. Water splashed around the pool and all over the concrete deck as they collided. Trent wasn't a great swimmer, but he knew his way around the water and had wrestled once or twice in his life. Ian was obviously experienced, and so much stronger, but Trent was faster. He ducked beneath Ian's arms and slammed into the taller man's torso. They landed close enough to the wall that Trent was able to reach it with his feet and use the solid surface to overpower Ian.

With a yell of his own, Ian tipped back. They grappled in the water and the smooth surface turned turbulent. Trent tried to keep himself up by using Ian's body as a ladder, but Ian fell away beneath him, only to resurface behind him and drag him back down.

They broke the surface again with Ian still holding Trent tight to his chest. Trent flexed and tried to wiggle out of the hold, but there was no breaking the drummer's grip this time...not that he wanted to. There was nothing better than the addictive feeling of being hopelessly powerless.

He ground his hips as the emotion sent a surge to his gut. Ian moaned against his ear as Trent pressed his ass against the bulge there. It made him realize that his cock was swelling, despite the chilly water around him. It pressed against the soft seam of his swim trunks in an obvious tent.

The door slammed shut as the stranger had finally had enough. They pulled themselves out of the hot tub and left. Trent glanced around as the bubble broke. Candace was staring at him from across the room, with her head peeked over the side of the hot tub and her chin on her crossed forearms. There was a flush across her cheeks from the heat of the smaller pool and her hair was haphazard after a night of dancing and fucking.

"You guys are really hot together," she yelled across the rooftop. Perhaps the flush on her cheeks wasn't from the heat of the tub. "Oh, don't mind me at all. Please continue."

The intruding stare didn't seem to bother Ian, who ground against his ass even harder. The tip of the barely covered cock pressed at the seam of Trent's ass, where he was still slightly loose from the previous evening's activities. A hand snaked down into his swimsuit and clutched his cock in a hard grip.

For a moment, Trent forgot himself. That hand knew him so well. The grip was just on the side of too harsh, and the heat was a huge contrast to the freezing pool water. It was so much stimulation that his brain went offline and he could only hope that Ian would look after him.

"Wait," Trent whispered quietly. He flashed his eyes between a flushed gaze to his right and the cerulean sky above. The door could open at any moment as other couples woke up and decided to take their turn in the tub. He shuddered as the eyes watching them grew half-lidded. It wasn't an attraction to his friend that drove him higher, but the mere thought of being watched.

"Let me have this," Ian groaned into his ear as he ground his hips hard. "I've never had this, T. I want to show you off to everyone I know, but I can't. Just let me have this." His grip tightened on Trent's cock until it was nearly painful.

Any second thoughts Trent had about getting off in front of his best friend were immediately swept away as Ian started to stroke him in earnest. His large hand moved from base to tip with smooth confidence, before he squeezed the head and ran his thumb over the pierced tip.

"I want you inside me." Trent groaned as Ian's hips bucked up and the hand on him momentarily stuttered. A part of his mind knew that it wasn't possible. The water would not offer the type of lubrication that he would need for it be pleasant for him, especially when he was already sore. Ian's cock was too big to take dry, even if he wanted to.

Trent squeaked as he was suddenly dropped into the water when Ian's hands fled from him. The heat at his back disappeared as Ian pulled himself over the edge of the pool. He offered his hand and hefted a shocked Trent out a moment later. Trent tried to smooth the front of his swim trunks, but it was no use. His cock was jutting out proudly at a ninety-degree angle, only slightly weighed down by the water-soaked trunks.

"Come on," said Ian as he slipped his hand into Trent's and dragged him across the cement. He moved away from the entrance of the pool and over to the hot tub that Candace was watching them from with rapt attention. The tub was set into the wall just a bit so that it wasn't the first thing someone looked at when they came up on the roof. Their gaze would go to the pool, the skyline, then the little hot tub set back against the wall.

The heat of the pool was shocking against his skin and he groaned as he settled into the water. His gaze caught Candace's flush, before he looked away in embarrassment. He couldn't believe they were doing this.

"May we join you?" Ian said as he settled into the middle and away from the benched sides. He pulled until Trent was against him, with his back pressing to Ian's front.

Candace nodded, speechless, as Ian pushed Trent closer to the edge of the tub. He placed his hand on Trent's back, gently forcing him down until he was leaning over the hot water. Trent caught his weight as Ian tipped him over. He crawled up onto the bench with his knees as he was pushed even closer to the edge. That brought his ass flush against Ian's groin at the perfect angle.

Trent let out a little gasp as Ian tugged at his waistband until it was slipping down past his hips to his knees. It held his legs together in a trapping embrace as Ian hovered ever closer. He was exposed in front of his lover, his best friend and the rest of the world.

He jolted as something wet pressed against his already-damp hole. A finger, slick with something that must've been saliva, pressed past the tight ring of muscle to the first knuckle. There was a dull ache that made him whine high in his throat. The heat of his belly pushed sounds past his lips that he never would've let out in any other circumstance.

"It's okay, T. We'll take it slow. I know you can take it. You're already so loose and ready for me. I could just push it all in and you'd take it, wouldn't you? You'd be so good for me." He worked his finger from side to side as he tried to loosen Trent.

Trent heard Candace let out a groan as Ian spoke and he managed to make himself look at her. She was staring at the place where Ian was pressed so intimately inside him. Her gaze was dark and flushed and her hand had disappeared beneath the water.

A second wet finger pressed into him and the sting was suddenly harsh. He let out a second whine, louder than the last, and the fingers withdrew all at once. The hands disappeared and suddenly Ian was pressing his tongue to Trent's entrance instead.

It was wet, hot and so fucking good that it made his arms tremble as he struggled to keep himself from face-planting onto the concrete. Ian pushed his tongue inside and swirled around his slightly loosened muscle with single-minded intent. The fingers pressed back, and they slid all the way home as he relaxed around them.

"That's it, T," Ian said as he pulled away before plunging back in.

Spit dribbled down his thighs to mix with the pool water as Ian sloppily licked his rim inside and out. A third finger pushed in with no resistance other than a broken moan that forced itself out. Trent rocked back against the fingers to try to get them to push against that spot that he loved and hated so much, but Ian refused to oblige him. He skimmed around the sensitive bundle as if he were purposefully avoiding it.

Trent groaned with loss as the mouth and fingers disappeared with a wet slurp. A second later, something hard and blunt was pressing its way inside him like an unstoppable force. There was a moment of hesitant resistance that made Trent think that Ian wouldn't fit after all. He was too wide and too big, but he was also unyielding. He pressed his hips forward and Trent's body gave way.

Trent could feel every ridge and vein on the thick cock as it slid inside him. As powerful as Ian was, Trent knew he was still holding himself back with every ounce of self-control he had. The stretch was nearly excruciating, but the satisfying feeling of finally being full was even better. It grew almost unbearable until, at last, Ian's hips settled against his ass.

Trent panted and gripped the edge of the hot tub as he waited for the flare of pain along his spine to diminish. He was feeling every thrust from the night before. Even with the slick saliva banishing the burn, there was still the unyielding throb of Ian's heavy cock.

"You okay, T?" asked Ian. He moved his hands over Trent's hips before gripping him tight so he could grind that last bit inside.

Trent nodded before pressing his head down to his hand braced against the concrete. The change in position pressed Ian's cock even deeper inside and he tensed automatically. Ian swept his hands up Trent's sides and one pressed against the ache of his lower back. The heat of the palm was enough to let him relax, just a bit, but the heavy weight of the gaze on him had him tensing up all over again. Some of the appeal had lost its edge. It was fine to be seen in the heat of passion, but this intimate moment of vulnerability was something that he wanted to himself.

"Ease up, T," said Ian as he leaned in close to whisper against the shell of his ear. "It's just you and me here. Nothing else matters. You're the only one I want, but I need you to relax. Let me make you feel good like you know only I can."

Trent responded automatically to the words. His muscles slowly unwound until it felt like a cock inside him and not a steel rod. His back arched and sagged as his hips lined up with Ian's. The warmth of the water tickled against the lower half of his thighs and the little jets soothed the muscles even further. He tried to spread his legs farther to sink back onto the heat, but they were still trapped in his swim trunks.

"You ready, T?"

It only took a nod before Ian was pulling out and easing himself back in. It wasn't frantic fucking like the night before, but the slow slide of two lovers embracing simply because they could. The thrusts were driven by passion, not mere lust and heat. It made Trent's toes curl as he panted into his hand.

The water splashed awkwardly between them until Ian adjusted his motions so he was thrusting up slowly with a heavy grind, before withdrawing in one quick motion. Every thrust was different and staggered, like a never-ending chorus fading away to a drum solo. The staccato beats of Candace's tiny moans only added to the song.

Heat pooled in his groin as Trent started to peak. His orgasm rushed in on him with the force of a bull as Ian rammed his prostate repeatedly. At the moment of his crescendo, when Ian's hips stuttered and thrust deep one last time, he had a sudden moment of clarity. It was a thought that had slipped from his mind as soon as a hand thrust into his swim trunks. There was no condom between them, only the slide of slickened skin.

There was a confusing mix of arousal and disappointment as Ian pulled out at the last moment. Ian jerked his cock twice before he was spilling over Trent's ass and lower back. Trent was pulled close again as Ian's cock started to soften and cum smeared between the two of them, even slicker than spit, before Ian took Trent's weight and lowered them back into the hot tub.

It was a long moment before Trent was able to open his eyes again. He met the aroused, yet satisfied, gaze of his best friend. Her hair was even more askew than it had been before, and one strap of her bikini had slipped off her shoulder to expose the soft mound of the top of her breast. There was a smile on her lips that would make a prostitute blush.

Her face went suddenly serious. "How much jizz do you think is in this hot tub? Do you think I could get pregnant?"

"You are so fucking weird," said Ian as he took the words right out of Trent's mouth. "But we should get out. You owe me breakfast, and a bonus Danish as a thank you for the show."

"What do I get then?" asked Trent. He hoped it was coffee, at the very least. He had not had nearly enough sleep the night before.

"I'll buy you everything on the menu if you want," said Ian as he nuzzled at Trent's neck. "Then I'll take the bottle of syrup and drip it over your cock. I'll spend all day cleaning it off you."

"Ugh, guys, I already came three times," said Candace, "I am too tired for four. Get out of the tub before I change my mind." Candace was already lifting herself out. She fixed her strap on the way to the door and grabbed a towel off one of the lounge chairs.

"You sure there's no chance of a three-way?" Ian asked as he nibbled against Trent's ear.

"Not happening again." Trent lifted himself off Ian and stepped out. His legs were still shaky from the heat of the tub and the powerful orgasm. He grabbed his own towel and wrapped it around his waist to hide the red smudges on his hips from Ian's hands. The marks would fade soon without even a bruise, but the memory wouldn't.

"You coming?" Trent called back over his shoulder as he started out of the door. "I was hoping for a quickie after breakfast." He'd never seen another living being move as fast as Ian did as he scrambled out of the hot tub.

Chapter Eleven

The two of them shared a glazed Danish and a cup of coffee before they stood from their table and left Candace alone with the bill. She didn't even look up as she waved them away, still perusing the extensive breakfast menu. Despite the three other people waiting to be served, Ian clasped Trent's hand and didn't let go until after the restaurant was behind them.

Trent didn't care about the hollow grumble in his stomach. He was too hungry for something else. Every clock they passed between the restaurant and the room glared at him. Even the little green bedside clock in their room reminded him that there was only an hour before Ian was going to leave him again.

Trent pushed Ian back against the door as soon as it shut behind them. He licked the scent of chlorine from the pulsing column of his neck as he rucked up his T-shirt. His palms smoothed over Ian's flat stomach and the little indentations of his ribs before he flattened over defined pecs. His nipples were already peaked and pressing insistently against Trent's thumbs as he circled the sensitive buds.

"Bed or shower?" Trent asked as he pulled Ian down for a kiss. He ground his awakening cock against the man in front of him. A bulge met his thrusts. *Christ, we're both insatiable.*

A startling ring broke the heat between them. It was the high-pitched sound of a cell phone followed by a second of humming as it vibrated across the nightstand.

He shrugged once, completely content to ignore the ring, and turned back to Ian. He reached up for a second kiss, but his lips met the bottom of Ian's chin instead of his mouth. Ian wasn't even looking at him. Instead, his gaze was drawn to the phone.

"Just leave it," said Trent as he leaned harder into the other man before grinding against him. Ian didn't answer his thrust this time. He pushed at Trent's shoulders until he had to take a step back so he didn't fall on his ass, then steered past Trent completely to rush for the phone. It left Trent cold in more ways than one.

"Hello?" Ian asked into the phone as he picked it up. He turned away from Trent, and his broad back was like an impenetrable wall between them.

Trent could hear the loud, tinny voice on the other end, but he couldn't make out the words. He could hear the tone, though, and whoever it was, they were pissed.

"I was busy," Ian growled back into the phone, glancing back at Trent for a moment before he looked away again. "You said ten. I've still got an hour." There was another pause as the voice on the other end grew even louder. "Why does it matter where I am? I'll be back before ten. Fuck you, man. It's not my fault you decided to change the plan last minute. I'll be back in an hour." Ian clicked the phone shut and tossed it in the middle of the bed, where it bounced once before settling on the sheets.

"You should go," said Trent as he struggled to remain standing with his back pressed against the door. His knees were suddenly weak beneath him. The clock loomed across the room. The time didn't matter now.

Ian sat down on the edge of the bed and ran his hand over his scalp before he finally looked up at Trent. His blue eyes were narrowed and pinched with a look akin to grief. His hands gripped at his legs like he didn't quite know what to do with them.

"It was nice seeing you again, Ian. It really was." Trent's voice wavered. There was so much he wanted to say.

"I don't want to go," said Ian as he shook his head. The phone buzzed on the bed again and the same ring tone split the air. Ian looked at it with clenched teeth before he scooped it up and accepted the call. With a second click, he put the call on speaker. A loud male voice, muffled by wind, sounded in the room.

"Ian, the bus is leaving in ten minutes, whether you're on it or not. I don't care where you went last night, but get back here *now*. I'm not kidding." The man was breathing hard and the sound of wind buffeted the speaker again.

"I'm in the hotel." Ian looked straight at Trent as he spoke. Blue eyes pierced into Trent's soul with a fierce expression.

"Finally got sick of sleeping in the van?" The voice huffed again and suddenly the wind went silent. "I'll come get you then. Which room?" The ding of the elevator sounded in the background, along with the distant murmur of a few voices.

"Four-thirteen," Ian answered before he reached for the phone and ended the call.

"I thought you didn't want anyone to know about us?" Trent's stomach clenched in nervousness, surprise and no small amount of joy. The biggest reason for the nervousness was the look on Ian's face and the unease in his entire frame. The silence stretched as the bigger man refused to answer.

A knock sounded at the door right next to Trent's ear and he jumped in surprise at the sudden noise.

Ian smiled, just the barest hint before it disappeared again. "He's a fast fucker when he needs to be. Can you get the door for me? It is your room, after all."

The handle was heavy in Trent's hand as turned it. The lock clicked open and the latch slid wide as he pulled the door towards him. It resisted in a way that only hotel doors seemed to do.

In the hall stood the flushed form of a very attractive man. His hair was cropped short on top and buzzed along the sides in a military cut. He was skinny, and only a few inches shorter than Trent, but his frame was wiry, firm and covered with a black T-shirt and slacks. He looked like he could fight dirty and come out on top in any bout he might choose to enter.

It was a few moments before recognition kicked in and Trent realized that he was looking at the same man who had been singing up on the stage the night before. Without the music surrounding him and the band T-shirts, he just looked like a man, not the performer that everyone wanted.

"Oh," the singer took a step back, "I must have the wrong room." He looked Trent up and down and his hand clenched into a fist.

"I'm in here, Mac," Ian called from within the room. Trent pulled the door wider and took a step back so Mac could see past him. The singer's face lit up in shock when he saw Ian sitting on the side of a bed that looked like it had gone through an orgy and back.

"Have a fun night?" Mac laughed awkwardly, refusing to look at Trent at all. "Are you ready to go?" He took another step back from the door, as if stepping into the room might somehow contaminate him.

"Nope." Ian crossed his arms over his chest. "I'll be down at ten, as agreed. Until then, I'm fucking busy."

Mac swallowed. His gaze swept the room again as if he was looking for someone else to come out of the woodwork. He clearly spotted the bra thrown over the back of the chair by the upended suitcase and he relaxed.

"Where's the chick?" He smirked at Ian and nodded as he still refused to meet Trent's face.

Trent was gripping the door handle so tightly that his knuckles had turned white and his palm ached. His gut was getting tighter with each passing moment that Ian sat there and said nothing. And the way Mac was ignoring him rubbed him the wrong way. *Fucking homophobe.* He wanted to let the door go so it slammed on his perfect fucking face.

Ian shrugged. "Don't know. Don't care. Like I said, I'm gonna be fuckin' busy." Ian looked like he was starting to get pissed at his friend's behaviour.

"I don't get it." Mac took another step back. He stopped only a few inches away from the door across the hall.

"You're a fucking idiot, Mac. This is Trent." Ian's crossed arms flexed as his frustration started to set in. His forehead was wrinkled as he glared at his friend.

Mac looked at Trent with a small sneaking glance before he shook his head again. "I still don't get it." His eyes had narrowed at Trent, though. He obviously did get it but refused to face the reality of the situation.

"Let me spell it out for you." Ian stood from the bed, his expression going dark. "This is T, the guy I'm fucking in love with. The same T who I told you about months ago when I got back. You are going to leave so I can finish fucking him — or maybe I'll just suck his cock and call it a day. Either way, I won't be down there until ten o'clock. It might even be later now that you've spent the last ten minutes wasting my fucking time. Now fuck off."

With every word, Ian had stalked closer to Trent. As he told his friend to fuck off, Ian gripped Trent's chin and pulled him up into a kiss. Trent was drowning in heat so quickly that he hardly felt the door handle slip from his hand before it slammed shut. He did manage to catch a glimpse of utter surprise and horror on Mac's face before he was cut off by the closing door.

"Your friend's a dick," said Trent as he pulled back from the kiss.

"Nah, he really is that fucking dumb." Ian leaned back in and nibbled at his lip. "He's lucky he can sing, otherwise he'd be homeless."

Trent hummed and tilted his head back in for another kiss. He didn't want to fight, not now, when Ian already had one foot back on the bus.

They stripped their clothing in record time and soon they were both panting and sweating on the bed. Ian slid a condom onto his cock and coated Trent's entrance with lube before he was slipping back inside. When he was all the way in, Trent was filled with the sudden feeling of being home.

He came slowly as Ian took him apart piece by piece, clenching around his cock as it spurted inside him. Even then, Ian kept thrusting as if he never wanted to leave. He only pulled back when Trent whined from overstimulation.

They made out like lazy teenagers until Ian finally lifted off him. He dressed, still smelling like sex and cum, and grabbed his phone from where it had tumbled to the ground. He slipped out of the door with one last goodbye.

Trent glanced at the clock and had to smile. It was ten-thirty-two.

Chapter Twelve

Dragging himself to work on Monday was one of the hardest things that Trent had ever done. He'd asked for the day off originally and had been hoping for a blissful late morning where he would still be in his pyjamas at eleven. When he checked his phone in the early hours, his voicemail was already full of complaints about equipment that didn't seem to be working properly. He could ignore them for the week, but he was only a short walk away from the office. If he was at home, they would find him.

He'd lain in bed, cold and alone, for hours on Sunday night before he'd finally drifted off to sleep. He dreamed of Ian slipping out of the hotel door without looking back.

He tried to recall the image of Ian bending him over the side of the hot tub and sliding inside. His memory felt dull compared to how the real thing had felt, and his rim ached as he tried to press his own fingers inside. Even a hand on his cock was chafing and unwelcome for the first time in his life.

His go-to on restless nights was to jerk off hard and fast. It always put him into a deep sleep moments after he wiped himself clean. But there had been no relief for him in the dark of Sunday night, just the scratch of his blankets and the soft whirr of the fan that rocked on his bedside table.

So, when he woke to his alarm a few hours later, it felt as if he'd just closed his eyes. His eyes were gritty and sore as he rubbed them with the back of his hand, and his body was stiff from the repeated nightmares.

He rolled out of bed and dragged himself to the bathroom. As he was brushing his teeth, he heard his phone ding in the bedroom, but he ignored it in favour of coffee. He looked like hell in the mirror and it wouldn't do well to put off his morning brew. He drank it straight up black, despite the cheap, bitter blend. The hotel coffee had been so much better.

He only remembered his phone almost an hour later, after he'd gone out to check on the ladies. He rushed back inside to grab the phone from the nightstand and ended up pulling the cord harshly out of the wall. He fumbled with his password and had force himself to move slower after he mis-typed it on the first two tries.

Morning, T

…the text read on the slightly glowing screen. All at once Trent felt himself flush at the same time his stomach sank. The text was over an hour old. It had been sitting here, waiting for him to reply, but he'd snubbed it in favour of coffee. He replied quickly.

Morning! Sorry. I was feeding the ladies.

He waited for a reply, but it never came. He packed his lunch, glancing at the screen every few seconds, but it remained silent. He even checked and double checked that his ring tone was on — which, of course, it was.

He was just about ready to give up by the time he started to walk to work. He trudged up the stairs and into the building and wished he was walking up his front porch instead. He would do anything to bury himself back under the covers — and preferably not alone.

His head was hanging low when he approached his desk. He skimmed over the grey chair, flat wooden desk and dull computer screens coated in a thin layer of dust. His phone was flashing red, which indicated that there were even more voicemails waiting for him here. He paused as he reached for his computer monitor to turn it on. Something massive and yellow was blocking the power button from view.

The largest yellow lilies that he'd ever seen were spilling out of an immense crystal glass flowerpot. Each petal was lined with vibrant red streaks and an orange blush that made them look almost surreal. The smell of sweet flowers and rich earth assaulted him as he stepped closer. There was a small white card tucked amongst the stems. He gripped it in his fingertips and pulled it out.

Thank you for the lovely weekend.

It was written in the neat cursive that must have belonged to someone at the flower shop.

He leaned in closer to take a deep breath of the blooms, filling his lungs with their sugary pollen. A massive sneeze roared out of his chest, which made him rock back on his heels. His eyes watered as a second sneeze threatened behind the bridge of his nose. It burst out with a rush of wind.

Sniffing, he pulled out his cell and typed out a text to Ian.

Thanks for the flowers! They made me smile for the first time today.

He wanted to write more. He wanted to ask the man when he was coming back to Canada and when he would be able to see him next. He forced himself to slip his phone upside down on his desk instead. He wasn't sure he wanted to know the answer.

He moved the lilies so they were far enough away that he didn't sneeze every few minutes, and got to work. His mind wandered, even as he tried to focus on his delicate work. Every once in a while, he would glance up at the yellow flowers now perched on the little windowsill in his office. They brought a smile to his lips every time.

It was a little past noon when his office phone rang. He set his salad aside and perched the fork on the edge of the dish before he reached for the receiver.

"Trent here," he called into the phone formally. He didn't bother looking into the display. The majority of the complaints had been taken care of, so there was only one person who would be calling now.

"You, my friend, are in for a treat," Candace called from the other side of the line. "Are you sitting down?" She hadn't taken vacation for the week either, seeing as she'd already blown all of her time by mid-spring.

"No, I'm juggling. What do you want?" he said sarcastically. He picked up his fork again and shoved a glob of salad into his mouth. It had too much dressing and toppings and not enough lettuce…just the way he liked it.

"Well, mister grouchy, maybe I'm not going to tell you now." She sighed dramatically. "Nah, I can't hold it back. So, guess who has a date with a certain brunette tonight?"

"What? No. Concert lady?" Trent laughed in surprise. "I had no idea she was a local." He shifted in his chair and the worn frame groaned in protest. He would never replace his comfiest chair. He'd just managed to get the ass groves right.

"Yeah, me neither, but apparently she's a social media stalker and she looked me up. She saw that I worked here and texted me that she lives just down the road."

"Tonight already? That seems really soon for you." He picked at a poppyseed lodged between his teeth and managed to get it free with one tine of his fork.

"I don't know if I should."

Trent stifled the automatic laugh at his friend's forlorn sigh, thinking she was just kidding with him. "Wait! Are you serious? What was wrong with her? She seemed nice for the ten minutes that I met her. Was she bad in bed?" If Trent were honest, he could hardly even remember what she looked like. He had been a little focused on someone else in the room.

"Nah, she was awesome. I've never come that hard in my life. Well, maybe one other time, but I think we won't talk about that if we want to stay friends."

Trent's cheeks heated as he realized what she was talking about. "Shut up," he hissed into the phone.

"You were totally into it." She laughed.

"Maybe, but don't avoid the question. What's so bad about her that you don't want to go out?" Trent tried to recall what her face had looked like. She'd had a piercing, he remembered that, and shoulder-length brown hair. The rest was a dim haze that would never be recovered from the depths of his mind.

"She was perfect," Candace replied. She sighed again before he caught the sound of fingers tapping against keys.

"Okay?" He paused, wishing that he were next to her so he could see her face. There was probably a reason she was doing this over the phone. She always tried to hide her emotions from him.

"I just don't know if I'm ready for a relationship like that. I could really see myself settling down with someone like her. I feel like I should already tell her about my weird sex-toy collection, and I don't tell anyone about that shit." Candace trailed off.

"You have a sex-toy collection?" Trent shuddered as he thought back to the double dong they'd found in the silver bag. If she didn't consider a vibrating double-dong note-worthy, he wasn't sure he wanted to know what she wasn't telling him.

"I like collecting different things and trying them out. It keeps things exciting for me, and I like it. Everyone collects something, Trent."

"You're comparing dildos to stamps?" He shouted into the phone before looking back over his shoulder and lowering his voice. "How many do you have? It can't be that bad."

"Like three hundred or so." She sighed. "And they aren't all dildos. There's other stuff too, and some things that you might like. Some would probably make you never want to talk to me again." She went quiet and the clacking of keys stopped. "Just forget I said anything. I just don't know if I want to date this woman. Am I not allowed to be unsure?"

"You're afraid you're going to get hurt," said Trent. Candace's grunt of affirmation was enough of an answer. "I'm afraid too, Candace, but you know what? I think Ian's worth the risk, and so is concert girl."

"Debbie. Her name is Debbie." The sound of keys continued as Candace spoke. "We should make a pact, Trent. If either of us gets hurt, we'll take out the other one's ex. And no falling in love. We'll just have to love each other until the end of time."

Trent stayed silent a beat too long and the keys stopped again.

"Oh no, Trent, really? You love him? But you barely know him. He might be good in the sack, but that doesn't mean that you go fall in love."

"I didn't realize it until he said it first. I just thought I really missed him, but I think I was just denying it to myself." Trent slouched down in the chair and stared at the flowers on the ledge. Those flowers looked like love and they sure as hell felt like it too.

"Shit. You know what? You two are made for each other." She hummed once before she started typing again. "Fuck it. I'll call her back and tell her it's on. Just be ready to take her out if she breaks my heart. Bye, Trent."

The phone clicked and Trent slowly set the receiver down. He looked back at the flowers. They were the same bright yellow colour and completely oblivious to his internal conflict. He grabbed his cell phone and typed out a message before he could stop himself.

Call me when you can. We should talk.

He erased it twice before he retyped it and hit send. If he'd been the one receiving that text from anyone, it would've sounded like a breakup. He just didn't know what else to say.

Seconds later his phone was ringing. He slid his thumb across to answer and pressed the phone to his ear.

"T?" said Ian's voice on the other end. "Are you okay?"

Trent relaxed as soon as he heard the deep timbre of Ian's voice. There was something about it that erased every bit of worry and insecurity that had pierced him since he'd woken up alone.

"Hey," said Trent as he lowered himself into his chair. "I just wanted to say hi. That's all."

Ian chuckled on the other end. "Has anyone ever told you that you have a flair for the dramatic?" There was a steady dull roar and a soft murmur of voices in the background.

"When am I going to see you again?" Trent forced out the question that had been plaguing him since the hotel room. His stomach clenched at the sound of Ian's heavy sigh.

"I don't know, T." There was a burst of laughter in the background and muffled male voices. "We have to finish this tour and that's months. After that, who knows? We're already working on a new release and that usually means more tours."

"Don't you ever get time off?" Trent glanced at the rest of his abandoned salad before he tipped it over into the garbage bin beneath his desk. His appetite had disappeared.

"It's never really mattered before. None of us have families, or kids, except for Mac. I'm pretty sure he likes his wife better when he's not at home. We take time off for holidays and Christmas so we can go home to see our families, but the rest of the time we are usually working or travelling."

"I couldn't do that." Trent chuckled humourlessly and shook his head. He tried to ignore the irony of his cancelled vacation time. "I am a nine to five, Monday to Friday kind of person. Thank you for the flowers, though." He smiled as he glanced back over at them. "I've always loved lilies. Something about them just makes me smile." Perhaps it was the sneezing fits he had every time he drew close to one.

"Good. Look, T... I'm sorry, but I have to go. We're stopping for lunch in a few minutes. We have another show in two days, so I should be able to talk to you after that. I can call you when we're done. Would that be okay?" Ian's voice got even lower until it was almost a whisper. The voices in the background got louder as he lowered his voice. Trent recognized the even tilt of Mac's voice among them.

"Yeah, okay. Bye." With a whispered bye in response, Trent hung up his phone and set it gently beside the computer. The tears he'd been holding back tipped over the edges of his eyes, even as he tried to force them back. His nose burned as he pinched the bridge and hoped that he wasn't going to fall apart.

Chapter Thirteen

Late summer bled away into autumn, then the first snow was on the ground. The trees were heavy with a frozen burden of crystalized light, and the ground made its own symphony with each hurried step through the deep snow.

Trent's life went back to the monotonous repetition that had always existed before Ian. He would bundle into a thick jacket and warm boots as he trudged out to check on the ladies every morning. They huddled next to the heater and pecked at their water bowl that had gathered a thin film of ice, despite the heating element. He had to be careful to tuck their eggs close to his chest or they would shatter in the cold.

After a quick breakfast, he was off to work for nine hours. He dragged himself home through the slushy sidewalks before he had a quick dinner. He would watch the world news, and sometimes the entertainment news, before he was off to bed. When he woke up, he was rested and ready to repeat the same thing.

There was one thing that kept him from going mad. Ian was there in spirit as a constant tether in his life. He was the intangible strength behind the daily text messages and deep voice on the other end of the phone before bed. The ache of not being able to touch and hold him had burned away to a dull numbness over the months.

On days Trent was feeling especially down, he would often come into work to find a new little treasure at his desk. People in the office peeked around the corners in envy at the array of gifts that lined his desk. His home smelled of the sweet lilies that Ian had bought him on that first day. He'd stuck them next to the sill in the kitchen, and new flowers spurted forth every few weeks. He'd shared the chocolate-dipped fruit arrangement with Candace the day it arrived. It had been artfully shaped into a chicken, complete with a dipped strawberry as a pointed beak.

A small sand garden had arrived after a particularly rough week. It sat on the little ledge of his windowsill at work. The sand had been combed into many shapes, and the rocks arranged and rearranged too many times to count. The next week a tiny water fountain had completed the ensemble.

It was the first time that Trent had been treated to anything in his life. Sure, his friends and parents had bought him gifts before, but they often fell flat, even if they were heartfelt. With Ian, it was different. Trent had mentioned in passing in the fall that it would be neat to have a sand garden. Then, nearly a month later, after the week from hell, he'd found the wrapped package on his desk. The flowers were always his favourite, though.

Somehow, it was never enough. The sand felt coarse beneath his fingertips, and so unlike the callused skin of Ian's palms that he longed for. The flowers were too sweet when he only wanted the deep rich cologne of Ian's natural smell. The discreet toy that was sent to his house as a gift was awkward and hesitant inside him, and so unlike Ian's powerful thrusts.

The worst part of all was that he could send nothing in return. Ian's birthday came and went without even a card. Trent had tried to have a courier take a package to the moving entourage, but it was nearly impossible. There was a mail service that could forward it to them eventually, but it was scattered and delayed. A text was flat and useless, and a call wasn't much better. A video chat was almost always out of the question because of the proximity of Ian's band mates. Trent had tried to whisper sweet nothings into Ian's ear on his birthday, only to have the phone click and go dead as the drummer hung up on him.

The text came a few minutes later.

Sitting with the guys. Don't want to get a stiffy here.

Trent didn't reply that day or the next. By the time he was over his embarrassment and anger, Ian's birthday was a distant memory.

The worst part, as Trent had known it would be, was the secrecy. Trent had always shared certain aspects of his life with those that mattered to him. He had hoped, given time, that Ian would do the same thing. Every time he hoped, it would come crashing back down around him. Ian never broke a promise, because he never made any in the first place. It left a cold feeling in the pit of his stomach that would last for entire days at a time.

It was on one such morning that his phone rang while he was cooking bacon in the kitchen. It was a chilly but sunny Saturday morning, so he had time to spoil himself with breakfast. He hit the button to answer the call, then switched it to speaker.

"Hey, Candace, what has you up so early?" He smiled, knowing that his friend was anything but an early riser.

"I was worried about you," she said, with her voice coarse with sleep. "I heard last night, but it was too late to call. I wanted to make sure you were okay." He heard a shuffling in the background. It sounded like she was still in bed and shifting below the blankets.

"What?" He flipped the bacon, jerking back as the grease struck his forearm. "I'm fine, I guess. Lonely, and it's freaking cold outside this morning. But Christmas is here soon, so that's something to look forward to. And don't even try to guess your present or you aren't getting anything."

"Christmas?" Candace yelled back into the phone, her voice tinny and bursting with static over the speaker. "What the fuck are you talk about? I meant about Ian. I can't believe you aren't upset."

"What are you talking about?" He froze with his hand hovering over the splattering pan.

"His girlfriend. That's what I'm talking about. Where have you been? It's all over the entertainment news."

Trent's heart went as cold as his frigid toes. "What do you mean?" he asked quietly. His bacon was forgotten in the pan as it went from perfectly crispy to downright burnt.

"Shit, you didn't know, did you. He never said a thing to you." Her voice lowered into a soothing timbre. "I'm so sorry, Trent. I was rooting for you guys, I really was, but he was obviously too far in the closet. If he won't come out for you, it's just not going to happen. Don't watch the news. It will just upset you more. Just take it from me. He picked up some girl at his last concert, and someone leaked a video of them fucking in a hotel elevator. There are pictures too, and it's pretty clear. I guess some charges were laid. I'm so sorry, Trent."

"I have to go." Trent ended the call a second later. Numbly, he flicked the stove off and put the bacon over his buttered toast. He sat at the table with his head pounding and ate every bite of his breakfast. It tasted the same way a cotton ball would if it was rolling over his tongue and had the texture of egg shells. As he finished, the ringing stopped and Candace's words sunk in. He ran to the bathroom and threw up every bite.

He was still heaving over the porcelain bowl when his phone chimed with his usual morning text. He gripped it and read the words on the screen. He'd been expecting an apology or an explanation of what Candace had said. There was neither.

Morning, T! How r u this morning?

The cheerful lettering on the screen made his stomach lurch again. His temper bubbled as he wiped his mouth on the back of his hand, grimacing at the taste of bile.

Go fuck yourself, you lying bastard.

He hit send hard enough that the screen squeaked under his fingertip. His phone rang a few seconds later, buzzing and chiming in his hands like a cheerful hummingbird. He glanced at the screen, pondering for a moment before he accepted the call. He already had the words on his lips that he was prepared to say. He wasn't going to take this one lying down.

"T?" Ian's voice was so sweet and innocent, like it was his heart being ripped out, and not Trent's.

"Shut the fuck up," Trent snarled. His hands clenched into fists as he gripped the mat on the bathroom floor. "How dare you. You lead me along for all these months. Do you send me shit when you feel bad because you're out fucking some whore? She doesn't know what you need, but I do, even if you don't admit it to yourself. You're such a fucking coward." Every hurtful word dripped out of his mouth as his anger grew. His stomach rebelled again, but he managed to hold it down.

"What the fuck?" Ian asked quietly.

"I'm not finished." He cut Ian off. All at once his anger vanished into nothing. He was left alone, bent over his toilet, speaking to someone who had hurt him more than anyone before. His voice went quiet as tears gathered at the corners of his eyes. "I love you, Ian. I hope you know that. I would've waited forever for you. Now I wish I'd never known you." He cut off the call with a sick sob.

Candace found him like that an hour later. He was huddled around the toilet and shivering as the cold floor soaked through his thin pyjamas. She lifted him from the floor and stripped his clothes off his body. She stayed silent as she ran the shower for him and helped him into the warm spray, even though it soaked her in the process.

He stood against the wall, completely numb, as she passed him a toothbrush through the open curtain. She was speaking to him in a low tone, but he couldn't understand the words. He trembled as his sickness slowly washed down the drain. He washed himself automatically and violently, as if he could rid himself of his thoughts and feelings if he only scrubbed hard enough.

When the water ran cold, Candace was there, pulling him from the shower and wrapping him in a towel. She passed him clothes and he dressed in a blur before he was ushered to his living room. She wrapped him in a blanket and pushed him down on the couch. There was a cup of coffee waiting for him on the small side stand. It was bitter and sweet, exactly how he liked it.

"This is my fault, Trent. I never should've taken you to that stupid concert. If I just let it go, then we both wouldn't be here right now." She shifted close to him so she was pressed against his side. The feeling of her warmth was completely platonic, but it did soothe him, just a bit. That, and the second sip of coffee that scorched its way down his throat.

"It's my own fault," said Trent. "I just feel so stupid and used. Maybe that's how Ian felt when he left the house after that first weekend." He shook his head and stared at the crinkling paint on the far wall. "I just don't know what to do, Candace. I keep imagining what that video could've shown. Some chick with her legs wrapped around him as he fucked her in an elevator. I can picture the look on his face when he came in her, and it just hurts so bad."

"The video was super grainy, but yeah, that was pretty much the gist of it." She snuggled deeper into his side. "If it makes you feel any better, they are both being charged with public indecency after there was a complaint at the hotel. He was already gone, but they identified him by the video, so there is a warrant out for his arrest." She wrapped her arms around him.

It reminded him of when they would have sleepovers when they were younger. Their parents had been concerned, of course, when they'd found the two of them bundled into the same sleeping bag, even though they were both still clothed and unsullied. Trent's mother had realized, even back then, that there was nothing more than friendship between them. But it was a friendship so deep that it kept away the loneliness of life.

"It makes me feel a bit better." He laughed humourlessly and took another sip of scalding liquid. The anger that had blinded him now left him feeling emptier than he could ever fill with simple comforts. "Does it make me a bad person if I still love him, even if I don't want to?"

"No, Trent, it makes you human." She pinched at the thin skin over his ribs. "Can you sing for me, just like you used to?"

Something in her tone gave Trent pause. He wasn't the only one hurting here. Something was wrong with Candace, and from her tone, she definitely didn't want to talk about it. So instead, he sang.

The words started off cold and tilted as he tried to find the rhythm of the song. His voice stuttered as he swallowed the dryness in his mouth and the burn of acid in his throat. He started again, stronger and louder as the beat came alive in his mind. He could see each word of the song as if it were painted on the wall in front of him.

Every song he'd ever listened to was trapped in his mind like a useless eidetic memory. The words curved and swam together, just out of reach, until he started to sing. Then they all poured forth like a leaking faucet turned into a waterfall. He tapped his foot to the beat as Candace made chords on his belly.

His voice grew stronger until he was lost in the sound all his own. It was someone else's words, but the groove was his, and he twisted it in his own way. He realized after a few lines that he was singing a song from Ian's band — one that had made their debut album a particular favourite of his.

Candace fumbled for her phone and started up the camera. "Keep singing. I want to keep this one, just for me." Trent didn't hear a lie in her voice.

He sang. His voice drifted and his face fell in grief as the song progressed. It was a story, as any good song was. It was about a lost love hidden beneath layers of deceit and anger. But it was the ending that drew him in. The pause of hopeful lyrics that broke back into the chorus of longing and desire. It was about sex, good sex, in a way that only artists in their craft could portray.

As he finished, he let his voice linger in the air before he let out a huff. Candace clicked her phone off and slid it back into her pocket before she let her head rest against his chest.

"Was that one okay?" He didn't ask about the tears on her face or the way she bit her lip.

"It was perfect," she said. Her voice was thick.

"Do you have the video? I need to see it," said Trent. As much as he knew it would hurt him even more, there was something in him that needed to see the grainy picture. "I don't think I'll be able to fully accept it until I see it for myself."

"You don't want to, Trent." Candace wiped the tears from her eyes. "I've walked in on girlfriends who were in bed with other girls...or even guys before. It's not something you want to see. Just trust me on this one."

"I need to see it, Candace, or I'll never be able to let him go." He shifted on the couch and the leather pulled at his sweaty skin.

She shook her head against his chest once, before she dug her phone back out of her pocket. "It's grainy, but the one online is actually pretty graphic. They didn't show that version on TV, of course, but you know." She flicked through her phone and pulled up the bookmark. She ducked back down as she handed the phone over to him.

The phone was warm from resting in her pocket and the screen was smudged with fingerprints. Trent ran the corner of his shirt over the screen to clear away the prints and the video started up as it sensed his barely covered fingers scooting over it. He'd accidentally scrolled ahead until the video was already half over.

The picture was low-quality, but clear enough to make out two figures pressed against the back wall of an elevator. The elevator was a huge monstrosity with walls that were made entirely of mirrors so that anyone could watch themselves as they plummeted twenty floors to the lobby. The mirror across from the camera gave a second view of the entwined couple.

They must've hit the stop button at some point, or it was late enough that no one was calling on the elevator, because the video was five minutes long and no one had interrupted them yet.

The man's pants were halfway down his thick thighs, and the woman's legs were wrapped around his waist with her knee-high boots crossed at the ankle. Her skirt was hiked up past her waist to leave her completely exposed, although shielded somewhat from the camera by the man's bulk. A few buttons on her top had been pulled open and one breast peeked through the open fabric. Her hands gripped around his neck as he pushed himself into her over and over in quick jerks. His hands were gripped against her ass with his shoulders leaned into her to hold her against the wall.

The video was slow and skipped instead of showing a seamless picture. It made for a disembodied series of still shots as he slid his hands down along her legs as he began to tire, and as she threw her head back from the change in position.

He pulled back after only two minutes of video lapse. His cock looked small, but Trent couldn't tell if it was because of the angle or the grainy video. He looked into the mirror for the second angle, but the man was already tucking himself back in his pants. There was no movement to remove a condom.

The man moved in close again and pushed his weight against her. Her feet were flat on the floor this time and her back was straight against the elevator wall. Trent looked between the two of them.

He narrowed his eyes as he squinted at the video, trying to get a better look at the faces. Too many things weren't adding up. He knew that Ian was usually a stickler for condoms, and he didn't think he would make an exception just because he was with a woman. If anything, it would give him more reason. The last Trent had heard, Ian had not wanted anything to do with children.

And the heights didn't make sense. He'd never met a woman who was as tall as Ian that still looked that good in high boots and a short skirt. Her shirt was quite short and showed off her belly in a way that would be sexy on someone around five foot eight.

The man turned as the elevator door slid open for the first time since the video began. A young woman, who was actually taller than the man, took two steps into the box before she noticed the state of the couple. Trent imagined that she could probably see the flush on their faces and the cum dripping down the woman's thigh. Her skirt was still hiked up with her bare pussy on clear display now. The young woman backed up a step before turning and leaving.

Trent paused the video and zoomed in on the man's face. He'd frozen it a second too late when the man was already fully facing the elevator door. He noticed that something was missing from the blurry side of the bald head. It was something that was large and dark enough that it should've been clearly visible.

"Oh shit."

Chapter Fourteen

"It's not him," said Trent as he zoomed in even farther, just to make sure. The picture blurred into large square pixels of swirled colour.

"What do you mean it's not him?" Candace shot up beside him and grabbed the phone from his hand. "It looks like him, and the entertainment news said it was him. He got charged."

"No, you said that someone recognized him and reported him, and they put out a warrant. Well, they were wrong. It's not him. That guy, whoever he is, is definitely not Ian." He pointed at the naked scalp. "There's no tattoo there, and Ian has an American flag. This guy is short, too, probably five nine or so, and his dick is way too small. And as you well know, Ian is not a minute man. That guy came in less than three minutes."

"Oh, shit, I think you're right." Candace squinted at the phone as she brought it closer to her face. She scrolled back through the video and paused when the small cock was visible for just a moment before it was tucked away. "That's like five inches max. A good size if you have technique — or if it vibrates."

"I have to call him. What am I going to say?" Trent ran a hand through his hair and pulled his legs up onto the couch to wrap his arms around them. "I was so mean to him, Candace. I called him a coward and I screamed at him. He isn't going to want to hear from me again."

She wrapped her arms around his torso, squeezing him once before she let him go. "I'm going to give you some time to think, Trent. I can't tell you what to do, but I think you should call him and apologize. The least you can do is try. It's more than what he did for you, right?"

"I love how you tell me that you aren't gonna tell me what to do, right before you tell me what to do." Trent found himself smiling just the tiniest bit.

"That's what besties are for." She lifted off the couch and tucked her phone into her pocket. "I'll see you tomorrow. Call me if you need me, okay?"

"'K," he said into his kneecap. "Then you'll tell me what's up with you too, okay? I know you're hurting over something."

She shrugged with a sad tilt of her lips before she disappeared around the corner. Trent heard a rustling near the front door as she pulled her shoes on, then the quiet slam of the door as she left the house.

He was left in utter silence. Even the furnace was silent on the chilly day, leaving him alone with his thoughts. His phone was still lying on the bathroom floor where he'd left it. The taint of acidic bile was lingering in the house, mild now, but unforgotten, and it felt like a league stretched between himself and the phone.

He pried himself off the couch, knowing that if he delayed any longer, he wouldn't make the call at all. He had called Ian a coward, but right now, he felt as if he were the one who was too afraid. His stomach jumped and tossed as he made his way to the bathroom and retrieved his phone from the rug, where it had tumbled to from his hand.

He nudged the wet towels off the ground with his toe before closing the toilet seat and sitting down. If his stomach continued to whirl, at least he would be in the right spot.

Taking a deep breath, he glanced around the bathroom one last time as he hit the Ian's contact. Discarded and damp towels littered the ground, along with a soiled pair of pyjamas. A crumpled tissue had found its way into the corner somehow, but he didn't remember using one. It must've been from Candace. She was a great friend, but her housekeeping skills left something to be desired.

It rang only once before there was a click on the other end that told him that the call had connected. There was no greeting, just the distant sound of mumbled voices that were quieter than usual. There was a constant whirl of noise that was typical over the phone when Ian was travelling in the bus.

"Would you accept an apology?" Trent asked, barely more than a whisper. He waited for a response, but after thirty seconds of relative silence, there was still nothing. His stomach tumbled even farther and he gripped the phone hard. The toilet seat squeaked under his weight as he shifted and the cold bathroom floor numbed his toes.

"I'm sorry." He tried to hold back the tears, but it was like they'd never stopped. They were pouring down his face harder than when he had thought Ian had cheated on him. He sniffed and wiped the back of his hand across his face. His phone was still pressed hard to his ear as he refused to give up hope that he would get a response. He wasn't going to be the one to hang up. He didn't have that right this time.

"Say it again," said Ian after another long pause. His voice was thick and deeper than Trent had ever heard it, and he realized that he wasn't the only one who was crying. The thought of Ian with tears pouring down his face, trapped on a bus filled with his unknowing friends, just made him want to cry harder. Trent had Candace, but Ian had no one he could turn to – at least no one who would understand what he was going through.

"I'm so sorry, Ian." Trent sniffed hard again. He tried to muffle the noise with his palm over the speaker, but it was no use.

"You've never said it to me before. Did you know that?" Ian's voice trembled. "You've never said that you loved me. You've come close more than once, but it always sounded like something was holding you back. I had this picture in my mind of something cheesy from a chick flick. You'd sneak through security at a concert and find me backstage. You'd pull me down for a kiss like you always do. It's like you think my neck's a handlebar or something. Then you'd whisper it in my ear like it was a secret just between the two of us."

"I didn't realize. I thought I said it?" Trent combed through his memories. He knew he'd told Ian that he was falling in love with him, but Ian was right. That wasn't the same thing.

"Then I realized that I wasn't just dreaming. Even if you did say it back to me, it really would be our little secret. I don't want anyone to know, because I'm so ashamed…" Ian's voice trailed off.

"You're ashamed of me?" Trent couldn't hold back the sob. He could understand Ian's reservations. People were assholes, especially strangers, and Ian spent most of his life with strangers. There were a few people he could call friends, and the single person among them who did know was not accepting in the least. It was one thing to be afraid, but something very different to be ashamed. "I don't know what to say," said Trent after he was finally managed to find his voice again. Ian was condemningly silent.

"Haven't you ever been ashamed?" asked Ian.

"Maybe when I shoplifted when I was twelve, but not now," said Trent. "I'm proud of who I am and of what I've done with my life. I may not be the most exciting person, but I'm happy. I have a house of my own, and a family who loves me. I thought I could count you amongst those people."

"You can," Ian took a deep breath. "I love you, Trent. You have to know that. There is no way that I would be having this conversation if I didn't love you."

"What is that supposed to mean?" His shoulders tensed and his hackles rose. The cold porcelain seeped into his back and put him even more on edge.

"I used to fuck chicks," said Ian in a rushed breath. "I fucked so many that I lost count. I didn't care about getting them pregnant or getting STDs. It felt good, and I think I was starting to like it. I think I was trying to convince myself that nothing was missing." He let out a soft huff.

"But my drinking got worse and one night I found my way to the bottom of a bottle of whisky. When I woke up, I was so hungover I could hardly see straight.

I felt someone beside me and I reached over thinking I'd find a wet slit. Instead my hand wrapped around the half-hard dick of the guy I'd just fucked. And I liked it. I really, really liked it. He felt so perfect in my hand and even better in my mouth. After that, it was only guys. And there were more of them than the women." There was a pause as something thumped in the background and the bus went over a large pothole.

"It's easier than you think to get away with something like that. Girls like to talk, but guys keep things more to themselves, especially if they are in the closet too. It was easy enough to find people who didn't talk, especially when I already had a reputation on the other side. It just went along like that for a while, until Mac stumbled in on me when I was with another guy. I've never seen anyone more shocked and disgusted in my life. He ran out and I drove after him, but I was so fucking drunk. There was another car and—" Ian's voice trembled and he cleared his throat. Trent thought back to the vivid scar on Ian's side and the words scrawled along it.

"So I stopped. I stopped drinking and partying. I didn't take drugs anymore or anything else that could fuck with my head. I started looking at chicks again and imagining how they would feel under me. I convinced myself that it wouldn't be so bad. I tried to get with them, but when the time came, I couldn't bring myself to do it. Mac was pressuring me, and the band was asking for more and more. So I took off and drove for three days solid. That's when I saw you walking down the street looking like the most beautiful drowned cat, and something just drew me in. You were like a drug that night, looking at me with your cock already hard in your pants."

"So I seduced you, and now what? You want out?" asked Trent. His toes curled under the bathroom mat as he tried to draw some heat back into them. His whole body trembled.

"No." Ian shouted into the phone. Trent heard the pause in the voices on the other end, and a knock on the door a few moments later. "Fuck off, Mac. I'll be out in a bit." Ian started again, "Trent, I just want to see you. I want to spend Christmas with you, then New Year's too. I never want to come back to work, and that scares the shit out of me. This is my life, and I've worked so hard for it. I'm ashamed that I could throw that all away."

"For a fuck?" Trent was bitter with the sour edge of disappointment. "Ian, if you really want something, you are the only one stopping you. I want to wait for you, and I want to be able to love you. I can't love you and be your secret. I can't be someone who you see and fuck every year or so, then shove under the carpet like the bit of dirt you missed with the vacuum. I won't live my life like that."

"You really do think I'm a coward," said Ian. "You think I'm afraid of them and the whole world."

"Well, aren't you?" Trent took a deep breath and held back the other angry words that wanted to stumble out of his mouth. "Look, Ian. I called to apologize. I heard about the charges against you for screwing some chick in an elevator. When I saw the video, I knew it wasn't you. I shouldn't have said what I did without even letting you say a word. I should have trusted you. I'm sorry."

"But you meant it," said Ian. His voice sounded more like a statement than the question Trent knew it was supposed to be.

Trent couldn't answer. He couldn't lie to the man he loved. And he did love him. He loved him so much that he would do anything for him. But his heart was also being ripped into tiny shreds.

"What do you want from me, T?" Ian let out an explosive sigh. Trent could hear the building anger, even as Ian struggled to stay calm.

"I just want to be a part of your life. Is that so much to ask?" A second wave of tears started to creep down Trent's cheeks. "Do you know what it feels like to have your lover hang up on you because he's too ashamed to let his friends know who he's talking to? I look forward to hearing your voice every day, but you never want to talk to me if they're around. God forbid they find out that you're fucking some random guy…again," Trent said sarcastically. If the situation hadn't been so heart-breaking, he would've rolled his eyes.

"You aren't some random guy, T."

"What did you tell Mac about me after you left the hotel that day?" He ground his teeth so hard that they squeaked in his skull. He already knew the answer, but he needed to hear it from Ian.

"He didn't ask, and I didn't tell him." Ian's voice was soft and quiet.

It was exactly what Trent had expected to hear. Each word was like a fondue fork that pierced his heart and dipped it into sizzling oil.

"I have to go, Ian." He didn't. There was nothing else in his tiny world for him to think about except for the man on the other side of the phone. Not even Candace could soothe the reality of that.

"What? No. We aren't done talking." His voice grew loud enough that the voices paused again in the background. He sounded like a lion about to drag his prey to the ground. "Don't hang up the phone, T. We aren't done."

It was as if Ian could see Trent's thumb hovering over the tiny red symbol on the screen that would disconnect the line. He wanted so badly to end it, but he'd already promised himself that he wouldn't be the one to do so. He promised that he wouldn't shut Ian out like that.

It took every ounce of willpower that he had to bring the phone back to his ear. He bit his lip hard enough that his dull teeth split the seam of his lip and a drop of crimson slid down his chin. He didn't even feel the ache.

"Okay," said Trent. Ian paused as if he hadn't expected to hear his voice again so soon. The end went silent again and Trent heard the sound of a quiet knock at the door. Ian grumbled and must've pulled his ear away from the phone and put his palm across the speaker from the amount of static.

He heard a voice that was distant but still audible. "Why are you crying, Ian, and who the hell are you yelling at?" It was Mac's steady voice.

Ian replied, his voice muffled but still discernible. "Some guy impersonated me and got charged with some sex thing."

"But why does it sound like you are crying?" came Mac's voice again.

"Seriously, Mac, fuck off." The speaker muffled again as Ian's hand dragged over the surface.

"Who's on the phone? Shit, it's not the cops, is it? I know I talked about boosting sales, but this is not the way to do it." The man was louder this time, as if he had opened the door into the small bathroom at the back of the bus.

"It's no one. Get the fuck out." The phone muffled again and Trent missed the rest of the conversation. He didn't think he would've wanted to hear it anyway.

He pulled the phone away from his ear and stared at the little red button, longing to push it but stubbornly refusing. Instead, he set the phone down on the fake marble swirl of the counter. The corner dipped into a water spot and smudged the dark surface to black. He stood from his perch on the toilet and walked to the door. He flicked the light off and gently pulled the door shut, leaving his phone, and Ian, alone in the small, dark water closet. He couldn't help but think it was somewhat appropriate.

Chapter Fifteen

Trent kept busy for the rest of the day, keeping his hands moving so his mind would stay quiet. He avoided going back into the bathroom for as long as he could. By then his cell phone had gone dead. He dropped it into his bedside drawer and slowly slid the door shut. The glimpse of the sex toy hidden in the drawer didn't bring the usual flush of heat to his cheeks. Instead, it only made his chest tighten.

That night, he slept deeper than he had in months. His tangled sheets almost felt like a body against him. He dreamed of warmth and sweet caresses instead of the nightmares he'd expected.

There was almost a sense of déjà vu as he cooked two eggs in the shiny copper pan the next morning. The knife scraped across dry toast as he spread a thin layer of butter. The eggs had been warm to the touch before he broke them into the pan. It was early enough that the sun hadn't even thought about bursting over the horizon.

There was a soft knock at his front door before it was scraping open as someone walked inside. He never locked his front door. He could probably try any door in the small town and it would be open at any time during the day or night. It was the naïve security that he loved about his home.

"You naked?" He heard Candace call from the front room. There were two thumps as she removed her shoes and tossed them in the vicinity of the shoe mat. He knew he'd be finding bits of gravel all over his wall later.

"I love cooking in the nude," Trent answered just as the butter in the pan snapped and splashed on his arm. He hissed as the grease shot a split second of burning pain down his arm before it faded.

She popped around the corner in a whirlwind of colour and Trent squinted at the sheer depth of the tacky atrocity that assaulted his eyes. Her hair was pulled back in a loose, sloppy bun, where more hair had escaped than was actually held back by the thin black elastic band. She had on a bright pink pyjama T-shirt with the picture of a half-eaten gingerbread man. That gave way to plain red shorts that showed too much leg for the cold weather. Her ankles were warm, though, covered in purple leg warmers that stretched from ankle to calf.

"What the hell happened to you?" Trent glanced up and down as he looked for some clue to her disastrous outfit. She always took pride in her appearance, and he'd never seen her outside her bedroom with something that made his eyes burn so badly. Then he saw her face.

Bits of mascara were stuck to each side of her nose, as if she had been crying and desperately trying to wipe away the evidence. Her nose itself was red and swollen and her eyes were bloodshot and moist. She looked worse than he felt.

He didn't ask if she was okay when she very obviously wasn't. Instead, he slid the eggs over his toast before he popped another egg into the pan. He dropped another piece of bread into the toaster and cranked the settings down, just the way she liked it. Her toast was nothing more than slightly warmed bread, completely dry, and with an egg on the side.

When they were done, he slid the plate in front of her and sat down across the table, digging into his own meal. He was ravenous after sticking to small meals the previous day for fear they might come back up.

She stared at the egg as if it were a disgusting ball of slime before she picked up the warmed bread and started nibbling on the corner.

"OJ or coffee?" Trent asked as he took a breath from eating.

She shook her head and set her bread back down on the plate. The butter on the egg had started to congeal into a greasy mess. Trent couldn't help but frown at the wasted food, but at least it didn't cost him much. Keeping chickens was cheap, and he made his own bread.

"You want me to knife the bitch?" Trent asked. "We made a pact, and I'm not backing out." He swallowed the last bit of toast and wiped his hands on a napkin.

"No." She shook her head again as her eyes started to glisten. "She didn't do anything wrong. It's my fault." Her features crumpled and her shoulders sagged even farther. The bright clothing looked as out of place as a red car in a thunderstorm.

"It can't be that bad, Candace. You drive me crazy, but deep down I know you're a sweetheart. I'd even ask you out if I wasn't so fascinatingly grossed out by your boobs." He tried for a joke, but her lips stayed turned down.

"It's bad, Trent." She didn't even look up at him as she spoke. "I fucked up huge."

"I didn't think you guys were that serious," said Trent as he grabbed her plate. He tilted her uneaten bits into a bin to go out into the compost later, before sliding both plates into the dishwasher.

"Remember what you said to me when I was home visiting from my first year of college on the August long weekend?" she asked. She gripped the placemat and twisted the fabric out of shape.

He shook his head. He had no idea what she was talking about. That was years ago, and long enough that he scarcely even remembered those days at all.

"You told me that you didn't see any point in having a relationship if you were just going to cheat." She met his eyes and a stray tear rolled over her cheek.

Trent didn't remember saying that, but he could sympathize with the words. He'd never been one to settle down with someone. His biggest reason at the time was that he was horny as fuck and couldn't see himself staying with just one guy. He wanted something different every time he went to a bar. He always made sure that his partner understood that they were nothing more than a one-night stand.

"I was dating a chick named Sara when you told me that," Candace continued, "and I never imagined cheating on her. I didn't even love her, but it never even crossed my mind. But now, when I'm finally getting serious with someone and we're thinking about taking it to the next step, all I can think about is other women."

"Oh no, Candace, you didn't actually..." Trent trailed off.

"Yep. Twice." Candace shuddered and her head drooped even lower as she held up two fingers. "I guess once wasn't enough, so I had to try again. It wasn't even that great either. But I want to do it again. I want to go to a bar and finger fuck the first hot chick I see, just because I fucking can."

"Okay." Trent took a deep breath and forced his thoughts away. He knew how it felt to be on the other side of that fence, but that didn't matter right now.

She looked up, drawing her eyebrows together and turning her lips down into a deep frown. "What do you mean 'okay'? It's *not* okay, Trent. I'm a monster." She let out a long sob and curled even farther down into the chair.

"Monster is too harsh a word. I'd settle on bitch." He let out a tiny smile as she laughed softly at the joke. A flash of utter relief passed over her face before it disappeared again.

"You aren't helping. You're supposed to yell at me." She sniffed and wiped her nose delicately on a napkin before she folded it and set it to the side. Trent knew he would be picking the tissue up later.

"I'm your friend, Candace, and I'm always here for you, no matter what." He reached across the table and took her hand. She was cold and clammy under his palm, despite the layers of clothing.

"I don't know how you do it, Trent. Ian didn't even cheat on you, but you still have him eating out of your palm." She shook her head again and shifted uncomfortably on the wooden chair.

Trent pushed down the confusion and the ache from Ian's name. He wanted to ask her what she meant, but she was already moving on.

"I don't get it. I mean she's cute, she's nice and has the sexiest little face when she comes. Who wouldn't want her?" She glared at him through the tears, biting her lip in frustration. Trent had never seen her looking so small and powerless. She was always the terrorizing blonde who would be ready to take on the world for him. She'd never been so vulnerable.

"You know that guy in our TV show?" It was the one they binge-watched and stayed up way too late on weekdays to see. They would call each other the next day at work, just to talk about it. "The main character, Steve... I find him completely unattractive."

"But he's gorgeous," she said, pulling back from him with her mouth wide. "Perfect height for kissing and hair you just want to put your hands in. I could get lost in those brown eyes for days. I mean, if I were straight, he could have me any which way."

"Not me," said Trent as he shook his head. "I'd sooner fuck a dirty sock." He shrugged one shoulder self-consciously. "Sure, he's cute, but one hundred percent not my type. I'd rather grind navel lint." He waved away her spluttered exclamation. "My point is, maybe she's just not your type."

"I like chicks. That's my type," she deadpanned, her eyebrows creeping up into her hairline.

"Okay, but what if she was seven hundred pounds and had thirteen clit piercings?" asked Trent. That brought an image that made him shudder.

"Ew, no."

"Okay," Trent continued, "then what if she chewed gum every waking moment and wore a cowboy hat and boots, even though she'd never ridden a horse?" Now that was something that he could remember from his college days.

"I'd think she was strange. I don't know where you are going with this." She crossed her arms. "Just because I have standards, doesn't mean I have to have a certain type."

"Okay, I'll spell it out for you," said Trent, finally starting to lose his patience. "She's a fucking brunette. You hate brunettes. They make you feel inferior because you worry that they'll think you're that stereotypical blonde. You rile them up to try to prove a point and it always comes crashing down. The only person you've stayed with longer than a month was a redhead. In particular a tall, huge redhead that could probably beat the shit out of me. You like them hard, butch and the shyer the better."

"Shit," her face fell and a fresh wave of tears spurted from her eyes as the realization finally dawned on her. "I can't stand her, Trent. She's just trying to be nice, but every time she opens her mouth, I just want her to shut it. She's so slutty and needy." She looked up at him with hope in her eyes. "Can't we just share Ian? I can be your hands-off side slut."

His face flushed before he could stop his mind wandering to their voyeuristic ménage. The thrill that it sent through him made his cock twitch, even with his friend sitting so close. He cut back a groan, and it came out a tiny squeak instead.

"Fuck it," she pushed her chair back and stood, marching towards the door. She looked back at him. "I'm gonna go break a heart, and you call Ian. This is totally on." She laughed at the look on his face. The sound of it followed her out of the door until it was cut off by the slam of wood.

Trent looked at the folded tissue still sitting on the table and shook his head. "There is no way I'm living with that bitch." He laughed to himself, feeling better than he had in days. His friend was back to herself, but he only hoped that she was truly joking.

His better mood finally gave him the courage to plug in his phone, which had gone dead the night before. He pushed the cord into the plug closest to the couch, which was just long enough that he could still see the screen if he held his arm to the left. A rush of notifications from various social media apps flooded the screen with pings and beeps. It was way more than he would usually get in such a short time, so he hit the clear-all button without looking at a single one.

There was a single text message waiting for him. It was from Ian. He had honestly expected a virtual barrage of messages after he had so rudely left the other man hanging. One seemed almost anti-climactic. The message was short and consisted of only two words.

You win.

The two words only deepened his confusion. That, mixed with Candace's mysterious declaration of her sudden love for Ian after being furious at him the night before, set him on edge. Yes, she'd left on good terms, but not that good — not enough for her to say that when she hadn't even asked how their conversation had gone. There was something that he was missing. Something big.

He scrolled back to his social media notifications but he'd already deleted them, and the entire stack had disappeared. He desperately pulled up the app, shaking as it loaded. He'd never been more infuriated by a slowly spinning circle, and he fixed computers for a living.

As a devoted lover, he followed Ian on every platform that was available. It made conversations more interesting when he could ask how Florida was before Ian could tell him where he was. He could make comments on how hot Ian looked during a drum solo in Vegas when he saw a fan pic. And how cute the small kitten they'd found at a fast-food restaurant was. It was the most supportive thing he could do when he was so far away, and it helped him feel like he was closer to the man.

When the application finally loaded, he saw the post that Ian had typed the night before. The time was two hours after Trent had left him alone in the bathroom, and only minutes after the text message had been sent to his dead phone.

There was a video link — the same one that Trent had watched with Candace the night before. There was a picture too. A screen shot of the guy pushing the woman up against the side of the elevator. Her head was thrown back in the throes of artificial ecstasy as he rammed his below-average dick home with hurried strokes.

Ian's comment below made his mouth drop open. It started with a laughing emoji that rolled from side to side.

Saw this video of this guy impersonating me. Lol, sorry to disappoint, but I don't swing that way.

Following the declaration, there were several hundred shares and nearing two thousand comments. Trent scrolled through them quickly, ignoring the single-word comments. There were only a few slurs and come-ons, and a couple preachy verses, but the comments were mostly positive. The ones that were poking fun were laughing at the guy in the video, not at Ian.

Trent scrolled back to the text from Ian.

You win.

That was it. There were no missed calls or any other texts.

Those two words had the opposite effect than Ian had probably intended. Trent knew that he should be overjoyed, or at least grateful that his lover had finally taken that step in front of the world. Instead, he felt like he'd been dragged across hot coals by a runaway mule. The idea that he had forced Ian into the decision, even if it was the right thing for their relationship, made him shudder.

If someone had taken that choice away from him, he probably would've tried to crawl his way back into the closet. It was something that someone had to be ready for and something they needed support with. Trent realized that he had offered neither. He'd pushed Ian before he was ready and had acted like a whining bitch the entire time.

He hesitated over the call button. He could imagine Ian sitting on that bus surrounded by his friends, who were now pelting him with questions. He could see Ian's face go sour and his arms cross as he shut down to the people who thought they knew him. He was probably too worried to check his phone. He would be completely isolated. Would he want to hear from the man who had done that to him? And would he want to hear the apology that Trent longed to give him?

His phone pinged with an incoming text before he could make up his mind. He scrambled to read it.

You didn't tell me you could sing.

The text was from Ian. Attached below it was a video file of Candace and him sitting on the couch. He was belting out a song to the imaginary tune while Candace cried silently just out of view. His phone pinged again with another message from Ian.

Mac said we should sign you. He's been hoping to get a break anyway.

Trent blinked twice before he typed back rapidly, not wanting to lose the positive wave.

Haha, very funny. I can't sing that well. I just remember lyrics. That's all.

His phone was ringing in his hand a moment later.

"I'm sorry," Trent said automatically into the phone. He clenched the placemat that was already askew from Candace's fiddling.

"What for?" Ian answered in his deep, rich voice that never failed to send a shiver down Trent's spine. There was no trace of tears left in the tone, and he sounded good enough to eat.

"For being an immature brat," said Trent. "And for not giving you an out. I never should've forced you to come out like that." He glared up into the flickering light on the ceiling of his kitchen, wishing he could kick himself as punishment for his wrongdoings.

"You shouldn't have, no, but I'm glad you did." Ian laughed softly.

"Really?" Trent smiled, and every bit of doubt was swept away. He heard the warmth in Ian's voice, and it was positively infectious. "So, are you on cloud nine right now?" He could remember the body-sweeping chill that soon melted into an exhilaration like he'd never experienced when he'd first come out.

"Something like that," Ian replied. "But anyway, I was being serious. Mac wants to meet up and talk to you about singing in the band. I mean, you're already family anyway, right? Then we would get to see each other."

Trent sucked in a huge mouthful of air, choking as it stuck in his throat. "Are you fucking with me?" He pinched the thin layer of fat along his belly, just to make sure that he was, in fact, awake.

"Yep. I wouldn't joke about something like that. I mean, he'd have to hear more and see what your range is like, but he thinks you'd be great for lead or at least second."

It was something that every kid dreamed about as they'd studied their way through high school then college or university. Being a rock star was the pinnacle of the kind of dreams that made someone wake up hard—the energy of the crowd, the music and the way each sound was heard by so many others.

"Thanks, but I'll have to pass," said Trent. "I have a job, Ian—a great job that I love. I would love to see you more, but if we worked together, I think it might get old fast. I have some vacation time saved up, though, and I could bus it down to you over the holidays. I'll get Candace to watch the ladies." The flashing lights of grandeur dimmed away to an old flickering light on his kitchen ceiling.

"Just take a plane, then you could be here tonight." Ian's voice ramped up with sudden excitement, instantly forgetting about the job offer. "I get home later today, and we'll be taking a break over Christmas."

The difference between them felt suddenly stark and unreachable. "I can't afford a plane ticket, but I can ride the bus for a quarter of the price. I've already looked up the cost of the tickets." Trent shifted in his chair and the wood creaked. He'd picked the chairs up in a garage sale a few years before, and not a single one of them matched.

"But it would take three days for you to get here." Ian pouted on the other side of the line.

"Four, actually, but I could be there for Christmas and we could spend it together." Trent could picture them sitting by the Christmas tree with the scent of pine filling his lungs. The little Christmas lights would glow against the stockings pinned over the entertainment unit. "Do you have a fireplace?" he asked, ready to edit the forming picture in his mind. They could watch the flames together, curled up on the carpet, slowly making love over and over.

"I live in Miami. If you want fire, just sit out in the sun for two hours in the middle of August," said Ian. "Don't buy your tickets yet. Let me work something out. Maybe I can come up there to you?"

Trent glanced around the house. He had yet to hang a single strand of tinsel or string of lights. The tree stand was up in the living room already, but it was empty except for a few dried needles from the previous year.

He had been stuck in a rut without fully realizing it, and now he had so much to do. Christmas spirit hit him with the force of a blizzard.

"I'm so excited," said Trent as he stood from the chair and did a small dance. "I have so much to do. I don't even have a tree yet."

"Just don't go buying up the entire tree farm yet, T. I'm not a hundred percent sure I'll be able to make it. Just let me chat with Mac, and I'll see if he can get me a last-minute flight. Sometimes everything is all booked up this time of year."

"Ian?" Trent asked. The other man grunted over the phone line. "Thank you, for everything. You're the best thing that's ever happened to me." His arms ached with the need to hold the other man close and his heart surged with joy.

"You too, T. Love you."

The phone went dead and Trent shouted with excitement. He scrambled for a piece of paper, then began scribbling down the perfect menu.

Chapter Sixteen

Trent fussed over last minute additions to his already-over-done Christmas plan. He had tried, and failed, to keep his hopes from getting too high. Ian hadn't called since their last conversation about a week before and Trent still didn't know if he was going to make it for Christmas. Their texts over the last few days had been brief at best, and Ian had finally started to feel some backlash from his unexpected announcement.

Trent had watched the media outlets explode while perched on the edge of his seat. People could be terribly mean when they didn't really know a person but thought they could judge them anyway. There were a few accounts that he had unfollowed to support Ian, and a few others that he had started to follow. Ian's band mates had remained dead silent, and Ian had commented sparingly. Trent wished he could line up the ones that were cursing his love, and slam a fist into each of their faces. But since he couldn't, he did his best to focus on the good ones instead.

When Trent went to pick up a tree at the lot just down the street, there were only three left. One was barely more than a few branching twigs speckled with brown needles, and a stagnant trunk. The second was about six and a half feet high, which would be perfect for his ceiling height, but it was limp and almost completely brown. It also smelled like it had been the target of every stray cat in the township. The third was a glorious and overpriced monstrosity, that was probably only still there because it was over ten feet tall. Trent bought it anyway and dragged it up the street to his house. He was sweating and panting by the time he arrived, and his arms ached terribly. He cut off the trunk and trimmed the branches until it was down to a respectable eight feet while sitting in the tree stand. He lopped off the pointed top next and set the remainder of the tree up in the living room. It left a line of sap on the ceiling, and one of the ceiling tiles was now dented beyond repair, but it was beautiful.

The rest was easy. He spread Christmas trinkets around the house, including two stockings above the cold fireplace. He'd picked one up for Ian that had a picture of the little drummer boy's drums on the front. It was also large enough that it would probably fit Ian's massive foot. He stuffed it with chocolate oranges and candies — and hung candy canes from the rim.

It was as if Santa himself had taken a sparkly shit in his house. Every little nook and cranny were decked with things that he had accumulated over the years. Even the television had tinsel draped over the top.

Before he realized it, it was the twenty-second of December and the office was bustling with activity. Every time a special occasion or long weekend neared, every computer in the building put on the brakes. Trent had already spent three hours fixing the main server, which had somehow managed to crash four times. The normally toasty room where the server sat was almost stifling, between the circuit boards and the trickle of heat coming through the floor vent.

He cranked the fans and kicked the portable air conditioner that was attempting to keep the room cool. The small unit spluttered once, then idled before shutting off completely. The screen went blank and the buttons dulled as it randomly lost power.

His toe ached from kicking the stubborn unit twice already. The first time, he'd forgotten that he had used his shoes to prop the door open. The second time, with his foot throbbing, it was pure frustration that drove the kick.

"Trent?"

He heard a tiny female voice through the crack in the door. He peered over his shoulder to see Belinda peeking her head into the room. She looked from the mess of cluttered wires to his sweaty form with a mixture of unease and curiosity.

"Your appointment is here," she said in the shrill voice could only be found in secretaries. It was slightly more tolerable over the phone but awful in person.

He wiped the sweat off his forehead as it slowly made its way down into his eyes. He vaguely recalled a blocked time slot for the afternoon, but he'd thought it was a virtual meeting, not one in person. From the gaunt growling of his stomach, it was probably later than he'd thought too.

"Can you just send them in here?" he asked as he kicked the air conditioner yet again. This time he aimed with his heel, and the impact was much less harsh. The machine shuddered and hummed for a moment before it stopped again. Without cooler air, the servers were bound to crash yet again.

He crouched down and completely ignored Belinda as she strolled away. The drawer beneath the unit was empty, as was the thin hose that sucked moisture from the tray to drip directly into a drain. Flipping onto his back, he scooted into the machine until his head was just inside. The flashlight app on his phone came in handy for times as terrible as this.

He saw the shape of male feet clad in running shoes a few steps from where his body was prone on the ground. He rolled his eyes and ignored them as he dove deeper into the inner workings of the machine. The light caught the drainage tube that was completely crusted with lime and rust.

The feet moved closer until they were almost touching his leg. He saw the Nike symbol on the side of the sneaker and wondered what the hell was wrong with the person. It was snowing outside, and Nikes were not exactly winter proof.

"I'll be out in a second." His voice was loud in his own ears from the small space. He suppressed a flinch as the feet moved even closer. The snow that clung to the laces dripped down onto his pant leg and the shivering temperature crept through his pants like a candle wick.

The foot moved up into the air until it was hovering just a few inches off the ground. Water dripped over his leg as the foot lifted higher and nudged his thigh. The shape of a wet footprint was stamped along his jeans, creating a chilly spot.

"What the fuck?" Trent mumbled into the machine as he watched the foot retreat again. No matter how rude salespeople could sometimes be, he'd never had one actually kick him. Even if it was a glance, it had still left his pants wet. They were black jeans, and he knew that they wouldn't be drying for hours. He'd have to sit with the feeling of gritty dampness against his leg for the rest of the day.

He pushed his way out of the machine and prepared to let a politically correct insult fly. He looked up the black slacks to the thin black T-shirt stretched over arms that it could barely contain. A broad chin with a day's worth of growth led to blue eyes that could carve through his soul.

"Ian," Trent half-shouted as he pushed his way to his feet. The air conditioner rolled away from the force of his scrambling, striking the wall and kicking to life. He threw his arms around the broad shoulders that he missed so much and buried his face into the damp skin of Ian's neck.

"You're wet," Trent mumbled into his neck. There were a few snowflakes still clinging to Ian's scruff, and their crystalized forms were slowly melting.

"Not possible. Biology doesn't work that way." A broad grin broke over his face. "Fuck, I missed you, T." He pulled Trent even tighter, almost enough to drive the breath from his lungs. His voice was loud, too loud for an office where a manager or HR person could walk by at any moment.

"Keep your voice down," said Trent, pulling back to glance back at the door. He half-expected Belinda to still be there, snooping in on his 'meeting'. Trent strode to the door and pulled his sneakers out of the way so it shut with a quiet snick. Ian reached past him to push the small, circular lock into place.

"Will anybody come looking for you?" Ian asked as he dipped his hands beneath Trent's sweater. They were cold against his overheated belly and warmth pooled in his stomach like a flame.

"No, but I can't, Ian, not here." He looked back with wide eyes, but didn't pull away. He had missed the sight of this beautiful man and his stomach was bubbling from a mix of arousal, happiness and a touch of nervousness. Ian was close enough that Trent could smell the unique cologne that seemed to be part of his natural scent. Ian's pupils were wide and dark with growing lust. There was something else there too.

"I missed you, T. Please let me just touch you a little," said Ian as he pulled Trent's hips back to meet him. He was already rock hard against Trent's ass, and his cock twitched in its confines.

"I could get fired," said Trent, but he was already tilting his neck to the side. Ian touched his lips to the side of his neck before sharp teeth scraped the sensitive flesh. "No marks." He hissed softly as Ian tugged gently then smoothed the nipped area with his tongue. The touch sent a wave of electricity over his skin that made every hair stand on end. It was as if it was the first time Ian had ever touched him.

"If I get you fired, will you come sing with me?" Ian asked before he was back, nipping harder at the reddened skin.

"I won't let you come." Trent tried to say it as a serious threat, but it came out as a breathy moan that was too loud in his ears.

Ian pulled away and spun Trent around. He pulled at Ian's strong neck and forced Ian's head down to meet his lips in a blissful kiss. He plunged his tongue into the man's mouth, taking control like he never had before. He pushed Ian's broad shoulders until he was backed up against the smooth metal surface of the server.

Having Ian back in his arms was the best feeling in the world, and no matter what had happened between them at a distance, it didn't matter anymore. He poured every minute of longing and heartache into the kiss.

Ian melted beneath him like the most delicious ice cream left too long in the sun. A small whine came from his throat as he submitted. The sound spurred Trent on and he bit Ian's lower lip before sucking it into his mouth and soothing the bruise.

It was the best kind of high. As much as he loved being beneath Ian, he'd never felt such a beautiful thing as his submission. Ian seemed stunned at his own response, his hands frozen and his mouth almost slack as Trent plundered it.

In one swift motion, Trent dropped to his knees and tugged down the zipper of Ian's jeans. Ian's hard cock pressed against the seam of his soft boxers and there was a small damp patch from the gathering pre-cum. Trent had tasted it before, and he knew how thick and sweet it was. He buried his nose against the fabric and inhaled the scent deeply.

"Don't. I've haven't showered in two days," said Ian as his hands dropped to Trent's hair and tugged at the thick strands. Trent only hummed and pressed his nose harder to Ian's groin to take in the scent. It was the smell that he'd dreamed about, only to wake up achingly hard in his cotton pyjamas. The thought of tasting Ian made his mouth water and there was no way that he was going to wait another instant. If his boss burst through the door at that moment, it still wouldn't have stopped him.

"Don't talk or I stop," Trent whispered as he grabbed the elastic waistband of the boxers. He stretched the band and eased it down over Ian's cock.

The jutting shaft bounced free and arched towards his mouth. There was a smear of pre-cum that glistened against the small slitted tip that he couldn't resist tasting. Flavour burst over his tongue as he licked the head. Ian's taste and smell were thicker than he expected, but it was nothing bad.

Ian tightened his fingers in Trent's hair and pulled him down instead of back like he'd been doing before. Ian's hips twitched as he pulled and soon half of his cock was in Trent's mouth, threatening to bump the back of his throat.

Trent pulled back, freeing Ian's grip. "You're gonna stand there and take it, and you aren't going to make a sound." Trent watched as Ian shuddered and flushed dark red as his words sank in. His pupils were so wide that they almost swallowed the endless blue.

When Trent let go, Ian dropped his hands to his sides before bracing against the metallic surface behind him. He didn't reach for Trent again as Trent slid his mouth all the way down the generous cock. He gagged as it tickled the back of his throat, so he pulled back and swallowed the spit in his mouth before it could dribble down his chin.

"You taste so good," said Trent as he lowered his head to mouth at Ian's sac, which was soft and loose. His balls strained tight as he sucked one into his mouth, then the other, before he swirled his tongue over the soft flesh. Ian let out a pleading whine that was almost lost to the whirl of the server and air conditioner.

"Quiet or I stop." Trent reminded him gently before he ran his tongue along the ultra-sensitive seam of Ian's sac. Ian bit his lip hard and gripped his hands into white-knuckled fists. "Good boy." The praise slipped from his mouth before he could even think about it. The cock against his cheek twitched at the words, and a few drops of pre-cum wet the tip before Trent quickly licked them away.

Trent waited, licking and sucking with slow, measured strokes until Ian was trembling under the constant onslaught. All thoughts of a speedy orgasm were completely forgotten as soon as he started. A steady whine came from Ian's throat that was almost too quiet to hear.

Trent waited until that crucial moment that Ian almost snapped, before he finally plunged his mouth all the way down Ian's cock. The head nudged the back of his throat before it slipped farther back, past his gag reflex. He hummed, so low that it hardly made a noise, but strong enough that he knew Ian could feel every bit of the vibration down his cock. The cock pulsed and grew even harder before thick cum spilled from the tip.

Trent swallowed and swallowed, holding off his need for air as long as he could. He pulled back and sucked in a deep breath while the rest of Ian flowed over his tongue. He swallowed it quickly, managing a small grimace as the taste became overwhelming. Cum was fine in small amounts, but he'd forgotten that Ian always came in abundance.

When he finally pulled back and glanced up at Ian, the man was a trembling, blushing mess. His lips were bitten and raw, with an incisor still nipping at the sensitive surface, and a blush had swept from the bridge of his nose to his chest and belly, where a tiny peek of skin was visible from beneath his rucked-up shirt. He looked utterly and completely ruined.

"Fuck," was the first thing that Ian finally managed to say after his chest stopped heaving. His eyelashes fluttered and suddenly he was staring at Trent, pinning him with his gaze. There was more than lust and satisfaction in it. There was wonder.

"Let me," said Ian. He scrambled to try to lift Trent to his feet, but he was still weak from his recent orgasm. Trent smirked as the usually strong and coordinated man was reduced to a soggy mess.

Trent shifted and his hardness pressed against the seam of his pants. A line of pleasure and pain from being so confined lanced through his cock. He bit back a groan as all his thoughts suddenly went south. He was throbbing in time with his heartbeat, and so hard that he was surprised he hadn't come already. There was a moment, when Ian's release had first flooded his throat, that he'd thought he might come untouched like a horny teenager. Instead, he was left aching and wanting.

Trent wanted to pull out his cock. It would only be a few strokes before he would be coming over his hand and the laminate floor. With his luck, though, he would probably shoot his load all over his shirt or the circuit board. And the thought of his coworkers on the other side of the door, bustling around cubicles and sharing bits of Christmas candy, made him want to shrivel away.

Trent pushed himself to his feet and adjusted himself in his pants with as little contact as he could manage. He stifled the groan as he brushed the head of his cock when he forced it under the band of his boxers so it was a less-obvious line of flesh instead of a jutting bulge. He was unsteady and weak from the strength of his arousal. Even the slightest shift seemed to press just right and drive his pleasure even higher.

He grimaced and turned his back to Ian while he tried to think of something disgusting to wilt his erection. It was difficult while he was so hard, and everything was alluring in his mind. It made him think of his booty shorts that Ian had defiled, and the frilly blue G-string that was waiting in his side drawer for a special occasion. That and the strawberry-flavoured extra-long-lasting lubricant.

"T? You okay?" Ian's voice was still soft and quiet, with just a hint of a tremble on the lower notes.

"Oatmeal, green slime in puddles, porcupines," Trent said aloud as he turned back around to face the man. Ian gave him a strange look as he continued. "Gum stuck to the bottom of a shoe, dog drool with pieces of treats in it, sandwich bags." He shuddered and his cock finally started to deflate.

"T?" Ian ran his fingers over Trent's hunched shoulder. Each finger was its own pressure point that dragged over Trent's sensitive skin.

"Stop. I'm thinking of gross stuff." Trent glanced down the front of his pants. There was a noticeable improvement, but still too much bulge for the office at midday—unless one was the boss' secret lover tucked away in the broom closet.

"Sandwich bags? Do I even want to know?" Ian relaxed with a huff of air. He leaned back against the metal server cover. "I wanted to take care of you too." He sounded indignant, as if Trent had dared steal an orgasm from him.

"You're staying for Christmas, right?" Trent asked. He perked up as he imagined every scenario that had crossed his mind in preparation for the holidays. There were a few spaces that he'd left deliberately tinsel-free.

"Of course." Ian nodded. A beautiful warmth bloomed in Trent's chest and a smile practically beamed from his lips.

"Then make it up to me," said Trent as he moved in close. He risked another erection as he slid his lips against Ian's. "I really don't want to get caught by Belinda either. She's just nasty. I'd rather not lose my job right before Christmas. The boss likes her and she already holds it against me that I'm gay."

Ian hummed against his lips in agreement. "Can't imagine how that feels," he said sarcastically.

Trent pulled back and really looked at Ian for the first time. There were dark bags under those clear blue eyes and a red tinge to the whites. His kiss-swollen lips were dry and chapped, and his normally clean-shaven face had a scratchy dark growth. Trent ran his hand over Ian's smooth scalp. He must've been naturally bald, as there was no hint of growth there at all.

"Are you okay? You look…" Trent trailed off.

"Like shit, I know." Ian let out a tiny smile. "I'm good, really good actually. I'm just so fucking tired. My flight was supposed to land yesterday, but it was delayed for eighteen hours. Eighteen hours of sitting in the same lounge with some teenager who was going to see her dad. She spent half her time freaking out about who I was, and the other half complaining about her life. I swear to God that if I see her again, I won't be able to help myself. I'm gonna fuckin' strangle her." He let out a small laugh before he shrugged. "Busiest time of the year to travel and I barely managed to get a ticket last-minute."

"I'm so glad you're here," said Trent as he pulled Ian in for another hug. "I was so surprised! Why didn't you tell me you were coming? I would've taken the day off and picked you up."

"I wanted to surprise you at work," said Ian as he burrowed his face into Trent's hair. "I had the whole thing planned. I was going to come here with a bouquet that would make all the office bitches jealous. I was going to sing for you and pick you up and spin you around. Sweep you off your feet." Ian pulled back with a grin. "But I could never quite predict anything about you. The flowers wilted the second they got out of the shop and into the snow. I didn't know it got so fucking cold here. How do you stand it?"

Trent shrugged as his face heated at the idea of Ian doing something so kind for him.

"Then," Ian continued, "you aren't even at your desk. You're buried in an air conditioner in the middle of a room hot enough to be a sauna. You looked so good in there with your shirt rucked up around your waist and your feet kicking as you tried to pull yourself farther under there. I was speechless. You didn't even know it was me. So, I just poked you with my foot. Sorry... It wasn't very romantic."

"I loved it." Trent smiled and pulled away. "Really though, Ian, are you okay? Everything with the guys? I can kick their asses if you need me to." He smacked Ian's chest as the man looked him up and down with a raised eyebrow. "Hey, I was wrestling champion when I was in high school. I was also the biggest guy in my class, but that doesn't matter. I would defend you because I love you."

Ian's smile was so pure that it wiped the look of utter exhaustion off his face. "They're good, T. They each took it their own way, just like everybody, but they know me. I think they were actually relieved that I finally told them what was up. I felt bad keeping something like that, like you, from them. I love you, but I love them too. It feels really good for them to know."

"And your mom?" Trent cringed internally. He remembered what Ian had said about his family. A part of him hoped that it was an exaggeration, but he'd began to doubt that the longer he knew him. Ian hardly ever exaggerated.

"Let's hope she never fucking finds out." He let out an explosive sigh. "The rest of the family is easy. I don't care about what they think, but my mom is my mom. She can always hurt me, even if I try to ignore it. I'm lucky that she doesn't do social media, or even the news. The rest of the family wouldn't want to be the ones to break the news to her either."

Trent pulled him back in for a hug and placed a kiss on Ian's chin with a small wince as the scruff bit into his sensitive lips.

A knock sounded at the door behind them. Ian's arms tightened just a fraction before they fell away. The knock came again, impatient and immediate in a familiar pattern. Trent waited while Ian scrambled with the last of his pants, slipping them up his hips and buckling them. Despite the slightly bruised lips and the flush on his face, he looked presentable. The flush could be blamed on the heat of the room anyway.

"Trent, are you in there or not?" a familiar female voice said from the other side of the thin door. "My whole screen is frozen and blue. It wasn't even my fault, Trent. I was out of the room when it happened." Her voice was escalating, like it always did when she didn't get an immediate response. Trent doubted that she'd ever heard of the word patience.

After flipping the lock, he pulled open the door just a crack and Candace pushed it open the rest of the way before she moved into the room. He narrowly missed the elbow that would've struck his solar plexus if he hadn't been paying attention. As the door slid shut, she stuttered to a halt. Her eyes caught Ian, leaning against the server with his arms crossed, before they snapped to Trent. Trent flushed even more as her eyes widened.

"Oh my God, are you fucking in here?" Candace hissed just a fraction too loud.

Trent shook his head as his flush spread down his face to his neck, while Ian burst out laughing. His shoulders rolled as he bent over and clutched his gut. His laughter was warm and loose in a way that only happened after sex.

"Oh my God, you did!" Her voice dropped into a high-pitched whisper. "Trent, you are such a slut. At work? What if you got caught?" Her lips spread in a wide smile, even as she condemned them. She let out a long groan. "That's so hot." She peered around Trent's shoulder to Ian. "Love the post, by the way, Ian. This little shit doesn't deserve you."

Trent knew she meant it in humour and light spirits, but the words made him flinch. It was true. He didn't deserve Ian. The man was the best person he'd ever met. He hardly ever asked for a thing, and he gave everything in return. Trent had never gifted him flowers on a sad day or made declarations of love to anyone who would listen.

"You're wrong." Ian cut off his line of thinking with a shake of his head. "T changed my life for the better. He's the one who made me into a good man. Without him, I'd still be some asshole too close to the edge to care."

Trent's mouth fell open at the same time as Candace broke into a smile. "Good, I'm glad you see that." She turned to Trent and pulled him into a hug. "Get out of here, Trent. I'll cover for you. Have a Merry Christmas."

"Just don't touch anyone's computer," said Trent as she pulled the door back open and disappeared. He hoped she didn't actually try to cover for him. The place wouldn't be standing by the time he got back. "Just give me five minutes," he said as he turned back to Ian.

Trent propped the door back open, this time with an actual doorstop, before he rolled the AC unit close to the computer server. Ian strolled out of the door and to the front desk, looking much more put together than he had any right to be. Every eye in the office was drawn to him as he strolled through the tight quarters. Some looked in open appreciation, and a few in recognition.

Trent could only watch him and wonder how he'd managed to snag this beautiful man. And how, with every eye on him, Ian managed to look back and give Trent the barest of winks. It was like he didn't even see the others looking at him from behind their glass doors.

It was easy to make his excuses when he approached his supervisor. The man only grunted once and shrugged. Trent hardly ever took time off or even asked to leave early. As long as the sever was fixed, the man couldn't care less. Trent left his office with a cheery 'Happy holidays'.

He rushed past the door where Ian was leaning over Belinda's desk. A small crowd of people, most of them women, had gathered next to the water cooler that just happened to be across from the workspace. Suddenly they all had to fill their glasses at the same time. They whispered to each other as they cast fleeting glances at Ian, who took it all in stride with a nonchalant ignorance.

Belinda was basking under the attention as Ian spoke quietly to her. No one would ever have known that she was married by the way she leaned over to show off her bosom to the attractive stranger. Her thin lips curled up into a smile as she forced out a laugh that was too long to be real. She kept her left hand hidden beneath the desk the entire time.

Ian's eyes lit up as Trent approached, and he pushed himself off the desk. He rolled his eyes just enough for Trent to see as he glanced over at Belinda and the steadily growing crowd. She frowned when she saw Trent approaching, her narrow eyes criticizing every bit of him in a few calculating seconds.

"Ready to go?" Ian asked as he reached out and slid his hand into Trent's. He tugged hard, throwing Trent off balance and pulling him in for a chaste kiss. Trent melted into the soft gesture that gave him more butterflies in his stomach than was strictly necessary. He heard Belinda gasp with a sound of absolute horror as she rocked back in her chair. He suppressed a snort at the shallow woman.

"Good to go, love," said Trent. The words slipped out of his mouth like they were meant to be there. If Ian's positive reaction was anything to go by, Trent would be saying them much more often. "Happy holidays, Belinda. Say hi to Peter for me." Trent let out an innocent smile at her glower. He couldn't imagine what her husband saw in her. Maybe it was the fake nails, fake tits and fake ass. That much plastic made Trent want to shudder.

"Happy holidays, everyone." Trent turned and waved at the small crowd with more warmth. A few waved back, but most were standing in open-mouthed shock.

Trent pulled his coat over his shoulders before he noticed that Ian was still in just a T-shirt. "Where's your coat?"

"I have a sweater in the rental car, but I didn't exactly get a coat. I didn't think it would be this cold." He shrugged.

Trent pulled the coat right back off before he handed it to Ian. He waved away the other's protests before he could get them out. "It should fit you. I bought it on clearance and they only had too-big sizes left. It works, though." He shrugged and Ian reluctantly pulled it on. It fit perfectly over his broad shoulders. "I've got another one at home anyway." The other one was worn and had three good-sized holes in it, but that didn't matter.

"Thanks." Ian flushed and lowered his head just a fraction. It was the same submission he'd shown in the server room. Trent couldn't help the thrill that ran through his belly. Other partners had given him that same look before as he took control in bed. It was the look he'd tried so desperately to get away from when he'd first found Ian. Somehow it wasn't the same this time. He wanted it from Ian more than anyone else in the world. Maybe because he knew he could do the same thing and Ian would snap to his side and sweep him off his feet in an effort to look after him.

Ian's rental was parked right in front of the glass double doors. The front windshield was covered in fresh snow and the black paint was almost completely obscured by gathering wind-swept drifts.

Trent shivered in the sudden wind and hurried behind Ian. The temperature had dropped as the day had moved on, and the snow had got deeper. The powdery white stuff made its way over the top of his shoes and worked down his ankles. His boots were still under his desk where he'd forgotten them. His socks were bound to be soaked in minutes, but he hoped it didn't matter. He was planning on being naked sooner than that.

He wiped his bare hands over the windshield and side windows quickly as Ian climbed in. A glance at the make of the car had him smirking. The last car he'd seen Ian driving had been worth more than Trent made in a year. At least the colour had improved.

He was shivering and out of breath by the time he tumbled into the passenger seat. He moved the bouquet of flowers from beneath him to the centre console. They had probably been beautiful before the winter chill had struck the tender petals. Now they were stained brown and wilted to almost nothing.

The seat was stone cold, but the first whisper of heat was blasting out of the tiny air vents.

"A Hyundai? That's a far cry from a Corvette," said Trent as his smile spread wider at Ian's blush.

"It was all they had left."

Trent burst out laughing. "I guess that means car sex is out. If we are going to fuck in a car, I require leather seats."

"That's it!" Ian slammed the gas too hard and they lurched backwards. "I'm returning this piece of crap and getting a hummer. Nothing is keeping me from fucking my willing lover in a car. It would be so hot," Ian groaned in longing.

"Yeah, it would be great to get twisted into a pretzel and be afraid that any minute, I could slip and end up with a gear-shift up my ass. I'd get a concussion if I tried to ride you. I think I might break my neck trying to give you head," said Trent as he shook his head. They would need a limo to make it work.

Ian pulled out into the dismal holiday traffic that was nearing rush hour in town. That meant that there were two other cars on the road between the office and Trent's house.

Trent popped the button on his jeans and pulled the remaining bit of tucked shirt out of his pants. He was already hard again and pressing insistently into a thin zipper. The zipper eased down one tooth at a time with almost-silent clicks. The cool air of the car soaked through his boxers and into his heated cock, and the change in temperature had him biting back a moan. Ian's eyes flashed to his and dipped to the opening in his pants before flickering back to the road. The engine gave a deep roar as he pressed the accelerator.

They were at Trent's home in record time. Trent snapped off the buckle of his seatbelt, but Ian was already free and climbing out of the car. The passenger door swept open and the cold wind cut Trent to the bone.

"Get the fuck out of the car," said Ian. His voice was so low that it was nearly a growl, and his eyes were blown wide with the edge of arousal.

Trent half expected the man to simply pull him out of the car and throw him over his shoulder. Perhaps if Trent was a foot shorter... The dark look sent a thrill up his spine all the same, though. He knew how powerful Ian was, and how he could wring every bit of pleasure from him.

He pulled the top of his pants together so he didn't risk freezer burn. Then he was moving out of the car and to the house. Ian was a looming heat at his back that cut through the wind and kept him warm.

The doorknob turned under his hand and Ian huffed under his breath as he pushed close to his back.

"You mean it was unlocked this whole time?" asked Ian with a shake of his head. "Never in my life have I met someone who left their door unlocked all the time. I could've come here and made myself at home between your sheets. You would've come back to find me hard and waiting in your bed."

Trent's shiver had nothing to do with the cold. He could imagine what it would be like to come home to find Ian there.

"I'd like that," he said genuinely. "Even if you were just in the kitchen when I got home or sitting in the back yard. I'd love to come home and find you here." He left two words unsaid—the 'every day' that was echoing in his mind.

The moment he was through the door, he let his pants splay wide again. The material was smooth and slid down his hips to the top of his thighs as he removed his soaking shoes. He toed off his socks next. The material was damp from the brief moment in the snow.

He went to pull his sweater over his head.

"Please, let me." Ian said as he moved in close and nuzzled against his neck. The scruff on his cheeks and chin scraped against the sensitive flesh and made the tiny hairs stand on end.

"Take me to bed."

Trent turned his head and their lips met with a press of heat and a line of slick sweetness. Ian moved even closer, from hip to shoulder, against his back. Trent's neck strained from the angle, but he refused to break the hold that they had on each other. If anything, he moved back to pull Ian closer.

Ian pushed and dragged him from the front door to the kitchen, then at last to the bedroom. They passed decorations and Christmas treasures along the way, but Ian didn't even seem to notice. Trent turned at the last moment and his knees buckled against the mattress. He fell into the soft covers that had felt so lonely the night before.

Ian pressed down on him from above but kept his knees and hands on the bed to hold most of his weight. They scooted up the mattress together until the back of Trent's head struck a pillow and he was fully on the bed.

He tugged at Ian's waist, which was too far above for his groin to reach. "You can lie on me. I can take it." He tugged again at Ian's hesitation. "I'm not gonna break." All he wanted was to feel Ian pushing him relentlessly down onto the mattress. He wanted to rut up into that solid body that could dominate him in ways no one else could.

Ian lowered himself, gently at first, then hard as he dropped the rest of his weight. The air pushed from Trent's lungs and he struggled for a moment to catch his breath. Between the weight and the lips back on his, it was almost impossible to get a breath. It made his head swim in the most delicious way.

"Please fuck me," he found himself begging already. He frowned at the sudden chuckle vibrating against him.

"So needy, T." Their groins met in grinding thrust. "So good for me, but you were such a little tease when I was away. The things you'd say to me and whisper into my ear when you thought no one was around. I'd have to run to the bathroom to jerk off in a moving bus. You know what that's like? No fucking fun, T. So, I have to pay you back for every single thing." He punctuated the last three words with rolling thrusts.

Trent let out a whine, long and low. "I didn't mean to." It was a lie. There had been times when he'd known the others would be there, but he just couldn't help himself. Then there was the time Ian had hung up on him when he'd attempted phone sex. He'd been upset at the time, but his face burned as he thought of Ian jerking off in a tiny bus stall.

"I know you can't help it, T, but I gotta pay you back anyway." He mouthed down Trent's neck and sucked a bruise just above his collarbone. The shifting weight had left him free to wriggle and move, so Trent ground into the hard belly above as his cock ached.

"None of that." Ian's hands gripped his hips and pushed them back so he was pinned to the mattress. He tried to roll them, but Ian was strong, even stronger than he looked. Trent didn't doubt that there was no way he could ever actually overpower the man.

"Lie there and take it. You gotta learn your lesson," said Ian as his teeth scraped over the same bruise. Trent was already hot and sensitive, and it sent a bolt of sensation directly to his groin.

Ian slipped Trent's shirt over his head and Trent shifted his hips as Ian dragged his pants down with a quick tug. His boxers followed a moment later with a smooth slide of cotton. Ian's lips hardly left him except for when he dragged Trent's shirt off his chest.

Ian groaned against his chest he drifted his hands across his heated flesh. "I missed this so much." He latched over a pierced nipple. The bud went tense under his ministrations and Trent cried out as teeth tugged the piercing.

"I missed seeing every inch of you and being able to touch you whenever I wanted," said Ian. "I wanted to hold you so bad, and just keep you in my arms so I could wake up beside you instead of alone on my shitty bunk. I wanted to hear your voice, your actual voice, not the tinny, delayed voice on the other side of my phone. I —"

Ian's voice cracked and he suddenly went quiet. Trent lifted himself and rested his hands on Ian's shoulders. Ian was shaking and there was something wet dripping onto Trent's belly.

Trent froze when the first sob broke from Ian's lips. Any thoughts of sex disappeared faster than snow in summer. With unknown strength, he pulled Ian to him and crushed the man in the force of his embrace.

"It's okay, Ian. I'm here." Trent smoothed over Ian's back as the man cried. Tears ran down his neck and shoulder as the crying grew louder. "Hold me now, Ian. Hold me while I fall asleep, and I promise I'll be here when you wake up. I'll be here whenever you need me, no matter what. I love you."

They fell back in a tangle of heavy limbs and a sweet sorrow that stole the breath from Trent's lungs. Ian's sobs slowed as he pressed his face into Trent's chest. His arms clenched so hard that it was nearly painful, but Trent ignored the discomfort.

Despite the early hour and the winter sun peeking through the window as the gale passed, Trent fell into a deep sleep with Ian in his embrace.

Chapter Seventeen

Trent pushed at the blanket that was across his shoulders as he tried to roll onto his side. The air was thick with something smoky and sweet that he couldn't quite place, and sweat stuck to every part of his skin. The seam where his legs met was sticky and damp, making him dread throwing the weight off himself completely. The winter air seeped through the thin insulation of his house and coated the walls with a sheen of frost on the coldest days.

His bladder throbbed as he shifted again and brought his arm up over his head and into the cold. He kicked at his blanket again, but it refused to budge, as if it was tucked around him on all sides like his mother used to do when he was young. He shifted his legs apart and tried to pull them out and to the side of the blanket. He met something solid with his toes.

His eyes flew open and he twitched as he realized that his blanket wasn't a blanket at all. The heat lancing across his chest was Ian's cheek stuck to his skin. The sweat on the side of his neck was the warmth of his breath, and the throb of his bladder was made worse because of the heavy weight splayed across him.

Ian was buried against his chest with a tiny line of drool seeping from the side of his mouth. The man was still clothed completely, including the thin white socks that peeked from beneath his pants. The slacks had ridden up, displaying a stretch of fading tanned calves that looked thicker than Trent's thighs.

It would've been the most beautiful thing in the world if his bladder wasn't currently being crushed. There was an ache in his spine that he only ever had when he slept frozen in the fit of a nightmare. There was also a slit of light peeking through the blinds that spoke of the early hours of morning before the winter birds had awoken to perch fluffily on evergreen branches. His stomach was hollow from a day with little more than breakfast and a light snack before lunch. His bladder was much more pressing, though. If not for that, he could've tolerated the heat and the stiffness.

He shifted to the side, cupping his hands behind the back of Ian's head as he moved. He cradled it as he used his abdominals to slowly turn them both onto their sides. Ian snorted once in his sleep as he pulled away from Trent's chest, leaving a line of connection between them that made Trent smile. There was a red smudge of colour that covered the entire side of Ian's face and a matching one on Trent's chest.

He snatched a blanket and tugged it up over Ian's shoulders as he extricated himself from the bed. The air was just as cold as he'd thought it would be. The wind outside had gone silent overnight, but the temperature must've dropped even more. He could hear the hum of the furnace that was probably close to overheating from the strain.

He quickly relieved himself and pulled a housecoat over his shoulders. It was the blue fluffy one that he had received for Christmas years prior. It was something he rarely used, except in the dead of winter while walking around the house naked in the wee hours of the morning. His neighbours were probably asleep, and if they weren't, then they got a free show. He hadn't heard a complaint yet, and hadn't seen a video on any questionable websites either.

He snuck into the living room and switched the Christmas tree lights on. They flashed in a pattern of gold, blue, red and green before spiralling back to the beginning. The light caught the silver wrapping of a small box beneath the branches. Ian's name was scrawled on the tag taped to the top that was partially obscured by a glossy blue bow. It was the only thing beneath the tree this Christmas, as he had already given everything else away in preparation for Ian's arrival. He'd wrapped it quickly when Ian had first said he might be coming to visit. Two hours later he had it unwrapped again and shoved back into his drawer. In the end, after several rounds of struggling with delicate paper and tape, he'd set it back under the tree. The name could hardly be seen, so he could still back out at the last minute if he needed to.

He slipped back into bed and pulled the housecoat from his shoulders before he settled into Ian's side. Ian's forehead, furrowed in sleep, smoothed out as he shifted to wrap his arms back around Trent. The tears from the day before had disappeared into the sheets, but the black lines of exhaustion still remained. Ian mumbled softly against his skin before he let out a tiny, huffing snore.

A feeling bubbled up from Trent's core, so powerful that he could scarcely breathe. His gut clenched in longing to hold Ian close and never let go again, but he was terrified at the same time. He realized that he never wanted to wake up alone again, no matter what he had to do to make that happen.

As he tried to fall back to sleep, he kept opening his eyes wide just when he was on the brink. He would reach out to feel Ian's solid shoulders and the dip of his waist before he could finally relax. The little snores brought a smile to his lips, and he listened to and cherished each one.

He closed his eyes again, only to open them a moment later as the cold of the room seeped in. The warmth of his side had disappeared and had left the stale heat of cotton sheets that never reached his toes or fingertips. He pulled his legs up and wrapped his arms around his toes, treating the cold with the palms of his hands. He was alone.

A crash from the kitchen made him shoot up in alarm. He was out of the bed and in the kitchen before he even heard the curse that followed.

Ian was bent over a bowl that was lying in pieces in the middle of the floor. There was another piece missing that was currently pushing into the soft centre of Trent's foot. Something was smoking on the stove, with acrid clouds puffing above the pan, and the smell of burning protein was thick in the air.

Trent grabbed the blackened eggs and thrust the pan under the running tap. The pan sizzled and jumped to life, splattering against his naked torso and sensitive belly. He flinched from the heat of the handle as he dropped it into the sink. The flames were still curling high on the stove at the maximum setting. He reached for the switch at the same moment the smoke alarm went off. He was glad that he was already awake, otherwise he definitely would've had a heart attack at the sheer volume of the alarm.

The shattered bowl hit the floor a second time, but the curse was drowned out by the piercing alarm. Trent grabbed a chair in a practised move and slid it under the alarm. A few seconds later, it was disconnected and silent in his hands.

"Sorry," Ian grumbled from across the room as he bent to pick up the shards of glass for a second time. "I've never used a gas stove before, and to be honest, I don't usually cook breakfast for myself." He glanced up and down Trent's form at the same time as Trent realized that he was still naked

"It's okay," said Trent with a shrug, turning his face to hide his blush. "It's not like I don't set this thing off at least once a week." He set the detector on the table next to a haphazard array of mismatched forks and knives. "Were you making me breakfast?" He tilted his head as he spied two cups brimming with orange juice. His stomach fluttered with warmth. No one had made him breakfast since he was young.

Ian shrugged and snagged the last sharp edge of shattered porcelain.

"Thank you." Trent smiled. "Even if you tried to burn the house down, I really appreciate the thought." His grin broadened at the pale blush on Ian's cheeks.

"Come on. Let's shower first, and I'll make French toast. It's my favourite," said Trent. It felt so good to be able to cook for Ian again.

"Mine too. You made it for me the last time I was here. I'd never had it before then," said Ian as he followed Trent back around the corner to the bathroom.

The room was tight with both of them in it, but the water was quick to heat, despite the chill of the outside. Trent stepped under the spray while Ian was still stripping the clothes off his body. He tilted his head back to soak his hair, leaning into the warmth. The touch on his belly made him jump. Ian was already there, jammed into his space in the tiny shower.

"Can I?" Ian motioned to the shampoo.

Trent's mouth went dry as he nodded. He spun in the water and tilted the spray down the wall so it didn't hit him in the face. He heard the pop of the cap before Ian's hands were combing through the short locks of his hair. Dexterous fingers massaged his scalp and swirled the strands around.

"I haven't had hair on my head for so long that I almost forgot what it's like," said Ian as he massaged Trent's scalp. Trent melted into the touch, having to grip the wall so his legs didn't fold beneath him.

"Do you miss it?" Trent asked as he leaned back into Ian. Heat was rising on his cheeks as he relaxed beneath Ian's talented hands.

"No, not really." Ian shook his head, his breath brushing over the back of Trent's damp neck. "It was a pain in the beginning when I would have to shave it or wax it all the time, so I lasered it off. Haven't had to deal with it since. I never even really thought to miss it. Never really liked it."

Trent reached back and brushed a hand over Ian's scalp. It was completely smooth, without a hint of stubble or the dark flush of a five-o'clock shadow. It was slick and soft beneath the hail of water, with no trace of the greasiness that he half-expected after so much time since having a shower. It felt just like the naked skin on the inside of his wrist, only thicker and less delicate.

"I wish I could've seen you with hair, though, even just once," said Trent as he tilted his head back, careful not to let any soap drip into his eyes.

"Nope, not happening." Ian chuckled and shook his head. "Here, rinse." He guided Trent's head under the spray and carefully massaged the water through the strands. "It was red. Like 'holy shit, my head is on fire' red. Best day of my life was the first time I shaved it off."

Trent turned, his gaze dropping to the thin curled hair that dusted along Ian's chest. It was soft brown, almost blond, with no hint of red, and the farther his eyes dropped, the lighter the hair became. Ian's gaze followed his, simply shrugging. Trent squinted, trying to imagine a mop of curly red hair on top of his head. He came up utterly blank.

Ian swept his hands down his body as he spread soap over ridges and shallow valleys. The touch was soft and tentative as his skilled fingers flowed over every exposed inch. They stopped all together as they approached Trent's groin.

"Is this okay?" Ian's words were hesitant. Trent inclined his head, happy to oblige the exploration. There was heat pooling in his gut, and the familiar feeling of tension in his groin, but there was no urgency.

Ian moved quickly, pausing every so often as his fingers found something new. He paused first at the small ridge of the mole at Trent's hip before he dipped lower. Ian gripped the girth of his cock with one hand, spreading a thin layer of soap before it disappeared just as fast. He dropped lower to caress the smooth skin of his sac before reaching back to his opening.

A gasp worked its way through his lips before he could stop it, but Ian was already pulling back. He could feel the answering hardness, but Ian was still. He followed Ian's nudge as he moved him forward and into the spray before Ian leaned back ever so slightly and started on Trent's back.

The throbbing died down to a simmer as Ian caressed his shoulders and down his back. With sweeping movements. Trent tilted his ass as water seeped between his cheeks, followed closely by soapy fingertips. He pressed when there was a brief nudge against his rim, but the feeling disappeared again and he was being turned so he was facing away from the spray.

"I just want to remember how you feel." Ian answered his questioning gaze. They were both very obviously aroused, but Trent was beginning to understand what Ian meant. There was a thrill to standing naked together without the heat of sex between them. There was a deep intimacy instead, which somehow felt more penetrating than any sexual act.

Trent returned the favour, soaping up Ian and lathering every bit of him that he could reach.

The water was growing cool by the time Trent turned the knob to shut off the shower. The small bathroom was full of steam, the tiny fan in the ceiling having no chance to keep up. The room was cold, though.

"Why is your house so cold? Don't you have a heater or a fireplace or something?" Ian asked from underneath the towel on his head. His skin had broken out into an array of goosebumps.

Trent shrugged, looking off to the side to try to avoid the question. "I have a furnace, but I think it might be on the way out."

"But what about the fireplace? There's one up front, right?" Ian peeked at him from behind the towel. "I saw the stockings on it this morning."

"Yeah," said Trent, biting his lip. Ian paused in his drying, obviously waiting for an answer. Trent turned around to the mist-covered mirror, unable to look Ian in the face. "I didn't have enough saved up to buy wood this winter. My usual guy doesn't deliver anymore and the only one who will is really expensive. I used all my wood money on the hotel this summer. Things kept coming up after that, and I wasn't able to replenish the fund."

"Why didn't you tell me?" A look of grief passed over Ian's face as he let his towel fall to the ground. Trent bent over automatically to pick it up. "I could've given you the money."

"I don't want your money, Ian," said Trent, trying not to let his frustration shine through. He tossed the towel over the rack, looking for any excuse to avoid facing Ian. He knew Ian had money—and a lot of it, according to Google—but Trent didn't want the money. He only wanted Ian.

"Yeah, but you came to see me, T. It's not a big deal," said Ian as he grabbed for Trent's arm.

Trent slunk to the side and managed to narrowly miss the outstretched hand. He saw rejection spread across Ian's face and his expression fell like a shutter. Despite the moisture still clinging to Trent's chest, he wrapped his arms around Ian's broad shoulders and sank into an embrace.

"It was my money to spend, Ian. I would sell this house and live on the streets if it meant I could see you." He leaned back and met the man's gaze with a joking smirk. "And until there's a ring on this finger, I'm not spending your money. After that, all bets are off." Trent broke into laughter and turned back to the mirror. "I'm just joking. I know I'm not exactly marriage material."

He glanced up from the sink and into the foggy mirror as a wave of cold air swept against his exposed skin as the door opened.

"Fuck, it's colder out here," said Ian as he pushed his way out of the room and disappeared. "How do you keep your balls from shrivelling up like raisins? Fuck."

"You get used to it." Trent chuckled and shook his head, sending water droplets around the small room. He hung his own towel on the rack and quickly brushed his teeth. By the time he was done, the humid air had been completely sucked from the room, leaving his feet chilled and numb.

"Do you need a toothbrush?" asked Trent. "I think I still have that one from when you were here last." Trent rounded the corner as he licked the remnants of mint from his lips.

He stopped in the doorway, his body frozen taut. Ian was sitting on the edge of the bed with the mattress dipped low under his weight. One knee glanced off the dresser while the other nearly touched the wall. The man made the small room look like a child's playhouse. But that wasn't what caught his attention. Ian was looking at something in his hands. Trent followed his gaze to the slight glimmer in his palm.

He squinted against the low light, wishing that he had turned on the lights or at least opened the blinds. The dawn light was just enough to catch a shine of something metal in Ian's hand. Trent wondered distantly what the man was so interested in, his mind working slowly in the early hour.

"So, if I give you this, will you take it?" Ian asked as he closed his hand around the glint of gold.

"What?" Trent asked dumbly as he tried to get a better look. He expected Ian to hand him whatever it was that he was clutching so tightly, but instead, the man slid to his knee. Trent took a step back in growing confusion and with a hint of fear. "What are you talking about?"

Ian held his hand out and opened his fingers. In the middle of his palm sat a gold ring. It was simple and thin. There were no diamonds or platinum marring the surface with overlaid designs, just simple beauty. It was the most terrifying thing Trent had ever seen.

"Will you take it, T? I was going to wait until later and do it right, but I can never think straight around you. Please, say something." Ian's heart wasn't on his sleeve. It was etched into his face like the most beautiful piece of art.

Trent's mouth opened and closed several times, but no sound came out. He swallowed, but there were just no words, not even the hum of a whisper. He saw Ian's expression of hope slowly crumble until it was hidden behind a blank façade. His shoulders drooped and he curled his hand back into a fist.

"Yes."

Ian's gaze shot up to his face at the word, his mask tumbling away as quickly as it had come. "What?" he asked in a voice so low that Trent could barely hear it.

"Yes." This time it came out as less of a squeak and more like his normal voice. Suddenly everything moved. Trent grabbed for the ring in panic, thinking that Ian might somehow try to take it away. At the same time, Ian surged to his feet in an attempt at an embrace. Trent's face collided with the top of Ian's head with a loud smack.

"Ah, fuck!" Trent's head jerked backwards, and the sharp ache hit him immediately as his eyes started to water. He brought both hands to his nose, even as he tilted off balance. Ian was reaching for him, but he was too slow. With a groan, Trent landed on his ass in the middle of the vinyl-floored hallway.

"You broke my fucking nose," Trent yelled and let out a startled, high-pitched laugh. He thought he tasted copper, but it could've just been from the salty tears that were already pouring down his face as he gasped for air. The initial stun was disappearing, leaving only throbbing pain behind.

"Ah, fuck, T, I'm so sorry. I'm such a shitty lover," Ian said as he attempted to lift Trent off the ground. His hands were shaking and warm as they grasped Trent's arm.

"Fiancé," Trent ground out through the pain, as blood started to drip down his face. "Fuck, I'm going to pass out." He cackled again as his vision wavered and two thoughts stood out in his mind. The first was that the key he'd wrapped for Ian was definitely anticlimactic next to a marriage proposal. The second was that this had to be the best concussion in the world.

Epilogue

The ring on his finger still felt new, despite the pale line on the skin below. For a time, he'd been worried that it would slip off as he typed on his computer at work or that it would disappear to the bottom of a pool. But it stayed on, solid and strong—the perfect symbol of what it was meant to represent.

He slipped his hand over the one chicken's back as she snuck by, stalking a cricket. She scooted away, unwilling to divert her attention during the hunt.

"Fine, no more tomatoes for you," Trent called after her as he plucked a cherry tomato off the vine and slid it into his mouth. The skin burst under his teeth, sending sweet tartness over his palate.

"Give her a break, T. She's just grumpy that she got kicked out of the garden."

Trent smiled and looked back to his husband. Ian was sprawled across the lawn chair with a pad of paper in his hands as he quickly scribbled notes. Cadbury was nestled between his ankles with her feathers ruffled in sleep. She roused slightly as Ian spoke, only to shake her head and settle back down against his legs.

"Coming along okay?" asked Trent as he wiped the sweat from his forehead. The sun was especially bright for the warm September day, and he had left his hat inside. He refused to get it, knowing that it would rouse Ian from his concentration and Cadbury from his legs. She would probably peck Trent a few times in retaliation.

"Mmm, yeah. Better than yesterday, that's for sure." Ian nodded and flashed Trent a smile before returning to his notebook. "It's too bad that Mac can sing but can't compose worth shit."

Trent wiped his hands on his pants and rocked back on his heels. The garden was green and growing well, despite the lateness of the season. He had managed to plant everything from tomatoes to watermelons this year.

"You headed out tomorrow then?" Trent already knew the answer, but he asked simply out of habit. It wasn't the first time they'd been apart, but it was the first time since they'd been married. The ring he wore was the same one that Ian had used to propose to him. He'd only taken it off before the ceremony so that Ian could slide it right back onto his finger, followed by a kiss. A matching band, a few sizes larger, was sitting on Ian's finger, catching the light as he wrote. He wrote with his left hand today. It was the one he used when he was feeling more creative – his right hand when he was stressed or working on something particularly difficult.

"My flight leaves at eight." His pen dropped into his lap and he shut the notebook. "At least it's only eight weeks this time."

"Eight weeks and you're back here with me again. I think I can deal with that." Trent nodded once and turned back to the garden. It was the only favour Trent had ever asked of Ian's friends. They were glad to oblige, some of them already sick of working near non-stop for years. They would tour or record for two months, then he would have Ian at home for another two.

"Just try not to break anything while I'm gone this time," said Ian in mock seriousness. He sighed and leaned back in the chair before ruffling Cadbury's feathers.

"The lawn mower was not my fault," said Trent as he threw up his hands. "There was a squirrel's nest in the bottom. Those guys are supposed to live in trees, not in my mower." It was a good thing he'd checked before starting it up for the season. He never would've gotten over it if there were chopped squirrels all over the yard.

"Yeah, but did they have to live in the house after?" Ian chuckled over the argument they'd had many times. He'd returned home after a stretch of too many weeks away, to find Trent perched on the edge of the tub in the basement with three tiny squirrels in his arms. "Not to mention the roof," said Ian. "I was gone two days before you call me and tell me that the roof blew off." He motioned one hand to the edge of the roof, where a new layer of shingles lay with a slightly darker shade.

"It was only the corner," Trent squeaked with indignation. "There was a windstorm. I can't control the wind." He crossed his arms and leaned back on his heels.

"What about the kitchen fiasco? Was that the northern lights or the Loch Ness monster?" Ian shifted until he was leaning over the side of the lawn chair with a goofy grin on his face.

"Let's never speak of that again."

They both burst out laughing, disturbing Cadbury from her roost. The hen clucked aggressively before jumping down and running across the lawn.

"Love you, T."

Trent turned back to Ian with a brilliant smile. Their lives weren't perfect, but they were good for each other. Trent broke things so that Ian could fix them, and Ian came up with fantastical ideas so that Trent could try to create them. He would never get used to Ian being away, but it made him cherish the time that they had together even more. What mattered most was that they were both happy.

"Love you too, Ian. Now, get off your ass and help me weed." The garden was growing well, yes. That also meant that the weeds were invading like conquistadors.

Ian grunted and lifted himself off his lawn chair before kneeling beside Trent. He placed a single peck on Trent's forehead before he thrust his hands into the garden, gripping a green stem and pulling it up from the roots with a smile.

"Ian, those were my ghost peppers," said Trent, wondering if the plant was at all salvageable. Dirt speckled Trent's leg when Ian gave the plant a slight shake before tossing it behind him. Ian shrugged before he reached for another stem, pausing and looking to Trent before he pulled it.

"That's asparagus." Trent deadpanned.

Yep, life was pretty perfect.

Want to see more like this?
Here's a taster for you to enjoy!

Success: Never Too Famous
Thom Collins

Excerpt

A line of people stretched around the block as the black Mercedes turned in front of The City nightclub. Not yet midnight and the place must be on its way to being crammed. From the back seat of the car, Harry Alexander watched the queue through the tinted windows. The patrons in the crowd were typical of those he met at any weekend club night—young women in scanty dresses and men who looked as if they'd spent the entire day and a month's salary grooming themselves for the event.

And there, right by the entrance, he saw himself. A life-sized poster in which he wore a white shirt, open to the waist, and a sea captain's hat. 'Tonight,' the poster announced, 'Meet the Star of *Ship Mates*, Harry Alexander.' It was an old photograph, taken around five years earlier, when he'd been at the height of his fame. Mega cheesy. Harry had never liked that image, but the damn thing followed him everywhere.

"Look at all those people," Vanessa exclaimed from the seat beside him.

"Relax," Harry said. "They're here for the club, not me. I'm just a sideshow."

"The club thought enough of you to send this car, didn't they? You're a big deal here."

A big deal. He knew it wasn't true. Not anymore. True, someone still valued his celebrity enough to book him for this gig. Despite the saturation of reality-TV stars on the market, places like this were willing to shell out a few quid to have a well-known face on the premises. He didn't understand why but had milked it for all it was worth, prolonging his fifteen minutes of fame to a decent six years. The offers were a lot less frequent these days, but there were opportunities to be had, as long as he wasn't fussy, or too proud.

The Mercedes slipped into the alley at the rear of the club and the driver came around to open the door. Harry stepped out, followed by Vanessa and her husband, Ross. Best friends since childhood, Harry had seen little of Vanessa since she'd married and moved to Manchester. Now work brought him here for the weekend, it gave them the perfect opportunity to catch up, all at someone else's expense.

Vanessa and Ross were dressed for a big night. She had on a full, sequined evening dress with narrow straps, low at the front and even lower at the back. Ross, a vet in his mid-thirties, wore a black suit and white shirt, more appropriate for a formal dinner than a trendy city center club. Ross put his arm around his wife's waist, and they followed Harry through the back door of the club.

Harry Alexander was six-foot-two and every inch of him looked like a star. At thirty-two years of age, he had an effortless, old-fashioned look, at odds with the overly Botoxed, waxed, polished, buffed and styled images of his contemporaries. Brown hair — thick with a natural wave, cut short at the back and sides and full on top. Icy-blue eyes — like Franco Nero or Paul Walker in their prime. A straight nose and strong, handsome jawline. He had a wide-shouldered build, slim through the waist and powerful in the butt and thighs, all achieved through good diet and a healthy fitness regime. In an industry where many young men go to extreme lengths to reach unachievable goals of perfection, Harry was comfortable in his own skin. That comfort and confidence made him sexier, more desirable than all the others.

Tonight, he wore his regular uniform for this kind of thing. Narrow-legged navy trousers to show off those assets, and a slim-fitting, short-sleeved shirt, which revealed his strong, tattoo-free biceps and forearms.

The club security led them into a small waiting room. There were drinks laid out — wine, champagne, spirits and beer. Harry told Vanessa and Ross to help themselves.

"Is this what your life is like all the time?" Ross asked, opening a beer and dropping into a sofa. "People just give you free stuff."

"Not really," Harry said. "Only at times like this. Though other people play the game a lot better than I do. They rarely pay for anything. I don't like to take the piss like that. Some things should be paid for." All true. On a job, Harry had no qualms about taking the clubs for all they would give. But he didn't behave that way through the rest of his life, expecting freebies just because he was well-known.

Harry looked at his watch. It had gone twelve. He was due on stage at one. These things followed a format. A brief turn on the stage, followed by photos and autographs with anyone who wanted them, then a seat the VIP room, where he was obliged to stay for one hour. That was where the clubs made the real money from these celebrity appearances. Regular punters would pay upward of one thousand pounds for a table in the VIP just to be close to the famous guests. Once there, they'd be stung with minimum spending restrictions on the bar, at least another grand toward the club. The hotter the celebrity, the higher the prize of a table. Harry's days as a top earner were long gone, though he could still command a decent fee for a few hours of what he could never call work.

The club's manager appeared a few minutes later, while Ross opened his second beer and Vanessa got stuck into the free champagne. Marc Jenner, a guy in his early twenties, had a frozen, shiny forehead and an overfamiliar attitude. Though this was the first time they'd met, he greeted Harry with a brotherly hug.

"Harry, mate, so good to see you." He grinned, with the wide eyes and overconfidence of a seasoned cokehead. "Glad to see you're enjoying yourself," he said, clocking Vanessa's full glass.

"There's just one thing," Harry said, taking Marc by the elbow and guiding him to the outer corridor.

"Anything, mate, just say it. We can sort anything you want. What's it to be, bro? A cheeky line or two? Or a pretty face plucked out of the crowd?"

Harry held his patience. "My fee. It hasn't come through."

Marc laughed. "Don't worry about it, mate, we'll see you right. We're good for the money, you know that."

How many times had he heard that before? Harry maintained the cool, professional tone. "I made it clear when you booked me for this gig that you would pay me in advance of the appearance. I checked my account in the car here, and the funds still haven't come through."

Marc's smile and confidence wavered for the first time. "Harry, man, it's all cool, don't worry. You'll get paid."

"Now," he said, his voice firm and controlled.

"What?"

"I'll get paid now. Or I don't go on. That was the deal. That's always the deal."

Harry had learned his lesson the hard way. Organizers were always keen to say they'd pay up later, but he knew from experience that the money would be less forthcoming after the gig. Once he'd done his job, they were on to the next C-lister and didn't care to pay the one before.

"I'll tell you what," Marc said. "How about you and your friends take a table in the VIP, and I'll see what we can do? Have a few drinks, mingle a little, and I'm sure I can get this misunderstanding fixed."

With his smile turned up full, Harry said, "We'll wait here, until you get it sorted. I'll take cash or a Bacs transfer, whichever is easier. Then I'll go to that table in the VIP." He knew Marc's trick. The VIP area was a public part of the club, and once he stepped out there, he would work for them, free drinks or not. When he hadn't gotten paid for several gigs at the start of his celebrity career, Harry had adopted a motto he'd stuck to, without wavering, ever since — no pay, no play.

"What's going on?" Vanessa asked when he returned to the green room.

"Nothing. Marc needs to deal with a small issue and then we're good to go."

Harry poured a vodka over ice and sat in a leather chair opposite Vanessa and Ross. They were both pretty merry. All three had been out to dinner before the car had arrived to collect them for the club. While Harry had paced himself with two glasses of wine across the evening, Vanessa and Ross had polished off two bottles of white wine and one red. He didn't blame them. He had to work tonight, they didn't. Let them enjoy themselves. Once he'd done his bit on the stage and posed for selfies, he intended to get very loaded.

The thud of dance music reverberated through the floor and walls. The club must be livening up. All those people in line would be inside by now.

"Do you do this every weekend?" Ross asked, gesturing around the room. "The personal appearance and all that."

Harry shook his head. "No, but I used to. Sometimes I'd appear at two different clubs on the same night. Thursday, Friday, Saturday, I could do as many gigs as I wanted, traveling all over the country. Sometimes I went abroad. I used to do appearances in Ibiza and Ayia Napa a couple of times a summer."

"Why did you stop? Getting paid for nothing, who wouldn't want that?"

Harry laughed. "That's the problem, everyone wants it. I don't know how many TV channels there are these days, spewing out God knows how many reality shows. And those shows are filled with dozens and dozens of hot young things who are prepared to do anything for their slice of the fame pie. I'm old hat. A has-been. I can't compete with the younger crowd. Anyway, they play the game much better than I do."

"You're here tonight, aren't you? They've got your poster at the door. You're not that old hat."

"Believe me, I am. *Ship Mates* isn't even on air anymore. Most of that crowd won't know me. If they've heard of me at all, it's because their mum fancies me."

In an era of naked dating shows and full on-screen sex, *Ship Mates* was reality television from a different time. A fly-on-the-wall documentary series following the crew onboard *The Atlantic Star*, a luxury cruise ship, it ran for four successful years with a peak audience of six million viewers. Harry had been working as an assistant maintenance engineer when the film crew had discovered him and featured him as one of the key players in the docu-soap. His classic good looks and sunny personality made him an immediate hit with the audience as they watched him deal with problems around the ship such as blocked toilets and clogged Jacuzzis.

When the show was broadcast in a prime-time slot on the BBC, Harry became an instant hit. His fame exploded after the second series. Almost overnight a slew of lucrative offers came his way. Magazine interviews, calendars, endorsements, public appearances—a tidal wave of money came down upon him. Harry left *Ship Mates* and *The Atlantic Star* after three years when his work at sea prevented him from capitalizing on all these new opportunities. He presented his own travel show on the BBC for two years and appeared as a guest on countless celebrity panel shows. That in itself was a joke. Harry never took himself seriously as a celebrity. He had a hard time accepting his status as a reality-TV star. He hadn't set out to be famous. He'd gotten luck, simple as that.

He didn't fit into the celebrity/reality-TV culture. All those people with their cutthroat ambition and ruthless survival skills. He was an imposter, a charlatan. The glory days were ending. He'd enjoyed them while they lasted, but his world wouldn't crumble when the fame did.

Marc Jenner returned a few minutes later, veneered smile in situ, his eyes gleaming a fresh coke-blaze. "All sorted," he said, slipping an envelope into Harry's hand. "Let's get out there."

"One moment." Harry broke the seal on the envelope. It was stuffed with cash, used tens and twenties. He had an image of Marc tearing around the club, trying to cobble his fee together from the various cash registers. "There's only twelve hundred here," he said.

"The rest has been transferred into your back account," Marc said, a note of irritation in his voice.

Taking his time, Harry retrieved his phone and accessed the banking app. The remainder of his fee was all there. "Okay, then," he said, granting Marc his full Mister Showbiz smile. "We're good to go. Let's do this."

PUBLISHING

Sign up for our newsletter and find out about all our romance book releases, eBook sales and promotions, sneak peeks and FREE romance books!

About the Author

M.C. Roth lives in Canada and loves every season, even the dreaded Canadian winter. She graduated with honours from the Associate Diploma Program in Veterinary Technology at the University of Guelph before choosing a different career path.

Between caring for her young son, spending time with her husband, and feeding treats to her menagerie of animals, she still spends every spare second devoted to her passion for writing.

She loves growing peppers that are hot enough to make grown men cry, but she doesn't like spicy food herself. Her favourite thing, other than writing of course, is to find a quiet place in the wilderness and listen to the birds while dreaming about the gorgeous men in her head.

M.C. Roth loves to hear from readers. You can find her contact information, website details and author profile page at https://www.pride-publishing.com